Amis in Holmes County

A Granny Weaver Tale

Karen Anna Vogel

Contact the author on Facebook at: www.facebook.com/VogelReaders

Learn more the author at: www.karenannavogel.com

Visit her blog, Amish Crossings, at www.karenannavogel.blogspot.com

Edited by Rachel Skatvold © 2019

ISBN: 9781693865404

Dedicated to fans of Granny & Jeb Weaver who encourage me to keep tapping away at the keyboard about the Amish in Smicksburg, and now Holmes County. You are all so precious to me.

&

To AJ and Angela. Your love story inspired Rachel Weaver's beautiful romance.

&

To the real Sydney.

Yes, hairdressers are good therapists!

Amish – English Dictionary

How Pennsylvania Dutch overflows into Western Pennsylvanian slang.

"To be" or not to be, that is the question. Folks in Western PA, along with local Amish, do not use "to be". It's not "The car needs *to be* washed." We simply say, "The car needs washed." This is only one example. This book is full of similar "grammar errors" but tries to be authentic to how people talk in our "neck of the woods."

Ach – oh
Boppli – baby
Bopplin -babies
Daed - dad
Danki – thank you
Dawdyhaus – a small house built for grandparents
Dochder -daughter
Dochdier - daughters
Ferhoodled – Messed up, confusing
Gmay – community or church
Groosseldre - Grandparents
Grossdaddi - grandfather
Grosskinner - grandchildren
Grossmammi – grandmother
Guder mariye –good morning
Gut – good
Jah - yes
Kapp- cap; Amish women's head covering
Kinner – children
Mamm – mom
Nee- no
Ordnung - A set of rules for Amish, Old Order Mennonites and Conservative Mennonites. Ordnung is the German word for order, discipline, rule, arrangement, organization, or system.
Rumspringa – running around years, starting at sixteen, when Amish youth experience the outsiders' way of life before

joining the church.
Wunderbar – wonderful
Yinz – You all or you two, slang found in Western Pennsylvania among the Amish and those who speak Pittsburghese.

CONTENTS

Chapter 1

Granny set out to cast on forty-four stitches to craft another *boppli* blanket, but the notion that she'd be in Ohio for Christmas, not Smicksburg, made her lose count at thirty-something. Her wrinkled hands fell to her lap. Thanksgiving, too, she thought with exasperation. What would her "little women" at knitting circle do without her? And the more dreadful thought. What would she do without them? Not having a daughter of her own, these girls were hers by a spiritual connection. Cookie frolics and their annual Christmas party were traditions now. How could Jeb go and agree to visit their son for an extended visit?

As the late November winds rattled the windows, she pulled tighter the shawl her knitting friends made her last Christmas. Each picked a muted color, like Joseph's multicolored coat in the Bible. It was so eye-catching that she could only use it in the home, like a crazy quilt, not in public to bring attention to herself. This was the Amish way, and she'd been steadfast for some seventy years now.

Jeb trudged in with an armful of firewood weighing him down. "I smell snow." He gingerly put each piece in their black wrought iron fire ring. "Roman says the girls are crying already."

"About the cold weather?" she asked. "They love it. Remember their poem about snowflakes?"

He plopped down in his Amish rocker next to her. "*Nee*, about us leaving. They want to come, but I said it's special, just you and me."

She tried to make her voice sound gentle. "Jeb, I don't see why our *kinner* can't come here?" She let her eyes take in her beloved kitchen. Oak cabinets, shiny honey oak floors and her stove. Her Pioneer Princess wood cookstove. Past holidays spent right here, in her little corner of the world, became more precious as time marched on.

She froze. "Jeb, are you planning another one of your surprises? Are we going to Lehman's department store? If so, we can order online over at Suzy's. They deliver, you know."

Jeb's brows furrowed. "Well, Lehman's isn't far from Daniel's place, come to think of it. We could go shopping there if you want. I wonder if they carry fishing poles all year long. Of course, they must, since so many Amish ice-fish."

Granny decided that she'd stop fretting. Jeb obviously wanted to go to Millersburg, Ohio for Christmas. He never insisted on much, so she'd sacrifice her kitchen, her knitting circle party and cookie frolics for him. But would memories of her long-gone parents take her down memory lane a bit too much, making her melancholy?

As dusk settled in, Jeb lit the gas lamps and picked up his latest read. *Ach*, she did love the time after harvest when everything was in slow motion, and the winter birds came back. Her birds! Her feathered friends that they grew all those sunflowers to feed. Well, the twins next door, dear Millie and Tillie would get to learn more about being responsible for filling her plethora of feeders.

Feeling so fretful, she called for her little black Pomeranian, a stray she'd taken in years ago, and Bea jumped into her lap. "And the girls will take *gut* care of you, too."

Jeb lay down his book. "Deborah, do you want to leave after Thanksgiving? Make it a short trip? Only two weeks?"

She studied his face. Yes, she saw it. Disappointment. Did he miss their son in Ohio more than he let on? She was being selfish. "Jeb, I'm getting to be an old stick in the mud."

"I thought that's what I was, remember? You called me that back when we were courting." He blew her a kiss.

Granny grinned and set to cast on forty-four stitches. And she needed to do a casting off prayer.

Lord, you know I want my way, being human. I hold dear to traditions and I suppose at my age it frightens me to know how many years I have left. How many years I have with my knitting circle, but Jeb comes first. I give my anxiety to you. You said to cast our cares on you because you care about us. So, I give Thanksgiving and Christmas to you. Amen.

~*~

Fannie stopped by the next morning as promised, despite her sore throat. Nothing contagious, of course, but the ache in her heart seemed to rise to her head. *Jah*, a headache, too. She'd miss Granny's Christmas gathering, and not having a tight bond with her own *mamm*, she felt the void already. Would holiday cheer make her sadness clear? The line from a song Ginny Rowland wrote rang in her mind. Well, she'd ask Ginny for a copy of that song because it made her focus on the real meaning of Christmas; not everyone was having a holly jolly Christmas.

Never needing to knock at Granny's kitchen door, she did pause to look through the glass. Granny was hunched over her coffee, looking so forlorn. This was not the robust woman she knew. Where was her excitement over the trip? Cracking the door enough to poke her head in, she overly smiled to draw forth a grin. "Granny, nice crisp sunny day for packing, *jah*?" Sliding in, she continued. "We can take a walk when we're done."

Granny's eyes lit up. "Fannie. So glad you could come over to help, but I'm all packed. I did it last night. Couldn't sleep."

Now, this was a new situation to Fannie. Giving advice to Granny? It was always vice versa. "You've never had trouble sleeping. Everything okay?"

Granny sipped her coffee. "*Ach*, I did sleep a few hours, but it was about my parents and I got up and…well, Millersburg isn't the same as when I grew up. The family farm was sold off and…did I ever tell you about it?"

Fannie poured herself a cup of coffee and sat across from Granny at her oak table. A place she relished. "Tell me."

"Well, guess what's on the family land now. You'll never believe it."

Fannie ran many possibilities through her mind. "I don't know. A highway? That would be sad. I know that outlet on Route 30 in Lancaster took out many a farm. Dangerous to cross now, too. My pen pal complains all the time."

"*Jah*, nothing like Smicksburg," Granny said with a groan. "Our settlement keeps growing due to land prices being dirt cheap, but not a three-ring circus yet." She let her eyelids close like shades. "A Super Walmart."

Granny's eyes remained closed and Fannie

panicked. "Granny, you're falling back to sleep."

She batted her lashes. "A Super Walmart is on the family farm. *Ach*, Fannie, how could my *bruder* sell to a land developer and not another Amish farmer?"

Did Fannie dare ask? How could she help it? "He must have gotten a fortune. Did he split it with all your siblings?"

"*Nee,* he did not. My *bruder* left the People. He's shunned, but it's my big Christmas prayer that he'll return to the People. Hard to talk about…"

Fannie reached across the table and took Granny's hand. "I'll be praying for you. I came here full of self-pity again."

"What's wrong?"

"*Mamm* planned a shopping trip to Punxsy today, but when I told her I was helping you pack, she blew up and said she was thankful Eliza was a faithful *dochder*. *Ach*, Granny, her tongue cuts me just when we're making progress. We made all kinds of pies last week and had so much fun."

Granny sighed, turning her mug. "Is there still time to go shopping with her? When does the driver come?"

"I want to spend the day with you," Fannie exclaimed. "You'll be gone for six weeks! I may just hire a driver to come out and visit."

"*Ach*, Fannie, the *dochder* I never had. Old enough to be your *grossmammi,* but you know my meaning. Can you stop over and make sure the bird feeders are all filled? And my little dog is over at Romans. Can you check on her?"

Fannie's heart swelled. Granny needed her and thought her capable. "Can I come and sit in your rocker and knit?"

"Why would you want to do that for? You have an Amish rocker," Granny pointed out.

She could not control herself any longer. The tears spilled and feeling like a *kinner,* she yanked a handkerchief out of her apron pocket and buried her face in it. She was so selfish at times, like her *mamm* always told her. She only thought of herself. Granny was having a hard time leaving and here she was making it harder.

She felt arms wrapping her and Granny was hushing her, saying how special she felt to be missed. Fannie just kept gasping out "I'm sorry" but soon the two were both in tears. Granny said she was ever so thankful to have a special bond with a special woman. *Ach*, Granny's words were a healing balm.

~*~

Ella glanced over at Ruth as they fetched their presents out of the buggy. "I don't know if I can do this. Granny gone during Thanksgiving and Christmas!"

Ruth nodded. "I feel the same way, but she'll see her son and *grosskinner*."

"Teenagers out on *Rumspringa*," Ella added.

"Granny told me they're all doing *gut* except the oldest girl. Granny can help her, I'm sure. Look what she's done for all of us."

"For sure and certain," Ruth said as they ascended the steps to the wraparound porch.

Ella glanced into the kitchen to see Fannie. She stepped in and soon discovered Fannie was in low spirits. "What's wrong?"

Fannie looked up from her book. "Nothing. Just reading the part in *Persuasion* when Anne Elliot thinks she's lost her bloom. Sometimes I feel that way."

"Me, too," Ruth said. "We should read that book for knitting circle when Granny's gone. It makes me realize that time and distance doesn't matter when…" She inhaled and forced a smile. "When people who love each other are apart."

"I agree," Ella said looking around the room. "Where's Granny?"

"Taking a nap," Fannie said. "She's bushed. Couldn't sleep last night because her *bruder*, who's shunned, will have to be dealt with when she goes to Millersburg." Fannie threw up her hands. "Walmart, of all things."

Ella and Ruth waited for her to continue, but she told them coffee was warm and to grab a cup if they wanted.

"What's wrong with Walmart?" Ruth asked. "We shop there all the time."

Fannie's eyes bugged. "You don't know. Of

course. Granny's *bruder* got money lust and sold the family farm to Walmart and never split any of his fortune. Lives in a mansion and left the People. I suppose Granny could have used that money, but she's never complained." Fannie scratched her head. "Come to think of it, she's never mentioned her *bruder* or the money. Must be too painful."

Ella set her packages on the table as did Ruth. "Do you think she needs us out there in Ohio? We could hire a driver. Go visit and check up on her and Jeb. They have a *grosskinner* out on *Rumspringa* gone wild."

Ruth spoke up. "Granny can handle anything. Well, we all have feet of clay, like the Bible says, but sometimes I think Granny's clay has hardened?"

Fannie laughed. "That's a *gut* way to put it. With age comes more steadiness, I suppose. But she was sad this morning. And she never takes naps. Maybe a trip to Ohio would be *gut*...and fun."

The three sat at the table, mulling over the prospect.

"She needs us to visit," Ella declared as the cuckoo clock chirped three tweets. "Should we surprise her? Take these Christmas presents back home?"

Light footsteps could be heard and Granny moseying into the room decided Ella's dilemma. "Granny, we stopped by to give you your Christmas presents before you leave."

With outstretched arms, Granny embraced Ella and then Ruth. "*Danki* ever so much. I don't have yours. Was going to get *yinz* something special out at Lehman's."

"You're going to Lehman's. It's like the Amish Super Walmart!" Ruth squealed.

Fannie hushed Ruth. Granny's brows knit together. "Fannie, what's wrong? It is as Ruth says."

"She mentioned Walmart and, you know. I told them what your *bruder* did with the family land."

"Why didn't you ever tell us about that?" Ella asked. "We bear each other's burdens at knitting circle, *jah*?"

"It happened before I started a knitting circle. Before I started to really open up to my girls."

"And now we've all come out of our shells and opened up, too," Ruth said with feeling.

Granny replenished Fannie's coffee and poured two cups for Ella and Ruth. "Sit down. There's something I need to say."

They obeyed and were soon in a huddle, all ears.

"Now, I have been emotional over being gone, but I'm not sad. *Jah*, I'll miss all *yinz* girls, but I've neglected my son and his family out in Ohio."

"They come here quite a bit and you cook for days for them," Fannie informed.

"I know, but I don't leave my little slice of heaven too often. I'm so fond of Smicksburg, you see, and as you age, you don't like change."

Ruth put up a hand. "I don't like change at any age."

Granny threw her a loving smile. "Well, there is something you can do when I'm gone. Can you keep the knitting circle going? Lizzie, Colleen, Maryann…so many now. And the Englishers who joined. Can *yinz* all work out a plan?"

Fannie grabbed her book. "We can read *Persuasion* and have a Jane Austen tea party over at Suzy's!"

"Or a Christmas book," Ella suggested. "Or read *Little Women* again since there's Christmas in it."

"*Ach*, I'd love to read the Bible or poetry," Ruth said dreamily. "My poems are being published in *The Budget*! I think I forgot to tell you, Granny."

Fannie bellowed out a laugh. "You sound like Josephine March. I say we read *Little Women* again."

They all joined the mirth and hugged and kissed each other, as they discussed plans. Ella pushed down that gnawing void that welled up when she thought of a Christmas without Granny. She had her knitting circle 'sisters' and maybe they'd be spun closer than ever this holiday season, all having a common need: Granny.

~*~

Granny made thermoses full of peppermint tea for their journey. Today she should be at Lena and Jason's wedding, but Jeb was relieved of his duties as bishop for six weeks. Granny turned this over in her mind. Is Jeb tired of being their bishop? *Ach*, he needs this vacation to rest! How could I be so blind?

Come to think of it, Jeb's bowlegs were getting more bowed. His vision was getting worse, too, having to get more powerful lenses. Well, she needed to take *gut* care of this *wunderbar gut* man God allowed her to marry. Even though he'll miss his fishing hole, she chuckled. He was outside now staring into the little lake stocked with bass. She held back a white curtain to observe him. He was nestled on the pier, throwing bread to his fish.

He mentioned ice fishing supplies at Lehman's. That's what I'll get him. *Ach*, this could be fun, she reasoned.

She heard the van pull into the driveway and knocked on the window. Jeb turned and nodded, making his way around the house to gather his belongings. But it was the Baptist Church van! What on earth?

Soon, Janice, Suzy and Marge were in her living room, dousing her with hugs and kisses.

Suzy spoke first. "We got this for you. Guess what it is!"

Granny's eyes twinkled. "Janice and Marge! You learned to spin wool! It's yarn. Yarn and needles. A new pattern I can work at while gone."

Suzy offered a fake pout. "Are we so predictable?"

"Middle-age," Janice groaned. "We girls need to do something totally different this year for Christmas. Granny, I think you stay young in heart because you change it up. Going to Holmes County for Christmas is a *wunderbar gut* idea, *jah*?"

Everyone laughed as Janice fumbled a Penn Dutch accent.

Granny opened the bag to indeed see several large skeins of yarn and a crochet hook. Stunned, she studied Suzy. "So, you finally like to crochet?"

Marge patted her heart. "When Suzy wasn't looking, I slid in a crochet hook along with a pattern. So, you can choose. Like I've always said, crocheting is more relaxing."

Suzy grabbed the crochet pattern. "It's for intermediates to advanced. Granny can hardly crochet, right? I mean, is there some kind of revolution going on in town? A crochet circle I don't know about?"

Granny opened the pattern and nodded with delight. "I can do this. Marge has helped me from time to time." She opened her arms and they all fell into a huddle of a hug. Granny loved these dear trusted English friends and had come to not even see them as not Amish anymore. They had one faith in common that bound them tight.

"I think your van is here." Janice clasped her long black fingers together. "Have a happy Thanksgiving and Christmas. And don't worry one bit about the girls over at Forget-Me-Not- Manor. They send their love and will live without all the pies you bring."

Granny held on to Jeb who was coming to collect her. "Janice, I forgot to give those girls their presents. And their precious *kinner. Ach*, those single *mamm's* have so many needs."

Marge towered over Granny. "You need a vacation. I've seen how you doze off when I'm talking." She slapped Jeb's shoulder. "You do it all the time; I must be a bore, but Granny hangs on every word I say." She wagged a finger. "But lately, I've caught you snoozing." Marge hugged her so hard it hurt, but knew this vivacious, cheerful woman had spunk and did nothing in halves.

"Can *yinz* do something for me?" Granny asked. "Fannie was over yesterday in tears. Can you make her feel…capable? Put her in charge of something over at the Baptist church. How about you ask her to read to the *kinner*?"

"Consider it done already," Janice quipped. "Christmas is a hard time for those kids and Fannie's good medicine. And you taught her how to make pies, so I'll ask her to bring some over."

Granny tapped her fingers in applause. "*Danki*." She pulled a paper out of her apron pocket. "Here's our son's address. Write if you need me."

"Go have a good vacation," Marge commanded, and then tears welled up in her eyes. "Smicksburg won't be Smicksburg without you."

They all descended on her again for a hug, but Jeb pulled her to himself. "This sweetheart girl of mine needs a long vacation, *jah*?"

Granny's cheeks burnt. "You're embarrassing me…old man. Now, let's get into that van before the driver leaves."

Peals of laughter rang throughout the little *dawdyhaus* as Granny nudged Jeb toward the door. She turned to throw them a kiss. *Ach*, I'll miss everyone. Maybe we should stay for only two weeks. Jeb was acting *ferhoodled*. Bride? That was a definite change in behavior that Doc Pal said accompanied a mini stroke. Maybe it was best their son saw Jeb. *Jah*, she needed their opinion.

~*~

The van was filled after all Amish passengers were picked up. Since the settlement in Smicksburg came from folks out in Millersburg, they were most likely visiting kin. Granny got out her yarn to crochet. What a lovely pattern Marge picked out. A sampler of many stitches and she knew them all. But her head soon bobbed, and she leaned against Jeb, sound asleep. She heard chatter when they crossed the state line into Ohio, but soon fell back to sleep. Granny was shocked when Jeb nudged her. "Time to get out. We're here."

She looked out the van door to see her beautiful teenage *grosskinner*, Rachel. She could not hide her smile, but jumped up in excitement, not knowing her legs were asleep. She was grateful Jeb had her hand since she would have fallen. Sitting back down, she rubbed her legs.

Rachel flew into the van. "*Oma*. Are you okay?"

"My legs are numb. I'll be fine."

Rachel hugged her neck. "I'm so glad you're here. You'll talk to *Mamm* and *Daed*?"

Granny touched Rachel's rosy cheeks. "I've read your letters, and we need to talk. But first I have to be able to walk." She forced a chuckle, embarrassed that she appeared to be impaired.

Soon Benjamin ran into the van. "*Oma*, I can carry you." He scooped her up, despite her protests. "Charlie needs to get going." He handed the driver large bills and mentioned his tip was included. Jeb said he was paying, but Benjamin said his parents insisted.

Carrying her to the large, white farmhouse, she felt so light in his strong, sinewy arms. "Benjamin, how old are you?"

"Nineteen and liking *Rumspringa*," he said with a wink.

"Are you behaving yourself?"

"Of course. Go to Singings and…well it's a secret."

Within seconds, Daniel came running from his rocker shop. "*Mamm*, are you hurt?"

"*Ach*, only my pride. My legs are numb from the ride."

They entered the house and Granny smelled apples, cinnamon and cloves. Sarah, Daniel's wife, was preparing the Thanksgiving meal to be served tomorrow. She was deposited on the green sofa and Daniel hovered over her. Jeb had concern etched into his brow. How embarrassing!

"Deborah, all you said about Doc Pal giving you a *gut* report at your check-up is true, *jah*? You wouldn't hide anything from me?"

Sarah had a mug of warm cocoa before her in no time. "My legs go numb on long trips. And it's cold out, *jah?*"

"*Danki*, Sarah." It marveled Granny once again that everyone in the family had chestnut brown hair except Sarah, a beautiful blonde, some gray peeking through. "So *wunderbar* to see *yinz*. Where's the other *kinner*? School?"

"Jacob and Jonathan are at their apprenticeship, and Ruby and May are in school."

"Does Ruby like teaching?"

"Loves it and the *kinner* love her."

"Six *kinner* keep *yinz* busy, *jah*?" Granny asked Sarah.

Sarah glance at Rachel. "Busy with many things."

Granny saw the worry on Sarah's face, but knew teenagers were more adventuresome. Her five boys had given her many sleepless nights. "I can help in the kitchen," Granny said, wanting to lift the mood. "Rachel, can you help me with pies? I do love to make them."

Rachel's cheeks turned crimson. "I, ah, have

chores."

Daniel rolled his eyes. "You do not. You'll help your *grossmammi*." He pulled her off to the far corner of the massive living room for a talking to. This is where they must have church when it was their turn. No need to take walls down, but plenty of room. Daniel built as big a house as he could afford because he wanted a dozen *kinner*, but so far only six and they'd been married for twenty years.

Sarah's parents were from Millersburg, so they settled here. "Sarah, will your folks be over for dinner tomorrow?"

"*Nee.* They don't make a big deal about Thanksgiving," she said, face pinched.

She knew that Fern and Matthew King were here for many Thanksgiving dinners. Were they having troubles? Or, did Fern still think she was second fiddle to her as a *grossmammi*? Granny dismissed the thoughts. She wasn't going to borrow trouble.

Able to cross the room hand in hand with Jeb, she went on tiptoes to give him a peck on the cheek. "I'm right as rain. Now, you and Daniel can go do your men talk. Let us women folk bake and chat."

Jeb's eyes lit up. "Daniel, let me see your new pond! And where's the fishing poles?"

"I got lunch all packed up and the poles are by the lake. We have a fishing hut with a woodstove now."

"Yippy," Jeb exclaimed, raising his hands.

"New pond?" Granny's brows rose. "Jebediah Weaver, did you know about this stocked pond?"

"*Jah.* Daniel wrote to tell me." He patted her head. "Now, now, Deborah, I didn't come out here to fish, if that's what you're thinking."

She pursed her lips. She knew her man. And he needed time to relax and fishing was his medicine. "Have a *gut* time love. Catch something big so we can add it to our Thanksgiving meal." Granny smiled at Sarah. "Men, they do march to a different drum than us womenfolk."

"I guess," Sarah moaned.

Granny found it suddenly very tense in the kitchen with the men gone. Was Daniel a buffer between Sarah and Rachel? How could she not see they were blessed to have each other's company? "I never had a *dochder*, you know. Always wanted one to teach baking, cooking and whatnot. So, Rachel, how many kinds of pies have you made here in this kitchen with your *mamm*?"

Rachel showed no emotion. "Too many. My *brieder* eat like pigs. The twins are the worst."

"They're fourteen," Sarah chided. "And growing like weeds."

"Well, why can't they help in the kitchen?" Rachel challenged. "English men cook. I see them on their shows when I clean over at the hotel."

Sarah slowly closed her eyes. "We said you could keep that job if you didn't watch TV."

"People keep them on all day," Rachel defended.

Granny didn't want to start this visit off on the wrong foot, but something needed nipped in the bud. "Rachel, did your doubts about being Amish start when you worked among the English? Did you watch TV?"

"*Nee.* It made me more thankful I was raised plain. But I like the money and freedom money brings. I'm tired of living like pioneers when we could live better if we had more money. And more modern conveniences. *And a car.*"

Sarah left the kitchen, mighty downcast. Granny followed her and soon found herself in the chilly enclosed porch in the rear of the house.

Visibly trembling, Sarah wiped tears with her apron. "*Mamm,* someone is influencing Rachel, but we don't know who. She gets mail with masculine handwriting, but no return address. The other day I found two-hundred dollars in Rachel's room."

"She gets paid from her work, *jah*?"

"And we're supposed to know about it. We all put our money into the pot to run this place. We're a family."

Granny took Sarah's hands. "Rachel said she wants to talk to me in private. Maybe she'll open up."

Sarah embraced Granny. "I'm so glad you're here. Not just to help me with a wayward *dochder*, but it's been too long since you've had an extended stay."

Granny knew that as hard as it was to be uprooted at her age, this was something she needed to do.

Chapter 2

Jeb near drooled upon entering Daniel's fishing cabin. Being so near the shop, he knew his son most likely could hear the fish call to him. A cozy Ben Franklin potbelly stove stood before the lone window, plankboard floors were glossed, and hickory Amish rockers were pinned into each corner. "It's only eight feet by eight feet?" Jeb asked with a wry grin. "Small enough for you and Sarah to come to but not the *kinner*?"

Daniel plopped into a rocker. "*Daed,* Sarah and I don't come out here together. Built it so she might, but she's never come inside. All that I wrote you about is wearing me out."

His son's letters hinted at marital problems, and Jeb was determined to help. "Your *Mamm* and I have had our differences. She never comes to my fishing hole." He leaned his head on his hand. "Go on. Tell me. Maybe I can help."

Daniel let out a mournful whistle, as if to say, "Where do I start?"

"Take your time. Now, Sarah looks *gut* but nervous. We never raised a *dochder* and I'm thinking Rachel has *yinz* worried?"

Daniel squinted. "*Yinz.* I forgot," he said, attempting to lighten the atmosphere. "Do you go down to Pittsburgh much?"

"Don't change the subject, Daniel. I'm not so old I can't keep track of things. Now, tell me what troubles you."

"Sarah. I don't have those…romantic feelings anymore. Sometimes…I find my eyes wandering…and I feel so sinful."

Jeb wasn't prepared for this, since Deborah had been his sweetheart since the day they married. Differences, for sure, but their love had never grown stale. *Stale.* That's what Deborah called her old bread and what she threw out to the birds. She baked bread twice a week to keep it fresh. And it was work. "Daniel, you need to work on your love for Sarah."

Daniel darted a puzzled look. "Work? Work on loving someone?"

"*Jah.* Things can get stale, you know."

"Have you and *Mamm* ever gotten…stale?"

He didn't want to lie, but neither did he want to paint a bed of roses of marriage. How he got Deborah Byler to marry him was still a wonder. She was so easy to love. "I spice things up sometimes. Get her a gift. Surprised her one time with sheep, of all things. But you know that."

"I've seen how you treat *mamm* and I've tried over the years, but like I said, the feelings aren't there. It's like she runs to her family before me. I'm not…first." He shrugged.

Jeb knew Daniel was his son with the tenderest of hearts. Sensitive to almost a fault. He recalled his wedding day. Not many Amish men wept through their vows, but Daniel was so teared up, the bishop had to pause to let him collect himself. Did he expect too much? "Daniel, you and Sarah need to talk. Tell her what you told me."

"What?" he exclaimed. "Isn't that mean?"

"Well, say it real gentle-like. Say that you love her, because you do. Love is a commitment, and you're committed, *jah*?"

"I suppose so."

"You suppose so?" Jeb boomed. "What kind of talk is that?"

Daniel closed his eyes as if in prayer. "*Daed*, I'm committed. I'm a *gut* Amish man."

Jeb had never heard this tone from Daniel. He may as well as said he was Amish out of obligation, but his heart was not in it. He recalled his scripture reading during the Thanksgiving to Christmas season to prepare his heart. "Remember my yearly ritual of reading Isaiah every year before Christmas? That book cleans me out. Just yesterday I was reading that God can hate the Sabbath if we're doing it out of obligation, our heart not in it. And I had to confess, as bishop, I dread going to *Gmay*. I know all the dirty laundry and find some of it as smelly as rotten fish. Had to get on my knees and ask God to give me a heart for the People. You need a new heart for Sarah."

Daniel's eyes met Jeb's. "You're such a *gut daed*. How'd you do it with us boys."

Jeb wiggled his eyebrows. "I was a trapper back in my youth. I know how to catch a fox." He reached over to hit Daniel's knee. "I outsmarted *yinz*."They rose and embraced, slapping each other's backs. Jeb knew now why they were asked to come for six weeks. Daniel and Sarah needed help in many ways.

~*~

By the end of the day, worn out, Granny plopped down on Jeb who sat in a stuffed chair in their bedroom. "Need a hug."

As usual, his arms enveloped her as he tossed his book on the floor. "Me, too. Our son's in such a state."

"Sarah is, too. Is Daniel being a *gut* husband? Is he helping her with Rachel?"

Jeb lifted Granny's prayer *kapp* and started to unpin her hair. "Sarah's always been a nervous one, like her *mamm*. She's pushing Daniel away."

Jeb had let her hair down on many occasions, but it was always an endearing act, and she fought the urge to turn and kiss him. "If a woman pushes her husband away, he needs to lure her in, like you and Daniel do your fish."

He chuckled. "What could Daniel use for bait?"

Granny knew from talking to so many women that being truly heard and understood by their mate was the lure. The lack of it caused distance. "Daniel needs to spend extra time with Sarah. She may not share her heart if it's been bottled up. He needs to really listen."

"Take her prayer *kapp* off and brush her hair like I'm doing?"

Granny's pulse quickened. "*Jah*, Jeb, that would be *gut*." She could hold back her love no longer. She jerked her head back for a kiss, but soon yelped in pain. The brush was soon a tangled mess in her long gray hair.

He kissed her soundly and then instructed her to hold still while he unraveled her locks. They were quiet a spell until there was a knock on their door. "Come in," Jeb said.

Sarah popped her head in. "Do you want some hot chocolate? Making popcorn, too." She flushed while she waited for their response, and then she apologized for interrupting.

"Interrupting?" Granny prodded. "Interrupting what? We're just two old crows up here winding down for the day. We'll catch up *gut* with the *kinner* tomorrow. Too bad they had to all work in the shop with Daniel, only time for a short dinner."

Sarah crossed the room, pressing her slender hands to her burning cheeks, taking a chair at the desk. "Do you always undo her hair, *Daed*?"

"Sometimes. Not every night."

Pitter-patter was soon heard as sleet hit the windows. "It might snow tonight," Sarah said. "I best be getting more logs in the stove."

"Daniel can do it," Jeb stated rather bluntly. "He takes care of the stove, or one of the boys, *jah*?"

"I like it," Sarah said. "Something about a crackling fire is cozy."

"Well, you go on down then," Granny said. "Tell the *kinner* we said good night."

Sarah nodded but hesitated. "How long have you two been married? Isn't your anniversary coming up?"

Jeb pursed his lips. "Only fifty."

"Only fifty?" Sarah gasped. "Did you get married in November? Is it your fiftieth wedding anniversary?"

"We married in spring," Granny cooed. "Right here in Millersburg where my family lived." Heaviness filled her. "All long past or moved on except…"

"Her *bruder*," Jeb said, smoothing her hair.

Tears welled in Granny's eyes. "What does it profit a man if he gains the world but lose his soul…"

"We're still praying for him, love. Have been now for nigh thirty years." He hugged her. "And he's not rich, if you ask me. We are. We're two peas in a pod."

Sarah blinked back tears. "I didn't know love could be so strong when you're…ripe in years."

"Old as dirt?" Jeb snickered. "We've had more time for love to grow. You and Daniel have many *gut* years ahead of you, Lord willing."

"With so many *kinner,* we barely speak," Sarah confessed. "And he's so busy with that rocker shop. The UPS driver comes nearly every day now to pick up orders."

"He's like our Roman," Granny informed. "The Weaver men are of pure German stock, you know. Work, work, work, and when not working, fish, fish, fish."

"That's not true," Jeb said as he started to laugh. "Those fish call to me, Deborah. Can't you hear them?"

Granny wrapped her arms around Jeb and laughed until she cried. This old joke got funnier the more he said it. He squeezed her and then they looked up to discover that Sarah had left the room. Granny leaned her head against Jeb's chest. "Sarah and Daniel don't have what we do."

~*~

Sarah ran to her room, holding her pounding heart. What she'd just witnessed, the pure love between husband and wife, she'd rarely experienced. Oh, in their early years of marriage, there was lots of romance, but she didn't have her teenage beauty now. Daniel was always fond of her hair, but now with it streaked with gray...

Her mind drifted off to her *Rumspringa*, her running around days. Several men took her home from Singings, but Daniel was the most persistent. Was she part of a cat and mouse game?

She shook her head. Such *ferhoodled* thoughts. She'd courted Daniel for two years before marriage, and he had plenty of time to call things off. *Nee*, they were happily married their first year, for sure. When Rachel came along, it was then that Daniel became distant. Or was it before? Or maybe it happened so slowly that they didn't realize it, but their romance and closeness had died.

I don't want a marriage like yours! Rachel had screamed. Was this at the heart of Rachel's discontent? A loveless home?

Shaking her head again, Sarah rose, smoothed her apron. Her mind was *ferhoodled* for sure and certain. Why such negative thoughts? Comparison. The Bible said it wasn't good to compare somewhere. It only led to envy, and how she envied Granny and Jeb. Did they have troubles while raising their boys? She'd ask them after Thanksgiving.

She marched to the door and down the stairs. After all, someone had to tend to the fire.

~*~

In the middle of the night, Granny woke with a start. "Bea? Come here, girl." Her eyes slowly adjusted to her surroundings. She wasn't at home and her dream wasn't true. Bea hadn't run off from Roman's house. She exhaled, cleansing the memory from her mind. She was not the same without her dog. Funny how she didn't know it until she was seventy what a treasure a little dog could be. Bea had a real calming effect on her as she slept at her feet during the winter.

She turned and closed her eyes, but the odd sounds of distant traffic rang in her ears. It was more congested here in Millersburg than Smicksburg. She lived at the end of a long dirt road back home; here she was in an Amish tourist hotspot and Daniel was a stop on many a tourist list. Daniel gave demonstrations of making Amish rockers and wood carvings. Would he be open for Black Friday? Is that what all the non-stop work was about? *Ach*, she hoped not. Emma Yoder's Quilt shop closed that day. Surely Daniel would close since they were visiting.

Her mind went back to her first knitting circle and her first Black Friday shopping spree with Fannie and the other girls. Fannie had seen a full-length mirror for the first time, and it was there that she discovered that she had a distorted body image. Always thinking she was fat due to her beautiful full face; she couldn't see her good figure in the mirror. Praise be, Fannie had come a long way, having reconditioned her mind. Many scriptures had Fannie memorized, especially, 'I am fearfully and wonderfully made.' Yes, God had made her, and He didn't make junk.

Now fully awake, she slipped out of bed. She knew that lighting the oil lamp would not awaken Jeb. When he was out, he was out. She tip-toed over to her dresser where she placed her new scented stationery and picked the paper with lilacs. She inhaled the aroma. Summertime. She yearned for it, but knew each season had its benefit.

She set her pen the paper to write:

Dear Fannie,

I can't sleep. I know you'll laugh, but I miss Bea at my feet. The hustle and bustle of Millersburg will take some getting used to. Car headlights flash on the walls all night. Don't folks sleep at night? Well, I suppose the English think the Amish odd for rising as early as four in the morning, the middle of the night to most of them.

Fannie, do you remember when you had such a low opinion of yourself? When you poked fun at yourself and acted all cheerful to hide your pain? My dear Fannie, I'm so proud of you. God's Word and the women at our knitting circle changed you. We build each other up, jah? We're stronger spun together.

Please pray for me. I'm fearful for my son and his wife's marriage. I'm sure it's nothing. I need to cast it on God, but I keep taking it back. I want to enjoy my grosskinner here but am feeling rather downtrodden. Maybe it's the long drive out. And I miss Smicksburg and my girls. Funny, flesh and blood kin don't have the heart ties like I have with you. As you know, you're like the daughter I never had.

Anyhow, pray for Sarah and Daniel. Daniel is as lovable as Jeb, but Sarah can't seem to accept him. She complained of him working and fishing too much. I fear Sarah's becoming a dripping faucet. What scripture can I tell Sarah to be mulling over? Nothing comes to mind right now. I know God's Word changed you so much, and I want this for Sarah and Daniel.

I love and miss you,

Granny.

~*~

The next morning, Granny got up at seven o'clock. Jeb was snoring soundly, so she let him be. She slipped on the new mint colored dress she'd sewn just for this occasion, a color approved by the *Gmay* in Ohio. *Ach*, she'd worn this color as a girl, and truth be told, since knitting so many varieties of colors, she was acquiring quite an eye for color combinations.

Once downstairs, she was greeted with a kiss by eight-year-old May and sixteen-year-old Ruby. "*Guder mariye* girls. I'm so glad to have Thanksgiving with *yinz*. Are you helping your *mamm* in the kitchen?"

"She's talking to Rachel and wants us to stay out for a few minutes," Ruby said in a knowing way. "They have lots of 'adult' talks."

Excitedly, May led Granny out on the enclosed back porch. "Look what came! Our shoeboxes!"

A pile of green and red cardboard was stacked up against the wall. Ruby took one and began assembling it. "See *Oma*, they make shoeboxes and we fill them for children all around the world who've never gotten a present."

Granny had seen these boxes in the Smicksburg Baptist Church, but she never thought to ask what they were for. Her heart swelled that her *grosskinner* were so eager to help those in need. "How will you get the boxes to the children?"

May stood on tip toes, clapping her hands. "This is the fun part. Amish businesses are open all over Holmes County to pack the boxes. We have a party and it's so fun. *Daed* said we could be one of the fifty Amish stores to participate." She lifted her arms. "After five years of asking, he said yes!"

Granny chuckled. "Now, now. Your *daed* is busy and maybe he needed time to think about it."

"There's five buses going to North Carolina, Amish and Mennonites all together, to help fill more boxes, but I'm too little to go," May said with a pout.

"Land sake," Granny sputtered. She'd been ridiculed by some for mixing with the English too much, helping at Forget-Me-Not Manor, a home for single moms, and the soup kitchen at the Baptist Church. She didn't want Ruby and May to see her puzzlement, but it would be something she'd have to ponder and discuss with Jeb. The Amish in Holmes County were so plentiful and so they mixed with the English more, she supposed. Amish worked for English businesses, some having cell phones in their pockets.

Granny heard a crash. What on earth?

Granny ran to the kitchen. "What's going on?"

Sarah and Rachel were busy sweeping up broken glass. "I dropped a pie plate," Rachel said. "Had butter on my hands and it slipped."

Sarah fired Rachel daggers, but bit her lip, saying nothing.

"Here Rachel, you give me that broom and I'll you get back to those pies you're making. Smells mighty *gut* in here. Sorry I slept in."

Sarah's face was too flushed, but she forced a smile. "You're our guest. Go on out and relax in the living room."

Granny blinked in disbelief. She was the pie maker of Smicksburg, not an ancient fossil who rocked her day away. "I want to be helpful."

Rachel rolled her eyes. "She thinks you'll be like me and make a mess."

"Rachel, that's not true."

Daniel came through the utility door, arms full of firewood. He kissed Sarah's cheek and briskly went toward the massive woodstove in the living room. Granny observed the kitchen, as it looked too modern. A refrigerator and stove that appeared to be English. "Sarah, don't you cook with wood?"

"*Ach*, we have natural gas for all our appliances."

Granny's new Pioneer Princess stove sat back home, calling to her, like Jeb's fish did him. "I got a Pioneer Princess stove from Lehman's and I like how nice and cozy it makes the whole kitchen in the winter. Bakes real evenlike too."

"Well, we're allowed to have natural gas and I like it," Sarah informed curtly.

Rachel frowned at her *mamm*. "*Oma's* allowed to have natural gas, too. She just prefers wood."

The two glared at each other and Granny could take it no more. She clapped her hands. "What on earth is going on? Mary, Mary, quite contrary, how does your garden grow?"

They stared, jaws hanging.

"That's a line from *The Secret Garden*, a book our knitting circle read."

Rachel's chin quivered and ran to embrace Granny. "I'm sorry. I have been contrary lately. Lots on my mind."

Granny rubbed Rachel's back, her lips pursed, eyes intent on Sarah. "We all can be contrary at times."

Rachel slipped an arm through Granny's. "I'm so glad you're here. All those letters about your knitting circle are fun to read. How is...Fannie, Ella, Ruth...I can't remember all their names."

"You know they all didn't want to come to my circle at first. They were hiding problems, some small, some as big as a barn. But we were brave enough to be transparent and realized we're stronger together. I have to say all the major issues the women had are resolved, but you never know what tomorrow will bring."

"Do girls my age go to knitting circles?" Rachel asked.

"Of course. Becca was fourteen when she came. She's married now."

"How long ago was this?" Sarah asked. "Several years back?"

"*Nee.* She's one of those rare girls who are mature enough at seventeen to marry."

A smile spread across Rachel's face that she could not hide. "I'm twenty!"

"Do you have a beau?" Granny asked. And then she realized Rachel wasn't baptized into the Amish church yet. "Of course, you're only allowed to be engaged to a baptized member and you must be baptized, so it'll be a while, *jah*?"

Rachel's chestnut brown eyes danced and whispered in Granny's ear. "He's *wunderbar gut* to me."

Rachel wanted to confide something to her, but now wasn't the time. "Can we talk later? Tonight?"

"*Jah*, that would be *gut*."

Granny cupped Rachel's lovely face. "You're a real treasure, Rachel. A gem that needs to be won by a *gut* man. Don't let a charmer fool you."

She was still glowing. "He's not," she muttered in hushed tones."

Daniel entered the kitchen and plopped down on his seat at the head of the table. "I could have pumpkin pie for breakfast. What do you say, Sarah?

Amish eat pies for breakfast."

"*Gut* idea, *Daed*," Rachel chimed in, seeming much more at ease with her *daed* present. "We have four pies almost ready to come out of the oven. And, we bought Cool Whip."

Daniel rubbed his hands together. "Yum."

"I'm saving the pumpkin pies for dinner," Sarah informed. "After we eat the turkey."

"*Ach*, honey, you know how much I love pumpkin pie. Bought pumpkin whoopie pies over at the bakery the other day. Hid them so the *kinner* don't find them."

Granny chuckled. "I hide Christmas cookies from Jeb."

Sarah remained mum but appeared mighty agitated. When the timer rang that the pies were done, Rachel sliced her *daed* a quarter of the pie and made a mountain of Cool Whip. "Here you go. Big enough?"

"*Jah*, for my first piece," Daniel quipped. "*Danki*, Rachel."

"Can I talk to Daniel in private?" Sarah asked frigidly.

Granny and Rachel nodded in unison, leaving the room.

"When are you going to tell them?" Sarah blurted.

"About what?" Daniel asked, hands up as if under arrest.

Sarah was tired of going around this mountain once again. She recalled the Israelites in the wilderness, having to roam around for forty years. *Forty years.* "What the doctor told you."

"Sarah, you fret too much. Maybe it's you who needs a doctor."

She knew what he was thinking. Menopause. Hormones gone haywire. "I saw the doc last month and I'm fine."

"And I'm not?"

"You are borderline diabetic and will be using a pin someday if you don't lay off the sweets."

Daniel gingerly rose and went to embrace his wife. "You fret too much. What happened to my sunshine girl?"

She wiggled out of his arms. "Sunshine girl? You haven't called me that in ages."

"Well, I miss that girl. How about we go on some dates? My parents can watch the *kinner*. Hold down the fort, like the English say."

Sarah's heart raced. She'd prayed just last night about their marriage. Was this an answer? "You have projects lined up until spring. How will you get away? How can we afford it?"

Again, he neared her and cupped her cheeks. "*Jah.* Can't afford not to."

"What does that mean?" Sarah challenged.

"Honey, you know how birds migrate in certain patterns. They practice, you know. All those blackbirds that swoop in, covering the yard the *kinner* are fascinated with? They land for a rest. A rest from practicing."

Sarah always considered Daniel a chip off Jeb's block, but here was Deborah speaking. That woman loved birds and what they taught her. So, Daniel thought they needed time alone to rest? Why? So they could talk? "Okay. Daniel, I'll go if you don't ignore what the doctor said. You need to lay off the sweets."

Their eyes locked. Sarah thought she saw a spark. Was it her imagination? Or was it that she hadn't seen it in so long, she noticed it? Her mind raced as to where they would go. Did they have spare money? *Ach,* she fretted too much. Maybe she needed to be in a knitting circle. Was life easier shared with other women? If so, she needed to carve out some time to do just that.

~*~

The Thanksgiving dinner was perfect. Sarah made the traditional meal, and May recited writings of the Pilgrims and how they would have starved if Squanto hadn't shown them how to plant corn. The *kinner* were lively, the twins going on about their apprenticeship, eager to talk about woodworking. Wood was indeed in the Weaver bones, Granny knew. She wondered how Roman was today and her two sons in Montana and the one who planned to move clear out to Maine for cheap land. She was thankful that Roman lived next door and Daniel was only a three-hour drive.

As she ate, she kept thinking of her knitting girls.

Was Fannie getting along with her *mamm*? Did Ella and Ruth share a meal together? Being best friends and sisters-in-law, she reckoned they were. She imagined the Smicksburg Baptist Church dinner who served a turkey dinner to those in need. Would they miss her pumpkin pies? And was Suzy going to keep her promise to not open on Black Friday, like she said? She wondered what tomorrow would bring to this hustling bustling tourist town.

"Daniel, you'll be closed tomorrow, *jah*? You don't want to attract those customers who are in a rush for you to make them something by Christmas."

All eyes landed on her, some wide eyed, some squinting. Daniel cleared his throat. "Sarah will keep you company, *Mamm*. She wants to go to Walmart. She's always first in line since the English sleep in so late."

Granny gasped. "I've been Black Friday shopping and nearly got trampled. You know, some Amish close their stores because of all the pushy customers."

Daniel steepled his fingers. "*Mamm*, there's ten-times as many Amish stores here as back home. Lots of competition with other rocker makers."

Jeb sat erect. "I have an idea. Daniel, how about I work in the rocker shop and you take Sarah out shopping?"

Daniel was a deer in headlights. Sarah got up to

replenish mugs with hot apple cider.

"*Gut* idea, Jeb," Granny cheered. "Jeb and Roman crank out rockers mighty fast. It's a wonder to watch."

"I could teach the boys a thing or two," Jeb added.

"*Grossmammi*, can we bake cookies tomorrow if the boys are in the shop?" Ruby asked. "I want to make a big gingerbread house to take to school for my students."

Granny said yes but kept her gaze on her son and daughter-in-law. "Well, I think it's settled, *jah*? You two go out for the day. Let us have the *grossskinner* to ourselves."

Rachel, who was sitting next to Granny clapped her hands. "*Gut* idea."

Daniel sheepishly looked at Sarah. "Is there some place you'd like to go? Surely not Walmart."

Sarah was near beaming. "We could go out to dinner. I agree with *Mamm*. Black Friday shopping isn't worth getting a few sales."

Granny felt like she was witnessing a tiny miracle. Sarah was melting right in front of Daniel.

Chapter 3

Jeb was proud of Jonathan and Jacob's carpentry skills. As he put a hickory strip into a vice, he noticed Benjamin was over the top happy. Dreamy eyed like he was in love. In love at nineteen. What could be better. He motioned for him to come near, out of hearing range of Jonathan and Jacob.

"Need help?" Benjamin asked.

"What's her name?" Jeb asked. "Hope she's a *gut* Amish girl."

"What girl? Who said I had a girl?"

"Your face did. I know the look. I had that look and still do sometimes, I reckon. Folks say I still act like a schoolboy around your *grossmammi*."

Benjamin pulled up two chairs. "Here, *Opa*. We need to rest."

"You need to talk, you mean." Jeb winked. "And it's about that girl of yours."

Benjamin leaned over and twiddled his thumbs. "I don't know, *Opa*. I'm only nineteen, but I found the right Amish girl. You know I'm baptized and so is she."

"And now you want to get married, of course. Well, when will I meet her?"

Benjamin took a deep breath. "*Mamm* and *Daed* don't know her yet."

"And why is that?"

He twisted his lips to one side. "*Mamm* thinks I'm seeing a girl from our *Gmay*. Mary tells everyone she's going to marry me some day."

Jeb knew Benjamin was holding back. Surely, he could tell his parents he won't marry Mary but is keen on someone else. "What aren't you saying?"

"*Opa*, maybe you can tell my parents I want to marry a…widow…four years older than me."

Seeing Benjamin married was one thing, but a father? "Any *kinner*?"

"*Jah,* a two-year-old boy. Real cute kid. He's lots of fun."

"Raising *kinner* isn't fun at times, Benjamin. It's downright hard work. How long has this woman been a widow? And why would she go courting with such a young guy?"

"I begged her. She thought I was *ferhoodled*, so she let me muck out her horse barn in exchange for pie."

Jeb hooted. "*Gut* exchange on her part. So, you went over and became friends?"

"*Jah,* real fast-like. When she realized she loved me, she stopped seeing me. She thought I needed to grow up. Court other girls. But I told her I've courted plenty. No one compares to her."

"How long a widow?"

"*Ach,* a year. Her husband fell into the silo. Horrible accident, but Heather recovered right quick. We move on, *jah*?"

This didn't sound right to Jeb. He wondered if the woman wore black still, as was their custom. Was Benjamin a rebound? "Benjamin, give it time. Two years at least. The woman must be in grief. She may be lonely and you're *gut* company, easy to talk to. If she's the right girl, time will go by right quick."

Benjamin crossed his arms. "She wants to get married sooner than later."

"It doesn't matter what she wants, it's better to do what is wise. Now, wait at least a year. She'll need to have at least two years to grieve her husband. An illness gives someone time to prepare, but an accident is a shock to the system. It's traumatic. Be kind to...what's her name?"

"Heather."

"Be kind to Heather but give her time to heal. She may see things differently in a year when she comes out of her grief."

Benjamin slumped. "That's not very encouraging."

"It's the truth, though. Would you have me give you anything but?"

~*~

Granny smelt pumpkin spices wafting around the

kitchen as three pumpkin pies baked in the oven. "We'll take one of these to the church down the road having that dinner for those in need, *jah*?"

Rachel, Ruby and May smiled and nodded. But Rachel had been hankering all morning to have a word in private. "Ruby and May, you two finish cleaning the kitchen while I have a talk with Rachel." The girls were very obliging and soon Granny and Rachel found themselves in the living room sitting on matching Amish rockers. "Did your *daed* make these? Have them near each other to talk, like *Opa* and me?"

"*Jah,* he did. But Ruby and May usually sit in these chairs." Rachel gripped the hickory armrests. "*Oma,* I have something to tell you and since you're so open to Outsiders, having all those *Englishers* in your knitting circle, I know you'll understand. My beau isn't Old Order Amish but goes to a non-denominational church. You'll love him."

Granny pressed her hand to her heart. "What? Not Amish?"

Rachel's eyes grew round. "In your letters you always write about your knitting circle and what you've learned from friends from the Baptist church. Jared is more committed a Christian than many Amish men I know."

Granny reached for Rachel's hand. "*Ach,* you were raised to be Amish."

"And on my *Rumspringa* I discovered a lot and don't hold to the old ways. *Oma*, I don't want to offend you and list all the things I disagree with, but let's just say the list is too long for me. So, I won't be getting baptized and truth be told, I'm engaged."

Granny bowed her head to shoot up a quick prayer for guidance. *What should I say? Rumspringa* was to make the youth realize what they'd be missing if they didn't join the church. It was driven into an Amish child's mind that it's better not to take the vow than to take it and break it. If broken, the church member would be under the shunning.

"Well, Rachel, you know I'm plain through and through. But you're following the teachings of the church. Your *Rumspringa* settles matters in your heart. Of course, your parents will think they didn't raise you right and so on, but…I wish you much joy in your marriage, dear one."

Rachel let the tears flow. "*Ach, Oma*, I'm so glad you're here. We can tell them tonight."

"Why the rush? Why not wait until after Christmas?" Granny asked. "Your parents will take this hard."

"I've always wanted a Christmas wedding."

"Christmas?" Granny could hardly believe her ears.

"*Jah*. It's something Jared and I discussed. We've been planning the wedding and pulling our money together. We have quite a bit in the bank for a honeymoon."

Granny could not grasp it all. "Are you saying this Christmas?"

"*Jah,* I am. I hope you can convince *Mamm* and *Daed* to come. I have a feeling *Mamm* won't."

Granny yearned to hold her little Bea right now. How the dog calmed her. She felt too tongue-tied to talk. "Honey, I'm going to ask you to do something for *Opa* and me. Please don't be so set on a Christmas wedding this year. It's too sudden. If you eat a whole pie at one sitting, you'll get indigestion, *jah*? This is a lot for your parents to…digest." Granny wiped her brow with a trembling hand.

"You think we should wait until next Christmas? I can't," Rachel moaned.

"I'm saying it's too soon. Why not get married in spring, like *Opa* and I did?"

"Because I want a Christmas wedding."

Granny felt like she was getting nowhere. "Why Christmas?"

"Because the snow looks so pretty." Rachel clasped her hands. "We'll run out in the snow for pictures and let my long veil blow in the wind."

Long veil? Granny wanted to scream. *It's all vanity!* But she knew Rachel was determined. "Let me tell you something. The best time for snow is February. I get the most birds at my feeders during February because they're so hungry and cold. How about February and tell your parents after Christmas?"

Rachel stared as if in a trance. She slowly said,

"*Oma*, you're a genius. Valentine's Day! We can have our wedding on Valentines' Day."

Granny smiled. "*Gut* day. It's my birthday."

"*Jah,* it is. The perfect day. *Danki, Oma* and *jah,* I won't say anything."

Granny felt like a wet noodle. She rose to make a pot full of peppermint tea. *Gut* for the nerves.

~*~

That night, Granny and Jeb retired to their room earlier than usual. Granny had a hankering to crochet and Jeb wanted to catch up on the latest edition of *Pennsylvania Field and Stream* magazine. Snuggling under the wedding ring patterned quilt, Granny realized she made a mistake in her crochet and started to tear all the stitches out with a huff. "Can't concentrate."

"Me, neither," Jeb sighed, dropping his magazine.

"What's the matter Jeb?"

"*Ach,* Benjamin imagines he's in love. Told him to wait a while to make sure she's the right one."

"*Jah, gut* advice. Rachel has a special fellow and I told her the same." Her chest tightened just thinking of Rachel leaving the Amish and she had a coughing fit.

Jeb pat her back. "Catching a cold?"

"*Nee*, it's my nerves. Jeb, I need to tell you that Rachel will be leaving the Amish for a *gut* Christian man. Wants to get married in a wedding dress and veil. So hard to swallow, but we know that it's better this way. My *bruder* wouldn't be shunned if he'd followed his heart. He was a reluctant convert."

"*Ach,* Rachel's headstrong, not your typical Amish woman," Jeb said.

"She takes after me, *jah*? If we hadn't met, I may not be Amish."

They laced their hands together. "I'm glad you moved to Smicksburg to live with your Aunt Mary. She fixed it that we'd run into each other quite a bit." He snapped his fingers. "Maybe we can do the same for Rachel before it's too late."

Granny chuckled. "Are you trying to be a matchmaker?"

"I learned from the best," he said in jest. "I don't know. When I see Rachel, Freeman Yoder comes to mind. They'd make a *gut* match."

Out of the yarn strewn across her lap, Granny began twisting to create a ball. "Jeb, God puts people together. Truth be told, deep down, I never did see Rachel making her vow to the People. I asked her not to say anything to her parents until after Christmas. So, don't be saying anything."

"Deborah Weaver, you're losing your spunk. Don't you think we could have Freeman Yoder come out for a visit for some reason?" Jeb raised his hands. "I got an idea. There's money to be had in furniture repair and Freeman does all that, plus he canes chairs the old-fashioned way. He could teach Daniel like he did Roman. Come on. What do you say?"

"I've lost my spunk? You think I'm old?"

"Now, now. I didn't mean that. You just don't want to 'see people happy together' like you always say, another way of saying 'matchmaking' in my book."

Granny didn't want this entire visit to be overshadowed by her *bruder's* shunning but learning that he lived five miles away gave her a yearning to see him. She couldn't shake this feeling deep down that he needed help. "Jeb, my *bruder's* shunning still smarts quite a bit. Give me a few days to get back to myself."

He wrapped an arm around her. "I've been thinking about him. Like we should try to speak reason before he goes before the Lord."

"Me, too. But we're not supposed to talk to him."

"His shunning was long ago. We talk to shunned Amish now, just don't share a meal or exchange money and whatnot. Anyhow, I am the bishop back home and you're under my care. I'm supposed to lead the sheep gently and I say let's loosen your ban a bit."

"*Ach,* Jeb, I don't want to get special privileges because I'm the bishop's wife."

"*Nee*, you've never interfered and for that I'm grateful. But your *bruder's* shunning in my estimation was too harsh. I say we make a visit."

Granny had longed to see this *bruder* who she was

closest to for so many years. Would he recognize her? She hugged Jeb and kissed his cheek. "*Danki* Jeb. I hope Rachel's fellow is as sweet and understanding as you."

Jeb wiggled his brows. "I'm going to write to Freeman Yoder. Daniel needs to learn some new skills."

Granny laughed. Jeb was turning into a matchmaker. *Ach,* she couldn't' wait to tell her girls back home.

~*~

The next morning, Granny couldn't believe she slept in until seven o'clock. These old bones! She tried to nudge Jeb and soon found he was up, fully clothed, reading his Bible, rocking contently in an Amish rocker. "Why didn't you wake me up?"

"You've looked too tired lately. Wanted you to sleep." He yawned. "Kept me up half the night, though."

"I did? How's that?"

"Calling for Bea. Talking to her. Telling her to come up on the bed or she'll be cold. Talking in your sleep again and that tells me you're stressed."

She had to acknowledge that she was. As happy as she was to see her brother, she dreaded it. And she didn't know if Jeb sensed the tension between Sarah and Daniel when they got home yesterday, but women's intuition told her their outing was a flop.

She made haste to pin up her hair, attire herself in her Amish garb and make her way downstairs to help Sarah in the kitchen. And pans were clanging. "Is something wrong?" she timidly asked.

Sarah rolled her eyes. "Rachel and I quarreled again. She's so careless. Left an envelope from that man on the coffee table. Is she trying to give me a heart attack?"

Granny's brows rose. "Would the Rachel we both know do such a thing? *Nee.* She got careless. Jeb leaves his magazines around the house. No one's perfect, *jah*?"

"But, I'm afraid. A strange man giving her money? Why? I do read the paper, you know. Rachel could fall for a bad man."

Granny poured herself a mug of coffee and sliced a piece of pumpkin cheese pie and settled at the table. "Rachel and I talked when you and Daniel went out yesterday. She confided in me about something and let's just say that I know she's not in danger. This man and Rachel are working toward a goal."

Sarah's countenance brightened. "Someone's proposed. *Ach,* I never thought Rachel would accept any of the Amish fellows, but she has. Praise be. *Ach,* I'm so glad she could tell you. You two were always close. We're like oil and water at times."

Granny tasted the delicious pie and coffee and hoped for a quiet morning. "That happens sometimes."

Sarah gawked. "*Mamm*, are you okay? You're usually full of advice."

She lifted heavy lids. "Do you want some?"

Sarah got herself pie and coffee and sat across from Granny. "You never had a *dochder*, so maybe you don't understand how hard it can be. Girls are more emotional. Too emotional at times."

She cringed at Sarah's sharp tongue. Had she forgotten that Granny had a stillborn *dochder*? She supposed Sarah had forgotten. *Ach, why is the past haunting me?* It was her *bruder* living so near.

"No advice?"

"*Ach, Jah,* I do. Be a *gut* listener. Remember how the Bible says to be quick to listen, slow to speak and slow to become angry. Make special times for you and Rachel. Go for a walk or have a baking frolic, just the two of you. *Yinz* will bond over doing something together."

Putting a hand up in protest, Sarah shook her head. "I've tried that. We tend to fight."

Granny pondered this. They *were* oil and water. "Maybe do a group activity with a small circle of friends."

"Like your knitting circle?"

"*Jah,* like a knitting circle, although we crochet and embroider quilt squares too. Why not have a quilting bee once a week."

Leaning her cheek on her hand, Sarah grew pensive. "What are you making with that yarn you brought?"

"Well, nothing yet. I started to crochet the pattern Marge gave me, but I keep messing up. Right now, it's just a ball of yarn."

"I like how your fingers move when you crochet. I kind of have a desire to learn."

Granny's heart warmed. "I'd love to teach you to crochet. Invite two friends and along with Rachel, we'll have five. A *gut* number."

"I'll ask my *mamm* and sister," Sarah said. "They'll be stopping by today.

Granny was truly delighted. "*Wunderbar.* It's nice that you have family nearby. There's lots more Amish in Holmes County than Western Pennsylvania."

"*Jah,* we have a larger population now than Lancaster, can you believe it? But it comes with a price. The large number of tourists makes many an Amish man greedy of gain, not content with what they have. Some become workaholics, you know."

Sarah's tone implied that she was talking about her husband, but Granny dismissed the thought. Her mind was on yarn and the prospect of a knitting circle. "What would you like to make at knitting circle, or crochet circle?"

"Well, if Rachel's courting, she'll be getting engaged soon and planning a wedding. Maybe we could make doilies for wedding presents." She clasped her hands in delight. "Or we could make doilies to sell at market."

Sarah just said that Amish men were eager to make money from tourist, but here she was wanting to make something for tourists. "Sarah, back home, we knit for charity. Once we made a quilt for a wedding, but usually we knit for charity. Keeps our greed in check. Now, we do sell things from time to time, but the groups purpose is fellowship, not greedy gain."

Sarah flushed. "Of course. We all need to be on guard for that. Always trying to make money, I suppose. With a wedding coming up, we'll need to pinch pennies. It's the bride's family who hosts and pays."

Jeb came in the kitchen. "Any pie left?" he asked as he eyed the pie on the counter. "*Gut*, one big piece!"

"You're chipper today," Granny said. "But then you always get your wings in the morning."

Jeb sat next to Granny. "*Jah,* I do."

"Wings?" Sarah questioned.

"'They that wait upon the Lord shall renew their strength, they shall rise up with wings like an eagle, they shall walk and not grow weary, run and not faint.' That's one of my favorite Bible verses." He licked his lips. "This pie is so *gut*."

"Jeb, how many pieces have you had? How much Cool Whip?"

He grinned. "Deborah Weaver, are you saying I'm gaining weight?"

"*Nee*, old beanpole. Just that Doc Pal told you that we Amish eat too many sweets."

He sighed audibly and slid his plate toward her. "Go on. You can finish it."

"*Danki*, Jeb. I was hoping for another slice."

Jeb rose. "Sarah, where's your phone shanty?"

"*Ach,* Daniel has a cell phone to use only for business. You can use his."

Jeb held on to the table. "Cell phone? My son has a cell phone?"

"To use only for business."

Granny met his gaze. "We're not back home, Jeb."

"*Jah,* I suppose not. Well, I'm going to make that call to Freeman, since he is a free man."

Granny chuckled. "*Ach,* Jeb, you do what you need to do."

Jeb near skipped out of the room.

"Now, what was that about?" Sarah asked.

Granny couldn't tell of Jeb's plan to bring one of Smicksburg's most eligible Amish bachelors out to meet Rachel. Sarah thought her beau was Amish and would discourage it. "Jeb has a friend back home who taught Roman how to repair antique furniture and cane chairs. He'd like Freeman to come out and teach Daniel."

Sarah cocked an eyebrow. "It must be Daniel's idea. He and Roman write like clockwork. Another skill to learn so he can spend more time in the shop.

Greedy gain."

Granny winced. Sarah's disrespect for her son was dreadful. This was not the Sarah that married her dear son.

~*~

After wetting his whistle with another cup of coffee, Jeb headed over to the rocker shop on the side of the house. He was proud of his son for building this white clapboard house, just like the one he grew up in, and the woodshop was so like the one he built along with his son, Roman, he felt right at home. Except for the sound of traffic and many tourists. He felt mighty blessed to live on a quarter mile dirt road off the main highway in Smicksburg.

Sometimes he wondered if Daniel was homesick for Western Pennsylvania. He always had Phillip nearby, but he moved further west, out to Indiana for more land. Why Phillip hadn't come back home to Smicksburg still smarted, but he'd never hold his sons back. No, they had their lives to live and he wouldn't be getting in God's way, trying to manipulate or change their minds.

Entering the shop, he was surprised that his son seemed so cozy with the pretty blonde woman about his age. She was ordering an Amish rocker for her mother for Christmas, but something seemed mighty fishy. That twinkle in Daniel's eyes. How he wished he'd look at Sarah that way.

He cleared his throat, and the two stared at him,

startled. "Daniel, when you're done taking that order, I need to ask you something."

"Sure *Daed.* Melody and I are done. Just talking."

Melody extended a hand to Jeb. "I'm Melody Kane. I come here all the time. Can't get enough of Amish stores."

"Well, this is a workshop, not a store. Lots of nice shops for women in these parts."

Melody stroked her shoulder length silky blonde hair. "I'm an antique dealer and am always wanting to learn more about how furniture is built. Daniel should be a teacher, he's so knowledgeable."

Daniel was blushing to beat the band. Jeb felt defeated. He'd had such a peaceful morning, waiting on God to get his wings, but they were falling off but quick.

"Daniel, I need to talk to you. In private."

Again, Melody stroked her hair, arching her neck like a cat. "I'll stop by again soon."

Jeb had it. He needed his fishing pole and spun around and darted out the door. Spitting mad, he marched to the fishing shed, shaking all over. And not from the cold.

He grabbed some kindling and wood in the corner of the little house and got a fire going mighty quick. "Lord, I'm too old for this. Everywhere I go is *stress.* Stress in the church, and now stress here." He paced across the eight-foot room, which allowed him four steps at best.

Inhaling the scent of burning wood always calmed him, and he took a seat in one of the rockers. He closed his eyes, mulling over and over what he just witnessed. Daniel had told him he had a wandering eye, so he had reached out for help. *Ach, Lord, Amish men know not to be alone with women.*

Soon Daniel opened the door, ushering in a cold wind. "*Daed,* what are you doing in here? You looked so angry at Melody."

"Sit down right now!" Jeb bellowed.

Daniel obeyed and Jeb bit his lip, not sure what to say. Speak the truth in love, the Bible said. Could he do it in a loving way right now?

"Go on *Daed,* if you have something to say."

Jeb leaned over, biding for time. He didn't want to accuse Daniel of wrong if he was too blind to see that that Melody woman was flirting with him. The image of her low-cut shirt disgusted him. It was cold outside, for Pete's sake. "Daniel, you do realize that woman was flirting with you, *jah?*"

"What? *Nee,* she just likes to come visit and ask questions about the Amish. She's writing a book about us and wants to get the facts right."

"So, do you talk to her a lot?"

Daniel shrugged. "Maybe she'll stop in twice a month. Depends on what's going on with her book."

"And why doesn't she talk to Sarah?" Jeb challenged.

Daniel seemed puzzled. "Well, you heard her. She's an antique dealer and wants to know more about wood."

Jeb sprang up and paced again. "What does woodworking have to do with antiques?"

"Well, she can't tell if she has a solid piece made of wood or if it's cheap veneer. So, she brings in a drawer or something and I tell her. *Daed,* why are you so upset?"

Jeb opened the pot belly stove and threw in a stick. "Son, you never did think yourself handsome if I recollect right. So, you don't know that women are attracted to you. Does telling me that you've developed a wandering eye have something to do with Melody?" He asked, neck craning. "She flirts with you."

Daniel bowed his head. "She's in a bad marriage, *Daed.* She said I give her hope that men still act decent."

This was worse than Jeb thought. His son was paying attention to this woman's emotional needs while his marriage was wilting from lack of water and sunshine. "Daniel, you have an emotional attachment to that woman, it's clear to see. And most affairs start with emotional attachments. You need to cut her completely out of your life."

"I confess. She's the one that I've struggled with; started to compare Sarah to her. But, *Daed,* Sarah is so critical of me. Our day out yesterday was a disaster. You don't know what it's like."

Jeb didn't know, that was true. Deborah had always been so supportive and kind. But Sarah hadn't been. "Daniel, what happened to Sarah? She seems depressed or overly anxious."

Daniel threw his hands up. "Rachel's *Rumspringa* has been hard on her. She thinks she's a bad *mamm* deep down."

"Does she blame you? Think it's your fault that Rachel has never been baptized and leans towards fancy things?"

A lightbulb seemed to go off in Daniel's mind. He slowly turned to his *daed*. "Maybe she does. Raising these teenagers has been a challenge."

Jeb leaned his head back on the rocker. "Okay, we're getting somewhere. Confession is *gut*. It cleans us out. But you must turn from your sin. Flee from evil, the Bible says. Pursue that which is right, just, holy. Now, you can't see Melody anymore. If she comes to the shop, you send her over to Sarah. Women minister to women. If she has a problem, let Sarah help her. As for your marriage, you need to confess to Sarah any shortcomings. Your *mamm* and I do this all the time. Like I said, confession is *gut* for the soul and relationships.

The wooden floor creaked as Daniel rocked. "*Danki*, *Daed*. Wish you lived here. Wish I could be as *gut* a *daed* as you were to us boys."

A lump too large to swallow formed in Jeb's

throat. He tried to talk but failed. He sat quietly, waiting on God to give him back his wings. Eagle's wings.

Chapter 4

Dear Granny,

I wrote this as soon as your letter arrived. Do you know I kissed it? I miss you so.

I feel mighty proud in a gut way that you're asking me to pray and share scripture to help your daughter-in-law. I know scripture changed me. But it seems like what Sarah needs is correction. Like she needs to 'put on kindness,' like the Bible says to do. And her mind needs to see the best in her husband. Her tongue can destroy him. You know how it says in the Book of James that the tongue is a small part of our body but can do a lot of damage. A spark can set a barn on fire, like you know. Have her ponder James 3:8-12.

I also like the part about a spring can't bring forth fresh and salty water. Now, I'm not saying I'm perfect or anything like that. I fail a lot. But I try to bring pure spring water into my marriage. Salty water kills fish.

Your pond is fed by that spring of yours. Could you imagine Jeb getting up one day and find his pond salty? Nee, it couldn't happen because he'd take care of his fishing hole. Nee, it would be from neglect, don't you think? Like he didn't care and gave up on his fishing, which we know will never happen.

Am I making sense? Hope so.

I went to visit your grosskinner. They cut out snowflakes again and sang their snowflake song. I just love them. They're happy to have Bea with them, but I can tell that dog misses you. Or, maybe I miss you and it made me think she misses you. Like I'm imagining things.

We started a knitting circle and are changing houses. We're reading Little Women because the March daughters' miss their Daed, being away as a chaplain in the Civil War, and we know how they feel. Only our marme is gone! There's a lot of Christmas in Little Women, too. Not the materialistic Christmas many English have, but the real humble type, giving to the poor Hummel family and whatnot.

Well, I need to tend to some chores. I'll write a longer letter later.

Love you like a mamm!

Fannie

~*~

Jeb returned to the fishing cabin with a pen and writing tablet. He knew for sure and certain that Freeman Yoder was to be here for more than one purpose. The twenty-seven-year-old bachelor had such outstanding character, he could be an example to his son to refresh his memory of Old Order Amish unspoken rules. Men ministered to men, women to women, for starters. Jeb had outright seen his son flirt and still shook his head in dismay. Freeman had ample opportunity to flirt, being single and all, yet he seemed to be waiting for that right girl. Like he'd cast the whole matter on God and wasn't worried about settling down and having a family.

Jeb scratched his cheek and chuckled. His wife was wrong. He could play matchmaker and he was sure once Freeman came, Rachel's eyes would be off her fiancé. She'd see his shortcomings compared to Freeman. As he recalled, when Rachel came to visit for a few weeks three winters ago, Freeman had stopped by most unexpectedly, asking Roman if he'd needed help with caning chairs. But, then again, it was Christmas time, and maybe Roman had asked for help. But Freeman knew Rachel was out here and if he showed up, he might be interested. *Jah,* the more he thought about it, Freeman seemed mighty keen on Rachel. How could Deborah not see it?

Dear Freeman,

Hope you had a gut Thanksgiving if you celebrated the holiday. With so many Amish working for the English, many have the day off and have a turkey dinner. The food here was mighty gut. Rachel prepared lots of pies and has such a way with baking. You remember Rachel, jah? She's the pretty grossdochder who comes and visits us. Funny how she still isn't married.

Anyhow, my son Daniel needs to learn new skills. Too many Amish out here and I hate to admit, but it's competitive. Daniel needs to learn to do more than Amish rockers. Furniture repair, especially antiques, is what he needs to learn. You taught Roman caning and carving. If I pay for your driver out here, do you think you could come out after the Christmas rush is over? Most likely you're busy with Christmas orders. You can call my son's cellphone. Jah, he has one for business. I'm writing his number on the back of this paper real big, so you don't miss it. My handwriting isn't too legible.

God bless you,

Jeb Weaver

~*~

Daniel found himself sitting across the table from Sarah at Miller's Café, memories of being disciplined by his *daed* when he was a *kinner* rippling through his mind. His *daed* had insisted that the two of them go out for breakfast and he take a day off work to set things right with his wife. He wondered if Benjamin, Jacob and Jonathan could make it a profitable day, or would they mosey around. Worse yet, horse around. *Lord, help my boys be disciplined today.*

"What's on your mind?" Sarah asked, after sipping her coffee. "You look troubled."

"Hope the boys can hold the fort down today."

Sarah surprised him by reaching for his hand. "Our sons are hardworking like their *daed*. It's time you relax a bit."

Daniel stared at her hand resting on his. He felt like a chameleon; one color around Sarah and one around Melody. Shame filled him and he knew he had to confess. Transparency in marriage was key, his *daed* had told him late last night when they talked further. His *Daed,* a real C.S. Lewis fan read him a quote about what was the most important thing in the world.

"Sarah, my *daed* and I have been talking—"

"I don't want to move to Smicksburg."

He cocked his head back. "What?"

"I'm sorry. I thought you took me out to soften the blow."

"*Nee*, my parents think we need time alone. They take special time to be alone and we should too. Like *Mamm* says, a plant will die if you don't water it." He studied his wife's face. She was afraid. "Sarah, my *daed* brought books with him and he quoted a favorite author, C.S. Lewis." He pulled a paper from his pocket to read:

'The homemaker has the ultimate career. All other careers exist for one purpose only - and that is to support the ultimate career.'

Daed said Lewis wasn't even Amish who have no modern conveniences. I want you to know I appreciate all you do to keep the house in tip top shape, sew clothes, cook, the whole nine yards. I don't say it enough."

Sarah blushed. "It's what my *mamm* did and it's all I know. Not like I was raised to run a business, like all those Klines who have quilt shops." She sighed. "Seems so appealing, but I'm sure there's lots of work to be done."

Daniel's mind raced. His wife had never expressed

this desire before. Visions of them working in a business together ran through his mind, and it would tell all the women who came to flirt that he was a married man. "Do you want your own shop?"

She laughed. "My own shop? What would I make? Pies?"

"Quilts! You're one of the best quilters in all of Holmes County. I could add on to my rocker shop and you could sell quilts," Daniel exclaimed. "And if I get a female customer, you could come over and help her pick out what she wants."

She squinted, puzzled. "But your business is doing *gut*."

He lowered his head. "Sarah, some of the women who come in are...Delilahs. You understand what I mean?"

Blinking to beat the band, she sat erect. "They flirt with you? Try to lure you into...Who? *Ach,* I can just guess. That Candace comes around quite a bit."

"*Nee*, Candace is happily married. It's Melody. She's been telling me how her husband treats her, and I feel for her."

"You feel what for her?"

"Like I care too much about her happiness."

Sarah cupped her quivering chin. "You don't seem to care much about mine."

Daniel knew she was right. "You're so strong, I never have to worry about you. Kind of wish I did, but you go to your kin if you have a problem."

Anger rose from deep within. His in-laws had taken his place, and they made him feel inadequate. "*Jah,* Sarah, your parents have made me feel like less of a man."

She swiped away runaway tears. "They treat you like a son."

"Like a young child," Daniel spat. "You know Sarah, something's been eating at me and I think this is it. I feel like your parents are a wedge between us. How many times have I had ideas, but you say your *daed* wouldn't think it wise or whatnot?"

"Well, we're supposed to look to the older ones. They're wiser."

Daniel was so shocked by his anger, but he figured he was a soda can shaken a little too much and when opened it exploded. But relief came as well. He'd discovered what was causing his marital problems. "Sarah, I don't want your parents coming over for a while. Tell them my parents are living with us for a change."

She gasped. "My parents don't live with us."

"They may as well be. If it's an Off Sunday, who do we see? Not friends, but your parents. Or your parents or your sister's family." Sarah fidgeted with her spoon. Daniel looked around and noticed that many eyes were upon them. Was he yelling? "*Ach,* Sarah, did I raise my voice? I talk so loud."

"*Jah,* you spoke up, Daniel. And I'm glad you did. I think you're right. My *mamm* can be belittling at times. I should know. I was raised under her…fist."

Daniel remembered the first time he visited Sarah's family. Sarah was not herself, but nervous. Like walking on eggshells. He looked deeply into her cornflower blue eyes. *Jah,* the girl he wed so many years was still there, and he needed to bring her back to life. Water this parched flower.

"I don't mean to speak ill of my *mamm*, but she always compared me to my older sister, Jenna. Truth be told, I was glad when she moved out west."

Daniel laced his fingers through hers. "You're worth ten Jennas. Nothing special about her."

"Well, my *mamm* thinks so." She met his gaze. "Your *mamm* had the strangest talk with me early this morning. She said Fannie wrote about the tongue, and how a spark can set a forest on fire. My tongue has been sharp." She lowered her head. "Your *mamm* thinks I need to memorize scripture to see my worth in God. Why do you think she wants me to do that?"

Daniel's heart sparked with a longing to help Sarah. *Jah,* she needed him, and he was oh so glad. "You don't see your value. Maybe *Daed* shared that quote about homemaking because he sees that you need it. All you do for the *kinner*, and for me, is so valuable."

She blinked back tears. "But Rachel isn't baptized

yet. And that's a reflection on me. I wasn't a *gut* example."

"Rachel is headstrong. She'll come around. And you've been a *gut mamm* to her. Is that what's been troubling you so?"

"Until recently. Rachel's engaged, so she must have plans for baptism. And Benjamin will wed, too. I think he has a sweetheart."

"I think he has lots of sweethearts," Daniel said with a wink. "Doesn't take after me. I only had my eye on one girl."

Their eyes locked and the feeling of broken chains fell from his heart. From her bright eyes, he knew she was free, too.

~*~

Granny rocked while crocheting next to Rachel. Laughter could be heard from the kitchen as Jeb, Ruby and May played a board game. Rachel was eager to get the knitting circle started and jabbered on and on about it. Someone came in the back door as a cold blast announced their presence. Rachel murmured, "It's *Mammi Fern.*"

A plump woman with ruddy cheeks was soon marching into the living room. "Rachel, I need to talk to you."

Granny was aghast. She'd met Fern King before, but a hello and nice to see you would be in order. Feeling irked, she said, "Hello Fern. Nice to see you. It's been over a year since we've been out to Ohio."

Fern muttered a hello and then pointed out of the room, eyes heavy on Rachel. Granny thought this so demeaning, like Rachel was a dog to obey a command. "Come in a take a seat, Fern. You look mighty tired. Do you want some tea to warm you up?"

She shook her face so fast her jowls jiggled. "Rachel. Now."

"*Nee, Mammi.* Whatever you have to correct me about can be said around *Oma*."

Fern had cow's eyes, too big for her face. Now they were gigantic, and the sight was menacing. She huffed and took a seat. "Maybe your other *grossmammi* needs to hear this, too. Rachel, I saw you in a little red car with an Englisher. A young man your age and you were mighty cozy."

"Where?" Rachel asked curtly.

"In the Walmart parking lot. Late at night. Things done in secret are evil."

Granny looked to Rachel for an explanation, but Rachel scarcely acknowledged what her *grossmammi* said. The wind beat against the windows, the rattle filling up the silence that ensued. Granny yearned for the sound of her pendulum clock. Tick-tock. Tick-tock. It soothed her soul. And her little dog, too.

"Rachel, you were raised to respect your elders," Fern went on. "Now, tell me what's going on with that fancy man. It's not the first time I've seen that red car. Saw it pull into your driveway a few times at night."

Rachel squared her shoulders. "I'm on *Rumspringa* and I have freedom to run around until I'm baptized."

"And when will that be?"

"Never," Rachel near whispered.

"What did you say?" Fern asked, hand on her heart.

"I don't know. I'm thinking there's other ways to worship God. I'm thinking hard on it."

Thinking it best to leave them alone, Granny rose, but Rachel protested. "*Oma*, stay. You understand me."

"You do?" Fern prodded. "How so?"

Granny reluctantly sat. "If I hadn't met Jeb, I would have turned Mennonite. Back in 1963, when everyone was getting a clothes dryer, I sure did want one. Jeb comes from a strict Amish sect and we clashed like the live-long-daylights, but he loosened up a bit, and he reigned me in."

"*Ach,* that is so romantic, *Oma*," Rachel exclaimed. "I want a marriage just like yours."

Fern let out nervous laughter. "You won't be getting what they have by flirting with the devil."

"His name is Jared, *Grossmammi*, and he's just the opposite. He's an angel."

Granny's heart did a flip. Fern would fuss to Daniel and Sarah. Granny was hoping this could remain mum so that she'd have time to drop advice into Rachel's heart, when the time was right.

"Rachel," Granny began, "don't worry your *grossmammi* unnecessarily. And Fern, Rachel is right. She's on *Rumspringa* to know her mind. Taking the baptismal vow is as serious as a marriage vow."

Fern's round body sprang from her chair. "I'll be talking to your *mamm*. I can at least make Sarah see reason."

Granny wondered why she didn't say Daniel as well. How much did she have Sarah wrapped around her controlling finger?

~*~

December's chilly winds ushered in a snowstorm. Through the morning light, Sarah suspected ten inches of snow had fallen overnight. She knew the *kinner* would need hot hearty lunches packed, so she set her mind to work in the kitchen. She was thankful for her natural gas stove, not missing her wood fueled one, no matter how much the Pioneer Princess stove was praised by many an Amish woman.

She took aluminum foil and tore off four large pieces. In each she placed sliced potatoes, sausage, green peppers and cheese, and then wrapped them up to bake. And then she set herself to cracking eggs and beating them to make breakfast. Sarah's mind was a jumble. Over the past week, her husband told her she needed to nip in the bud comments made by her *mamm* and rely on his judgement, while at the same time her *mamm* told her such unpleasant news about Rachel's so-called Englisher beau. *You'll handle it. Daniel may turn a blind eye, but you're the one with a strong sense of right and wrong,* her *mamm* had said. A jab at Daniel's character, for sure, but there was truth in it. She wanted a marriage like her in-laws, and she could see the respect they had for each other. If they disagreed, Granny was ever so humble to let Jeb make a mistake.

Inviting Freeman out from Pennsylvania was one such incident. She overheard their disagreement, yet Freeman was coming, since Jeb insisted. Granny said he was interfering, but with what? Daniel's business? He did need to learn new skills.

She felt chilly arms around her, and she jumped. "*Ach,* Daniel. You're so cold. Coffee's almost ready."

He squeezed her and kissed the top of her prayer *kapp*. "Got up extra early to shovel a path to the shop, although I don't think we'll have many customers today. This storm's a whopper."

"*Jah,* and my *mamm* said it may snow up to two feet."

"She was over?" Daniel questioned.

"*Jah*. Came for a cup of sugar. Said she never thought she'd see the day when she'd have to have an excuse to come over…"

"Well, we've had an open gate too long. Need to put up a ten-foot fence."

Sarah crossed her arms. "You can't do that."

"Fences make *gut* neighbors," my *mamm* always says. Comes from one of her poetry books. But then again, she doesn't need a fence because my *bruder*, Roman, doesn't meddle."

Sarah wanted to defend her *mamm* but held her tongue. This marriage was beginning to sprout. It was something she cherished more than anything, and she would do all she could to gain what they'd lost over the years.

"Are you mad at me?"

"*Nee*, not at all. Just thinking about how it took your parents coming out to recognize how far we'd grown apart. I sure do wish they'd come live by us."

Daniel poured himself a mug of black coffee and took a sip. "They'd be *gut* for the *kinner*. And closer to Phillip out in Indiana. I know they miss my *brieder* out in Montana."

"How can we persuade them?" Sarah asked. "Your *mamm* is so encouraging, I'd never be starting that knitting circle next week if it wasn't for her." Sarah decided not to invite her *mamm* ever since she was rude to Granny, and she came down too hard on Rachel.

"Well, my parents' love Smicksburg, that's for sure. I can see them coming out for long visits, but not move here. Let's enjoy them while they're here. Maybe they can stay through January."

Sarah prepared two plates of scrambled eggs and toast and sat them on the table. She even got out her homemade jelly that she was saving for a Christmas present, as a special treat for Daniel.

His eyes grew tender. "*Danki*, Sarah. You make the best jam. You should start a business."

This lifted her heart yet concerned Sarah. "Daniel, from my budget book, I see we're doing okay financially. Do you think we need more money?"

"*Ach,* I was just saying that because those Amish-made jams that supermarkets sell aren't as *gut* as yours. *Nee*, we're fine. Nothing to worry about."

"Then why is Freeman coming to help you expand your business? That UPS truck picks up orders daily."

Daniel stared into his mug. "Truth be told, I don't want to cane chairs. I like bending the hickory wood. What do you think about my new hickory porch swing?"

"It's right fine. Hope you can make us one someday." Sarah's eyes met Daniel's and pride, in a *gut* way, poured from him. She was respecting him, and he needed it. They looked at each other for ever so long, and her eyes welled with tears. "I love you so."

"Me, too. *Danki* for putting our marriage first. I don't want to cause problems with your *mamm*, but…"

"She does it on her own. She's too outspoken; never lets *Daed* get a word in and I was doing the same thing. No more."

He had that schoolboy grin smeared across his face; one he couldn't hide. To see her husband happy gave her more joy than she thought possible. It truly was better to give than to receive.

Chapter 5

Rachel set up the ironing board in the living room and then got the basket full of crisp, clean shirts, pants, dresses and aprons. This was something she would not miss once married to Jared. Granny wanting a clothes drier back in the 1960s she could relate to. She wondered if Granny ever regretted her decision not to leave the Amish on workdays like today.

A van pulled into their driveway and deposited a young man. An Amish man. Was this Freeman? She inched to the window and peaked out. *Ach,* he noticed her and was headed right toward the house. Didn't he see the rocker shop sign? By her first glimpse of him she saw that he was tall and lean.

When the rap at the door sounded, she hoped someone in the house would answer it, but no one seemed to be around. How odd. She gingerly went to the door, a lump in her throat. She hated meeting new Amish men. They all fell into two categories: boring or overbearing. But she opened the door and stared. This man was the most handsome Amish man she'd ever seen. It was like he could be on an

Amish romance novel cover. "C-come in," she stuttered.

"*Danki*. Awful cold. I'm Freeman Yoder." He extended his hand. "Do you remember me? I met you once when visiting your *Groosseldre*."

She briskly shook his hand. "I'm R-Rachel Leaver. I mean, Weaver." Her heart was pounding but *gut*. "Are you looking for my *daed*?" She didn't think she'd met him before. She'd surely remember this man.

The van blasted its horn and Freeman was gone as soon as he came. What on earth? She watched as the driver slapped Freeman's back while Freeman lifted his mammoth suitcase as if it was a feather. *How long's he staying?*

He came back to Rachel and asked where to put his luggage. She didn't know what the plans were. Where on earth were her parents or grandparents? "Well, you brought a lot of stuff, so I suppose the bedroom with the biggest closet."

He chuckled. "I have tools in here along with clothes for a week."

"So, you're staying for a week?" she asked.

"Well, it's all the clothes I have. One for each day and then wash day comes." He motioned to her basket of clothes. "I'm sure things aren't much different out here as back home in Smicksburg."

His eyes were like blueberries. Or maybe black

raspberries. Indigo? A dark blue that was so becoming with his shaggy long blond bangs. Transfixed, she just couldn't make it out. Sandy colored hair or light brown?

"Rachel, do I have food on my face?"

"What?"

He wiped his mouth. "You're staring at me and we had powdered donuts in the van. Do I have something on my face?"

How embarrassing! "*Ach, nee.* I'm trying to remember you, I guess."

"It's been three years," Freeman said. "I've changed, but you haven't."

"I, ah, think I'm just tired from all this laundry," she fumbled, kicking herself inwardly.

"That *is* a heaping stack. Do you need any help?"

Rachel felt her knees grow weak. "With laundry?"

"*Jah,*" he said with a laugh. "Jeb inviting me here to teach caning and a few carving skills, I want to earn my keep."

"You're teaching my *daed.* It's enough."

"It could only take a week, but Jeb asked me to ice fish off of Lake Erie in two weeks." He grinned. "Didn't pack my fishing pole since he said there were plenty here."

So, he was staying for over two weeks? Rachel was flabbergasted…but glad.

~*~

The snow never let up that day, the chunky flakes piling high. After supper, when the house was dark,

Sarah decided to get out all her oil lamps to have a soft glow. Granny was glad since the natural gas lighting was too bright, and she felt more at home.

She soaked in the cozy scene. The woodstove had a glass door and the flames flickered and sputtered, letting off a nice even heat in the big living room. Two long brown upholstered couches faced each other, making for good conversation. A round table Daniel built was in one corner and hearty laughs echoed off the walls as Dutch Blitz was played. She studied the interaction between Rachel and Freeman, and she started to hope Jeb's matchmaking efforts would pay off.

She remembered meeting Jeb in the autumn and accepting his proposal by Christmas. On Christmas Eve, her dear husband had filled the one room schoolhouse with flowers. *Ach,* how they'd butt horns about flowers. Jeb being raised in the strictest of the Amish orders, believed planting flowers was showing pride. He was taught to just be content with wildflowers. Well, she loved flowers and he found her carnal. But like iron sharpens iron, he finally came to see her way and she saw that she was plain. *Jah,* she was teetering like Rachel, but Jeb pulled her off the fence. Could Freeman do it? If he wasn't right for Rachel, maybe he would be an example of what a *gut* Amish young man could be.

Granny took up her basket of yarn that she'd

unraveled. Having decided to knit small teddy bears for the Christmas shoebox drive, she felt so happy participating in this event. The Smicksburg Amish settlement wasn't one-tenth the size of the Holmes County population, but maybe they could have Amish stores open and the English could do a tour, like they were planning on doing soon here in Holmes County.

Her mind drifted to her *bruder. Lord, when the roads clear, Jeb said we're going to visit. Soften his heart. Go before me. I am afraid, Lord. What if he doesn't want to see me after all these years? With all these wrinkles, will he see the little sister that tagged along, always his shadow? Wanting to be like him?*

The front door that led right into the living room rattled as someone knocked. She thought she heard someone calling for help, but was it the whistling wind?

Benjamin jumped up and opened the door. A woman, wrapped in a black hooded coat that bundled her from head to toe, stood shivering. Through chattering teeth, she asked to see Daniel. Was this a customer out in such weather? Granny made haste and put on the tea kettle. The poor woman was half frozen.

"My car slid off the road," she said. "Daniel, I'm so glad it happened here."

Sarah darted up and went to the woman. "Melody, is it you? I see you need help."

Melody blinked in disbelief. "Sarah? Daniel's

wife?"

The air was thick with tension, but Sarah managed to say, "We met in the workshop. We'll get you warmed up while my sons help shovel out your car. Benjamin, you and your *bruder* go out and help get the car…unstuck."

Freeman was eager to join the boys and Granny saw Rachel flash him a brilliant smile. *Praise be.*

~*~

Jeb put a firm hand on his son's shoulder when the boys went to task outside and the girls all drank hot cocoa and cookies in the kitchen. "So, you talked to Sarah? Confessed?"

"*Jah,* I did. Look at how she welcomed Melody. I'm amazed."

Jeb felt a weight fall from his heart. "And you and Sarah will be spending more time alone?"

"*Jah. Daed,* how could I have been so blind? I'm so afraid of losing all this. Taxes are going up and well, I know God provides, but I spent way too much time in that shop. I see in Rachel that she's headed towards the world because of me. I've been a poor example of what a *daed* should be. What a marriage should be."

Jeb shook his head. "*Nee*, no condemnation. Remember Romans 8:1. There is therefore now no condemnation to those who are in Christ Jesus. He knows we have our sinful nature to deal with and it was the right time for you to see it. It's God's timing. Always perfect."

Daniel inhaled and sighed audibly. "But Rachel is twenty. And I have a feeling she's seeing an Englisher. A red sports car's been seen by my mother-in-law, you know."

He slapped Daniel's back playfully. "And we're snowed in and Freeman is here." Jeb could hardly stop grinning.

Daniel stared at him. "You planned this for Rachel?"

Jeb leaned in to whisper. "*Jah*. Your *mamm's* a real matchmaker and I've seen many couples hook up due to her efforts. I've asked Freeman to go ice fishing while here."

"On my pond?"

"Nee, on Lake Erie." He nudged Daniel. "That was the big lure."

Daniel shook his head in disbelief. "Lake Erie doesn't freeze over until late January."

Jeb placed his hands behind his head. "Guess he'll have to stay for a while."

Daniel frowned. "You're kidding."

"Kind of. I thought the lake froze sooner. I'll have to tell Freeman. But I'd like him to stay and help with that shoebox charity. Thought he'd like to experience the Amish folks volunteering with the English. And I see there's every kind of Amish imaginable here. Do they all get along?"

"Mostly. We do pull together for volunteering and other outreaches. *Mamm* seems happier here. Don't you think with her personality being so friendly, she may just want to live out here? We could build a *dawdyhaus*."

Jeb was truly touched at his son's offer and unbidden tears sprang to his eyes. "Your *Mamm* loves Smicksburg."

"But, how about you and all your bishop duties? It's time to relax. Go fishing."

Jeb had to admit his son may be right.

~*~

Sarah took deep breaths while serving Melody tea, trying to push down the notion that this woman wasn't being truthful. She planned to slide off the road to see Daniel. But she was going to overcome evil with good, like the Bible said to do. She remembered also that Jesus said if you give a cup of water to anyone, you do it to Him. "Melody, this tea will warm you right up."

Granny and Rachel sat at the kitchen table, encouraging Melody. Sarah saw concern in Granny's eyes. What was it? "*Mamm*, is everything okay?"

She pursed her lips. "Melody, such a pretty name for someone so sad. What ails you, child?"

Melody's lips parted, but she was deemed speechless.

"Why are you so afraid?" Granny continued. "You're among friends here."

At this, Melody broke into tears. She covered her

face and kept saying, "no one understands." Granny assured her that whatever her problem was, it was better to air it out. Mold grows in the dark, Granny informed. Melody kept saying she didn't have friends, except Sydney and she didn't trust many people.

Sarah sat next to her. "We're starting a knitting circle next week. Would you like to come?"

Rachel guffawed and let her cheeks blow up.

"What on earth is wrong, Rachel?" Granny asked as more of a correction.

"I'm sorry, *Mamm*. You're usually not this friendly towards Englishers."

Sarah knew she was a poor example of a strong Christian woman. She tended to hide from the world, living in the comfort of her home and church, but the more she got to know her mother-in-law, she knew she was just plain afraid of life. Maybe Rachel despised the Amish because of her fears. "Well, with age comes wisdom," she finally said. "Can't see the gray in my blonde hair, but it's there."

"*Mamm*, you're in your mid-forties."

"You're right I'm not," Sarah said with as much cheerfulness as she could muster. "So, Melody, what do you say? Would you like to come and join a small circle of friends?"

"It's something I say all the time. I found this to be true in my knitting circles." Granny said, smiling at Melody. "Would you like to join us?"

Melody shrugged. "I can't knit."

"I can teach you," Granny said. "Do you crochet or do needlework?"

Melody shook her head. "Not very talented."

Sarah didn't want to take over Granny's circle but had to make a suggestion. "We have boxes to fill for children in need. Would you like to come over and help pack them up?"

Melody's emotions were hard to read. She straightened up and forced a smile. "I'd like to learn knitting from you. You seem like you'd be patient."

"*Danki*," Granny exclaimed. "I have a knitting circle back home in Smicksburg and us women are spun together, not all unraveled like we used to be. A three-strand cord is not easily broken, *jah*?"

Melody slowly nodded. Sarah was in awe of her mother-in-law. How she wished her own *mamm* would be kinder to Englishers. This was a prejudice she'd learned at home that needed to stop. She knew many that were prejudiced against the Amish, but she never saw that she had preconceived notions about them. But Melody? The woman who flirted with her husband?

Boots stomping on the large log soaker rug by the door echoed around the house. Freeman ran into the kitchen. "We got the car out of the ditch." He looked at Rachel. "*Gut* snow out there to make a snowman or have a snowball fight."

Rachel flashed a smile. "Let's build a snowman!"

Rachel rarely gave the time of day to any Amish young man, but she sure did take to Freeman. Praise be. Maybe the fancy man with the red car will stay away forever.

~*~

Rachel dug for stones buried a foot under the snow. Not able to reach them, she called for their Australian Shephard who loved the snow and asked him to play dead. The dog did, and getting up, flung up a lot of snow. Rachel hugged the dog, saying "*Gut* boy!" and then commanded the dog to do it again. Soon a patch of the driveway could be seen. She picked out two stones for the snowman's eyes. Freeman laughed throughout the whole episode.

"Do you like dogs?" he asked her.

"*Jah.* I can't live without a dog. *Mamm* won't let us have a dog inside, though," she complained.

"Not many Amish have inside dogs."

"My *oma* does. A little black Pomeranian named Bea. She misses her."

"I've held that dog," Freeman informed. "I go over and shoot the breeze with Jeb sometimes, him being the bishop and all."

"You get in trouble?" Rachel teased.

"*Nee.* Jeb can't figure out youth today and asks for my opinion." He winked. "Sometimes we fish, too. And Granny makes pies. They're the kindest people I know, besides my folks."

This took Rachel back. "You have a happy

family?"

"*Jah,* I do. I'm thankful I was raised plain. Want that for my *kinner.* Couldn't imagine raising them any other way."

Rachel's mind skipped down memory lane and fond memories of her growing up years filled her. "I had a *gut* childhood, too."

"But you're not baptized. How come?"

She wondered if everyone from Pennsylvania was this nosy. Or, were they just more open about their feelings? "I'm not ready," she said lamely.

Freeman stuck two branches into the snowman to make arms, and then pressed his black wool hat on its head. "Looks *gut* to me. Snowmen in Smicksburg don't have eyes. No faces on dolls either. This is the first snowman I've seen with eyes." He cupped his mouth as if telling a secret. "Looks nicer."

Rachel laughed. "Are you serious? Your snowmen can't have faces?"

"Nope. We're more old-fashioned, I suppose. But, Englishers say that Smicksburg has the friendliest Amish they know of. We keep to our ways, but don't judge others."

Rachel's *Mamm* asking Melody to join the knitting circle did something to Rachel's heart. Was it softening to Amish ways? "You say the Amish in Smicksburg are kind to the English?"

"*Jah,* they are. Now, you find a bad apple in every

bushel, but we try to keep the spirit of the law, not the law…law."

"What do you mean?" Rachel asked.

Freeman sat next to the dog and stroked his fur. "Well, like the eyes in the snowman. I could have been proud and said the Amish back home keep the commandment to have no graven images…faces, you know. But, the spirit of the law says there's a higher law. The law of love. And we all know what the greatest commandment is, *jah*?"

"Love the Lord with all your heart…"

"And love thy neighbor as thyself. If we're always correcting others, we're stirring up strife, discord and envy. You know, all those messy proud feelings. God looks at the heart, right?"

Rachel was eager for him to continue, but he said it was getting too cold and they'd best be getting inside. Rachel wanted to see the stars, so he left her to herself. The stillness of the night was magical. Few cars going up and down the road offered a holy hush. She chided herself for how she felt toward Freeman. She was being unfaithful to Jared for having such thoughts. But Freeman was the most unique Amish man she'd ever met. He reminded her of someone.

She spotted Orion's Belt and The Big Dipper and pondered matters. To her surprise, a shooting star arched across the sky. She gasped at the wonder of it all. "The heavens declare the glory of God," she whispered, her words piercing the darkness. She'd heard at the church she and Jared attended about the glory of God. As a Christian, she was supposed to live for the glory of God, to show others what the Lord's nature is like. But she knew she fell short. Very short. All her lies and secrecy. How she did not honor her parents. How she looked down on the Amish. *Jah,* she was prejudiced against them and this was not right.

Somehow what Freeman just said about the spirit of the law humbled her. She knew her Bible but in a proud way. Freeman could have told her not to make a snowman with a face, but he didn't. He was so kind. Kindness was a fruit of the spirit. *The spirit of the law*, she kept pondering.

She lifted her eyes to the heavens. "Lord, lead me. I want to be like *Oma* and *Opa*, two people I believe live the spirit of the law. Their hearts are so pure. Help me be like them…and Freeman. He seems to have something I lack. Something I want.

~*~

Granny was glad to think of the banter between Rachel and Freeman the night before. It still made her chuckle how Jeb found 'chores' for the boys to do and encouraged Freeman to go outside to be alone with Rachel. And she needed a light heart today as the driver dropped Jeb and her off at her brother's house. She'd prayed that covetousness wouldn't consume her, or anger over Noah not sharing one cent of the family farm with any Amish relatives.

"I don't think he lives in a public building," Jeb informed the driver. "There's no sign, but isn't this a library?"

The two-story redbrick building stood at the top of a blacktopped driveway. "*Jah,* there's a parking lot." Granny pointed to the many spaces to park and asked the driver to fix his GPS to the right address. She eyed the contraption from the back seat, and she had to admit, it was a marvel.

"This is the house," the driver said. "Do you want me to wait or will you be calling for another driver?"

Well, they hadn't yet thought of this. What if Noah didn't invite them in? "Can you wait a minute?" Granny asked.

"Sure," he said. "Glad the road is cleared off. No snowstorm in sight."

Jeb ran around to open the door for Granny and his steady grip told her she had someone to lean on. *Her leaning post. Jah,* they'd leaned on each other fifty years and she never let a day go by that she didn't thank God for him.

As they neared the large front door, she noticed that white curtains peeked out of every window. Did he miss the Amish way of simplicity? Even though it was *nippy* out, perspiration beads formed on her forehead. *Lord, help me.*

After the second doorbell chimed a tune, a woman in a white apron and hat came to the door. "I'm s-sorry," Granny stammered. "We've come to the wrong place. You go on back to your duties."

"My duties?" the thirtysomething blonde asked. "I'm doing my duty now. Answering the door. Do you want to see Mr. Byler?"

Granny found herself gaping. Was this Mrs. Byler? Surely not!

Jeb spoke up. "*Jah,* we'd like to see Noah."

She narrowed her eyes and then escorted them into a waiting room with plush leather chairs. "Who may I ask needs him?"

"His sister, Deborah," Granny said hoarsely, her mouth dry. The woman ogled at her even more and then exited the room. "Seems like Noah's an important man to have a waiting room like this," Granny said as she gazed around the room.

Jeb nodded as he took off his black wool hat. "Or has more money than he knows what to do with. Some of the Englishers live like this to show off, you know."

Granny nudged him. "Noah never wanted too much attention."

"Well, it's been ages since you've seen him. Maybe he married a woman who likes lots of fancy stuff."

Granny heard footsteps. She remembered Noah running after her while playing tag. He could outrun any kid around, so he always won. But when anyone teased her for being a slowpoke, Noah always defended her. 'Leave my little sister alone' she'd heard countless times. Even when her *daed* was unreasonable, Noah said the same thing, even if he got a thrashing. Why this memory was vivid, she did not know. But she knew the rhythm of his footsteps.

He appeared around the corner and she could not control herself. She ran to him, like she did so long ago. "Noah!" She embraced him. "It's Deborah, your little sister. How are you?"

Noah was rigid as a board, not embracing her. "Who are you?" he asked as he searched her face. "Debbie?"

Jeb extended a hand. "Nice to see you again, Noah. It's been years. We're out visiting our son and his family, and we thought we'd come see you."

Granny felt a light and quick embrace. "We're going to be here for a month, and we have time to visit. Most trips are only for a week." Her heart was a stone sinking in a murky pond. Noah was bone thin and skin sallow. "Noah, are you sick?"

His eyes softened just a tad. "Still playing *Mamm's* helper?"

"*Jah,* I suppose."

He kept his light blue eyes on her. "You look like her."

"*Danki.* You look like *Daed.* I guess we both look old, *jah*? I'm not the blonde-haired little sister anymore but just an old woman…who'd like to catch up with her *bruder.*"

He let his head hang. "For a short visit. Not

having a good day."

Jeb scooted outside to tell the driver to wait for half an hour. The woman came in and asked if Noah would like for her to serve tea. He gave a quick nod and she hurried out. With just the two of them in the room, Deborah had to say what was on her heart in private. Even from Jeb. "I still love you so and hold nothing against you for leaving the People."

His eyes clouded. "I was expecting that you were here to get me to repent, lest I die and go straight to hell."

Granny clasped her hands. "Noah, I've changed. I'm Amish, but I don't believe others who aren't are going to eternal hellfire like we were taught. The Amish have changed quite a bit on that matter."

"When I left, many came daily to break me, but I had to leave."

"Why?" Granny near pleaded. "Did you fall for an Englisher?"

His wrinkles deepened. "I never married. Too busy to marry. Traveled the world. Why I settled back here I'll never know. I love the Orient."

Jeb came in and sat next to Granny on the loveseat. Taking her hand, he seemed to be sizing up the situation. "Noah, how are you? Can you fill me in on thirty years?"

"Well, like I was telling Debbie, I never married,

but traveled the world. So sheltered as a child, I went on to higher education and being forbidden to see fine art, I studied it in college. Have my doctorate in Art History and was a professor for a while." Noah motioned around the room. "This is one of twenty rooms. This house is requested for weddings. It's historical, built in 1853. I have a gardener and the woman you've seen, Kimberly, helps with events…and other things. I also have two—"

"Then why are you so unhappy?" Jeb asked sincerely.

Kimberly came in with a tray of cookies and a teapot with dainty cups. "Tea is served," she said brightly.

As they sipped tea and nibbled on cookies, Granny prayed Noah would see that they had pure motives. That he'd realize she came simply to see her big *bruder*.

Chapter 6

That night, Rachel snuck out to meet Jared in their usual place, a short walk up the road where he parked his cougar. His car was toasty warm, not freezing like an Amish buggy. How she loved modern ways. They fell into a mutual kiss and she fastened the seatbelt close to him.

"I thought we'd talk a bit before choir practice at church," he said, voice strained. "Did you pay the balance on our bill to Landoll's Mohican Castle?"

Rachel's heart skipped a beat. She forgot completely. And then her words with her *oma*, promising to wait until Valentine's Day. She grabbed his hand. "I'm sorry. You know how my grandparents are here and well, my *oma* asked me to do something. She's a wise woman, and she has a *gut* marriage."

"*Good* marriage," Jared corrected.

"I'm sorry. My accent won't go away overnight. Anyhow, it's a long story really, but my parents seem to be having some marriage issues, and my *oma* thought a Christmas wedding was too much to put on them."

He withdrew his hand. "*Oma* means 'grandma' right?"

"*Jah*. I mean yes. And she counsels lots of women concerning marriage issues."

"Does she have a degree in counseling?" Jared chagrined. "Rachel, if you're having doubts, you need to tell me."

Rachel had never seen Jared act so rude. "Is everything okay? Have a bad day at work?"

He shrugged. "On a bad case right now. Being a divorce lawyer isn't too much fun around the holidays. Parents fighting for custody is rough."

Rachel leaned her head on his shoulder. "I'm sorry to appear fickle about our marriage. It's just that things have been tense around the house and when my grandparents arrived, they helped me see a thing or two."

"Such as?"

"Well, my mom needs to cut the apron strings with her outspoken *mamm*. I mean *mother*. It's helped my parent's marriage. And I like it. *Oma* says you have to put your spouse over parents, although you'll always love and honor them."

He seemed to warm at her words. "So, will you be cutting the apron strings when we wed?"

She leaned in for another kiss. "Of course. The Bible says for a man to leave his parents and cleave to his wife and the two shall become one."

He took her hands. "So, if I take a promotion, you'd be happy for me?"

She nodded. "I don't like you being a divorce lawyer. I see how it drags you down, and I don't believe in divorce either."

His brows shot up. "Some people need to get a divorce. The kids suffer being in an unhappy marriage."

All her life, Rachel never pondered this. Divorce was forbidden in the Amish church. Her stomach twisted and insecurity ceased her. "Couples have hard times. Like I said, my parents have been struggling, but they're going out alone more and nurturing their love."

A snowplow drove past, spitting up snow onto the windshield. Jared snapped on the windshield wipers and released the fluid. Rachel knew he wasn't upset that his prized car was sloshed up, but he was mighty nervous about something.

He stared ahead as the wipers cleared the window until she could clearly see the little chocolate shop across the road. "Rachel, we need to get married around Christmas, like we planned. I got a job promotion and we need to move to New York City." He smiled. "What would you say to living in the Big Apple?"

Leave Millersburg? Live in a huge city. Her eyes pricked with tears, but she was too afraid to say anything. Jared was beaming now with excitement.

"What kind of lawyer would you be?"

He comically arched like a proud peacock. "A corporate lawyer, dealing with some of the biggest businesses in the Big Apple. I'd make double what I make here in this podunk town."

Two-hundred thousand dollars? Before she could stop herself, she blurted, "Who needs that much money? My *daed* makes a fraction of that."

Jared rolled his eyes. "He's Amish with a low standard of living. I don't want that for us. I want our kids to have it all, without being spoiled. I even looked at the schools in the area that they may attend. Top notch."

Rachel's schooldays were so secure, carefree days. Walking to the one-room schoolhouse, knowing all her classmates, gatherings when the families came, it was what everyone today seemed to yearn for. She'd gotten quite attached to watching *Little House on the Prairie* while working at the hotel. What fond memories flooded her just today while she dusted.

"Rachel, you don't look very happy," Jared said with understanding. "I know you'll miss your family, but like you said, once married, we need to cleave to each other. Leave our parents. Grow up."

This was so foreign to Rachel; she could not hold back the tears. She pulled a Kleenex from her purse and sobbed. What was wrong with her? *Her grandparents!* Ever since they came, she longed more for the old ways of the Amish. Did she secretly hope that Jared would convert? She imagined living in Millersburg or some other Amish settlement her whole life.

Tension slowly filled the car. Rachel glanced at Jared and he appeared so hurt. "I'm sorry. This is such a surprise."

He blew out air, his shaggy bangs fluttering up. "You'll always be Amish," he groaned.

Rachel was happy going to their local church, as it was so accepting of everyone. "I just imagined we'd always go to Refuge Church. Settle here. I wouldn't be shunned, and we could visit my folks."

"Folks I've never met outside of buying a rocker from your dad." He mashed his lips together. "I'll drop you off in front of your house. I don't feel like singing tonight."

Neither did Rachel. No, she wanted to run into her *oma's* arms and tell her everything.

~*~

The next day Granny felt as light as a feather. For one thing, her talk with her *bruder* would not be the last. Being invited for dinner surprised her, but she knew deep down Noah would extend an olive branch to his little sister. *He still sees me as Little Debbie*, she mused. And knitting circle would start this afternoon.

Granny was glad to see Sarah and Daniel growing closer, but she advised that Fern be invited, along with Sarah's sister, Leah. Melody was bringing an Englisher friend, but Granny didn't fret. She'd learned to do her casting off prayers from her knitting circle in Smicksburg. She'd mention that today at circle. 'Cast your care upon the Lord because he cares for you', the Bible said.

The term came to her one day while knitting and casting off the finished garment. And the phrase stuck. Jeb told her that casting a fishing pole was hard work and you needed to do it repeatedly. She'd found this to be true. Casting a care seemed to boomerang right back, so she'd have to keep casting a care until she felt sure God was in control. Then she could rest, knowing He'd take care of a situation. How it helped not only her but her many girls who came to knit.

This morning she cast Rachel on the Lord. Truth be told, she was glad the differences between her and Jared came up before they wed. Rachel wilted under the idea of living in a big city so far from home. Granny told her that Jeb gave her the choice to live in Millersburg or Smicksburg, but she said she'd live on the moon if Jeb was there.

This made Rachel sob uncontrollably. She feared Jared would break off the engagement if she didn't marry him soon and move to New York. *Ach,* that was too pushy and not love. When she encouraged Rachel to reason with Jared, come to a happy medium, she cringed. Apparently, they'd never butted horns before. Or, Rachel had never spoken up.

Freeman coming had been a *gut* thing. An Amish man to his core, but as kind as the day is long, hopefully Rachel could see the contrast between Freeman and Jared. Hopefully more fond memories of being Amish would flood her like they'd been recently, overhearing Rachel and Freeman exchanging stories over a game of checkers. Her parents' marriage was on the mend, too, it was clear to see. Did their bickering make the world more appealing to Rachel? If so, Rachel was seeing a miracle unfold before her eyes, Daniel and Sarah holding hands while taking many a walk around their land, filling birdfeeders together, even building a snowman.

Redding up the noon meal with Sarah and Rachel, she set the rockers and benches in a closer circle. When Sarah asked what she was doing, she said it was better this way. A close-knit group needed to be physically close. Sarah said she hardly knew Melody and dreaded she'd really come, but Granny knew a secret. Women bonded over knitting or quilting or whatnot. Seemed like women calmed down enough to loosen their tongues, sharing their trial or joy, and bonds were formed.

The sun cast beams across the polished oak floor. Granny shot up a prayer. *Lord, help me be a light to these women coming today.* As she lifted her head, she turned to see Fern, and with her slip of a daughter, Leah. Fern towered over everyone or was Leah cowering under her *mamm's* presence. "*Gut* to see *yinz*. I mean you all. Take a seat," Granny said with a swoosh of her hand.

Leah bobbed her head, and thanked Granny. "Do you know how to crochet? I'm all thumbs and I hear crochet is easier, especially for baby booties." She rubbed her middle. "Need to prepare for a spring *boppli*."

Fern plunked herself in a rocker. "Leah, I have plenty of booties knit already."

"Do you want to learn how to crochet?" Granny prodded. "You can make doilies, you know. Oven mitts, potholders and whatnot. I do think *boppli* booties in a half crochet stitch would be lovely."

Leah smiled. "I like the hook. I'd like to try it."

Granny told her she'd be right back, going upstairs to pull out a pattern and get some extra crochet hooks. All things yarn gave wings to her feet and she near flew up the stairs. Seeing Rachel in the hall, eyes puffy, she reminded her that she promised she'd attend knitting circle. Rachel groaned but said she'd be down.

Granny rummaged through her tote of fabric, yarn, and sewing needles, until she saw the crochet hooks. Grabbing the needles, she dashed down the hall, reminding Rachel to put one foot in front of the other, carry on, despite her sour mood. Just what was ailing Rachel? She went back to stand in the doorframe of her bedroom. "Rachel, are you all right?"

"Not at all. "I don't want *Mammi Fern* seeing me

so blue."

Granny saw the fear in Rachel's eyes. Much like Ruth, Ella, Fannie and Colleen when they came to her many knitting circles. "Rachel, lots of women think that hiding will help them, when the opposite is true. Mold grows in dark places. You need to open up to other women."

"I do. To my *gut* friends, not Englishers."

Granny lowered her wire rimmed glasses. "You want to marry one. You may as well get used to them."

Rachel fell back on her bed, arms crossed. Granny went to her, reached for a hand and tried to pull her up. "Now, you come with me." She asked Rachel to carry her yarn and needles and linked her arms through hers, leading her downstairs, right into the circle.

~*~

Melody had arrived with her friend. She introduced Sydney to everyone, saying she was a beautician who had one thousand customers since she only charged eight dollars for a haircut. Sydney had blue makeup covering her eyelids, nigh up to her eyebrow. Her hair was puffed up so high, Granny thought it looked like a pileated woodpecker's plume. Yet, she'd learned not to judge by outward appearances. "Welcome to our circle, Sydney. I'm Deborah Weaver, but most everyone back home calls me Granny. Melody, you can call me that, too."

Fern huffed. "Why have them call you Granny when you're not their *grossmammi*."

Granny took a seat on one of the benches, Rachel sitting to her left. "Well, Deborah sounds so formal. Debbie sounds like a little girl. My knitting circle back home call me Granny, and it gives me great purpose. I like to take in lots of *grandkinner* who aren't kin."

"That's so cool," Sydney said with her eyes all lit up. "My clients tell me I'm their therapist. You know, when you comb hair, set it in curlers or cut it, women start to relax and talk. I think I've heard everything. It gives me a real purpose to get up in the morning. Plus, I have five kids to clothe and feed, although two are married and out of the house."

Melody spoke up. "I met Sydney when she did my hair and I can say she knows how to listen. Gives good advice and is a true-blue friend."

Fern was obviously irked. Was she staring at Sydney's heavy make-up or her tattooed wrists? Granny decided to ignore Fern's arrogance and start the circle. "We can knit or crochet. If you have a project, just work on it."

Leah mentioned discreetly that she'd be needing more *boppli* booties. Sydney squealed. "Me, too. My daughter's having another baby girl." She clapped her hands in glee. "I brought pink yarn to crochet a blanket."

Granny noticed Fern was blending into the background, so she told Rachel to sit next to her *grossmammi* to pick up some knitting pointers. "Fern, you're a *gut* knitter," she stated. "Sarah, can you teach Melody how to knit or crochet? Whichever she prefers."

The women paired up and Granny found this circle so different than her first, when everyone brought their Amish knitting looms. And everyone was Amish. She demonstrated how to make a chain stitch to Leah, and Leah practiced it while talking to Granny.

"I'm glad you put my *mamm* in her place but *gut*."

"What?" Granny gasped. "I'm the one who insisted she come."

"Well, *Mamm* got a clear message to not meddle in our marriages. Menno and I get along so much better, *Mamm* not coming over every day."

"She came over every day?" Granny whispered.

"*Jah,* she did. But, since Sarah had words with her, advice she got from you and your husband, she's been keeping to herself more."

Granny never wanted this to happen. *Jah,* Sarah needed to put Daniel first, but not neglect her *mamm*. How old was Fern, anyhow? Her age? "Leah, does your *mamm* live in a *dawdyhaus*?"

"*Jah. Daed* got all this land and Sarah's portion faced the road. I thought she was daft to have all that traffic so close to her house, but Daniel has a business and I suppose he wanted his store to have more visibility."

Granny said she needed to stretch her legs, so she got up and peered out the window to the vast open back field. She spied a red barn and white house, but no little house built for aging parents. What a mystery. And where was, Matthew, her husband? He hadn't come over to visit yet. Growing curious, Granny wondered if Fern wasn't a busybody at all, but a lonely woman.

She took the tray of sugar cookies and sat them on the coffee table. "Help yourself. There's hot water on the stove and tea bags and cups on the counter."

Everyone gave thanks, and Granny settled back into her spot, feeling sorry for Leah who was unable to make the chain stitch. "Wrap the yarn around your left fingers like I am. It stays stationary while your right hand does the work. It may take time, but with practice, you'll learn." She picked up her green yarn and proceeded to crochet. "Leah," she said in a near whisper, "where is the *dawdyhaus* for your parents?"

"It's attached to our main farmhouse. Why?"

"That's nice. Does your *mamm* have her own kitchen?"

"*Jah*. She's a *gut* baker. Has a kitchen nearly as big as mine."

"Do *yinz* eat together?"

"Well, we used to, but I asked Menno if he felt like Daniel, overshadowed by my parents. He said more time alone with me and the *kinner* would be nice. So, we told *Mamm* and *Daed* we'd eat with them on Sundays. Odd enough, they were fine with it, but *Daed* just booked a train ticket to Pinecraft Florida to visit his *bruder*."

Granny groaned. What had she done?

"I suppose he needed a winter break from all the noise. *Mamm* decided not to go. I think she's upset that *Daed* may want to retire down there and she's mighty peeved."

"I could never leave Smicksburg. It's been my home for ever so long," Granny said with feeling. "Wanting to redirect this unpleasant topic, Granny asked Leah the ages of her *kinner*."

"Well, Molly is ten, Jenna is nine, David is eight, Samuel is seven, Kelly is six, Lizzy is five and this wee one is on its way. We feared I couldn't have anymore *kinner*."

Granny whistled a weak tune. "I think the Lord knew your body needed a break. I lost track of what you were saying. How many *kinner*?"

"Six and this one on the way."

Granny mused and her heart lifted. Fern was never ever lonely. *Ach,* she hoped she was right.

~*~

Rachel kept eying Granny, motioning with her head to leave the circle. Rachel was in an outright panic. Granny was about to set down her crocheting when Melody asked Leah to switch seats to chat with Granny. She'd learned interruptions were God's appointments, since Jeb read so much C.S. Lewis. How often he quoted this when called out for an emergency, since he was the bishop.

Leah quickly obliged her, and Melody was soon seated next to Granny, appraising her. "You're all that Daniel says you are. So sweet and content."

Jeb told her that Melody flirted with Daniel, so Granny did not appreciate any talk of Daniel. "Well, he's a *gut* son who overlooks faults."

Melody grasped Granny's wrist. "I know I seem needy. Sarah talking to me is good of her. I was getting a bit too reliant on her husband and I hope I didn't cause trouble."

"Things are fine now," Granny assured. "Couples need to spend time nurturing their relationships like houseplants. Got to water them."

Melody stared at the floor. "My houseplants always die, and I do water them. But I get your point. You see, I moved here from Detroit. My husband lost his job and well, I can't get enough of Amish ways. I came into the rocker shop to look around and was stunned at Daniel's respect. His sons, too. They all have...what's the word?"

"Integrity?" Granny guessed.

"Bingo. Yes, that's it. And they never rush me out of the shop. The Weaver men have made me less content with my husband. He's so immature. All he does is watch sports or play video games."

Granny winced. "All the time?"

"Practically. It's like he's addicted. Oh, he goes to work and all, which I'm glad. We both have to pull together to keep our house." She huffed. "It's also why I peppered Daniel with so many questions. I'm writing a book on the Amish. Like I said, I find them fascinating. So, I'm trying to simplify my life. Hardly watch TV, make my own candles, cook from scratch, and it feels so good. But I'm so tired; running my business while writing a book is exhausting."

Granny knew Melody was writing about the Amish; she appreciated the writers who took the time to get their story correct. "I can answer any questions about the Amish. But I didn't know you had a business on top of writing. What kind of business?" Granny asked.

"I sell antiques out of our detached garage. Looks like a little shop, I suppose."

"Do you have *kinner*?" Granny asked. "My boys were expensive to raise. We had a cow, since they gulped down a gallon a day, and that's just one boy."

Melody grew pale. "I can't have children. It's just Kenny and me. And I think he plays games and is addicted to football because he's tired of me. Sometimes I wonder…"

"*Jah*?"

"Well, let's just say he wandered quite a bit in Detroit. Maybe I should be glad he's home and not at the bar."

Melody's loneliness was choking the life out of her. No wonder she came so often to talk to Daniel. "Would Kenny come over for dinner sometime? I'd like for him to meet Jeb. He has a way with men who seem to have no time for their wives."

Melody pressed a hand on her heart. "Amish marriages?"

"*Jah,* Amish marriages. Some Amish women are married to workaholics. It's been quite a problem, but it's called out and talked about. Some people change quick-like, mighty appreciative that you helped them see the error of their ways, others not so much, but we don't give up."

"I give up," Melody murmured. "I read in a magazine that I need to have a life of my own. If the husband is distant, have your own life."

Granny turned and took Melody's hands. "Marriage is a blessing. You just can't live like strangers in the same house."

Biting back tears, Melody said, "I don't know what to do. We were high school sweethearts, but I can't have kids. I think it rips Kenny apart."

"And you?" Granny asked. "Do you want *kinner*?"

Melody nodded. "I'd love to be a mom, but well, I'm pushing forty. Getting old."

Granny snickered. "You must think I'm a fossil if

forty is old. *Ach,* you're young. You have your whole life ahead of you. Now, you need to speak up and tell Kenny you want *kinner*."

Melody frowned. "I can't have *kinner*."

"Back home, there's a house for foster *kinner*. Lots of *kinner* need homes. Jeb and I adopted a teenager not long ago."

Clasping her mouth, Melody began to giggle. "You're kidding! You adopted! I don't believe it." She turned to Sarah and blurted out, "Did Granny adopt a teenager or is she pulling my leg?"

Sarah confirmed that indeed Granny and Jeb adopted a boy named Denny. There was a lull that hung in the air, the only sound was the pendulum clock. Everyone looked mighty uncomfortable. Sydney was the first to break the ice. "Well, I think that's wonderful. I hear many grandmas who come to my beauty shop. They're raising their grandchildren, and I think it's nice."

"What's wrong with the parents?" Granny asked.

"Denny was in foster care, signed over to the state."

Sydney's large blue eyes watered. "Well, there's lots of drugs in some families. Like mine. My mom is a junky and doesn't give a hoot about me. Haven't seen her in years. She's always out trying to get illegal prescription drugs. My sister died of an overdose."

Leah's large mother's heart moved her to get up

and give Sydney a hug. "Poor thing. Do you have a *Daed,* I mean father?"

"In Florida. He remarried, and I go down to visit him. But my cup runs over. My children fill the gap."

Leah appeared to be filled with admiration. "And you must have a wonderful husband, like mine."

Sydney laughed. "That's a good one. He left me with three kids. Went for a high-power job and younger chick. When I turned thirty, he came home less often, and then flew the coop. And he doesn't do a thing for his kids like he should." She inhaled and raised her hands, blowing out air. "I can't talk about him much or I'll get sick."

Melody went over to Sydney and hugged her. "This woman is so amazing. She owns her own beauty shop, charges the lowest prices in town, and supports five kids. She never did hook up with a real man. Granny says they exist," Melody said to Sydney.

Sydney blushed. "I'm sure they do. My sons are fine young men. Even though they're sixteen, eighteen and twenty, they're mature. We're all close, and I don't want any pity. My one thousand customers tell me their hardships and I count myself blessed."

"But you said you have five *kinner,* I mean children," Fern prodded, arching like a peacock. "Did you remarry?

Again, Sydney laughed. "Yes, but he left, too.

Wanted part of my shop and alimony. I will never, ever get married again."

Everyone was suddenly back to knitting or crocheting, no one knowing what to say. But Granny admired this young lady who appeared to be in her late forties. Two husbands leaving her with *kinner*? It was clear to Granny that women needed support more than ever. She felt fulfilled knowing that there was a reason for this knitting circle.

Chapter 7

The expression of joy on her grandma's face made Rachel realize she thrived on mentoring younger women. She was happy her circle was successful, but Rachel felt a bit put out. Granny was tired after all the chatter and was taking a nap. She needed to talk to someone about Jared's proposition. Move to New York? She couldn't fathom it. She thought of her *opa* and headed to the workshop, since he was out there with Freeman and her *daed* and *bruder*, learning how to cane chairs.

So, she slipped on her boots and plucked her cape from the wooden peg in the utility room. She looked around the room filled with hats, coats, capes and boots in all sizes, everything neatly in a row, as orderly as how they hung up the wash. Memories of her family running in, cold as icicles, *Mamm* running to the stove to heat up milk for cocoa. Such a happy childhood she had. How would she raise her *kinner* in a city? Truth be told, cities scared her. Too much noise and movement. She liked the slow pace in Holmes County.

She was glad someone put salt on the sidewalk leading to the workshop, because she was sure to fall on the ice. Upon entering the woodshop, she inhaled the smell of wood. The best smell besides the aroma of pumpkin pie, she thought. "Is anyone in here?" she asked, as the shop appeared empty. Four heads popped up, as her *daed, opa*, Benjamin and Freeman were all on their knees, working on a chair. To her utter amazement, her *opa* suggested that Freeman teach Rachel how to cane a chair. He said he had something personal to tell her *daed* and Benjamin. *Ach,* her *opa*! She was not so naïve. He obviously wanted her to get to know Freeman better.

Well, two could play his little game, she mused. "*Ach, Opa*, my fingers hurt from all the crocheting. I best be resting them."

Freeman smiled. "You learn from watching at first. Come on over."

Jeb chuckled and headed out of the shop with the men. Shyness enveloped Rachel. She took a chair near his caning project. It looked fascinating. "It's like weaving."

"This is the easiest pattern. This here chair is a ladder back and I'm doing a simple weave. When we get to real caning, there's more pattern options. Do you want to try?" he asked, holding up a thin rope.

"What's that made from? Looks like it would scratch up my hands. I tried to crochet with twine once, but my fingers got cut up."

He handed her the rope. "This is seaweed all twisted up. You can wear gloves, I suppose. I think Daniel has a few pairs around."

Rachel thought the chair mighty pretty and quickly nodded. Once she had work gloves on, Freeman showed her the pattern, telling her to go under the open seat sides, around the back, up under the front and so on. "It's like knitting or crocheting, *jah*?"

"Well, I wouldn't know," Freeman said with a chuckle. "But my aunt crochets to get her creative juices out, as she puts it. I do it with caning. So many patterns, but I'm doing this basic one because, well, no one's really catching on."

Rachel knew the work involved with steaming hickory branches and bending them into arm rests. It looked much harder than weaving this chair seat. "Maybe you should try a harder pattern. *Daed* is used to more of a challenge. I like the simplicity of this style. It looks Shaker."

His brows shot up. "You know about different furniture styles?"

Rachel continued to work on the chair as it reminded her of making a giant potholder made with a loom. "Well, I read a lot. The Shakers were some of the best woodworkers. And they hung their chairs up on pegs, like we do our clothes. *Daed* has all kinds of books on woodworking, but the Shaker style draws me in somehow. So plain and well, simple. Makes me feel…normal."

"Normal?" Freeman questioned. "Do you feel abnormal being Amish?"

She stopped and looked up at him. "Don't you? Some say we're backwards."

"And some are inspired by us like you're inspired by the Shakers." He knelt beside her. "Rachel, you have ten times as many plain folks out here compared to Smicksburg. Why do you feel out of place?"

She could not tell Freeman about how torn she was with Jared's world and her own. She shot up. "I forgot. *Mamm* expects me to help with supper."

"Well, come out and help me finish this chair sometime soon. Maybe it's too easy for rocker makers and I need to start showing them patterns they can cane. But, I'm eager to learn anything new about woodworking. Can I borrow that book you talked about?"

"*The History of Woodworking*? Sure," Rachel said, a smile forming on her pink lips. She crossed the woodshop and opened her *daed's* desk. Riffling through the deep drawer, she pulled out the massive book.

Freeman ran to take it from her. "It looks heavy."

Rachel could lift things much heavier, but she felt

that Freeman's offer was sweet. "*Danki*. See you at supper."

"Rachel? Can I ask you something?"

"*Jah*?"

"Do you ice skate?"

"Not on my *daed's* fishing hole, if that's what you mean. But my aunt has a pond. She lives right behind us, and we share it. And there's a sled riding hill not far away. Why? Are you bored here? Missing folks back home."

He winked at her. "*Nee*, I just like your company. You're so interesting."

The sincerity of his voice was remarkable. How she liked the feeling of feeling capable of doing something right. Rachel nodded. "I'd love to go ice skating. We have so many pairs of skates, I'm sure we have your size."

Freeman beamed with delight. "Maybe this Saturday?"

"Saturday? There's a full moon tonight." She clenched her fists. How forward to say such a thing. Skating by moonlight would be something a courting couple would do.

Freeman crossed his arms, a smile splitting his face. "Tonight then?"

Giving a shy nod, she spun around, hiding her burning cheeks. On her way back to the house, she could not hide a smile. Oddly, her *opa* was heading to the shop, followed by her *daed* and Benjamin. They said they needed to get back to work. Rachel's eyes met Jeb's and she burst into laughter. He did, too. They both knew he was trying ever so hard to play matchmaker.

~*~

When Jeb entered the workshop, he threw his black wool hat in the air. He whispered in Daniel's ear, 'I knew Freeman and Rachel would see what I see."

"Which is?" Daniel chuckled.

"They're a match made in heaven above. No finer Amish man than Freeman."

"Well, I hope you're right. No one in Holmes County has caught Rachel's eye."

Daniel's shop phone rang and when picking it up, Jeb soon knew it was Roman. And it wasn't good news. *Lord, give me strength.* If there was a death in the *Gmay*, he'd be heading right back home.

Daniel called him to the phone and Jeb gingerly made his way. Amish in Smicksburg used phones for emergencies, not casual talk. "Roman, is everything okay."

"*Daed,* no one's hurt. But Ezekiel and Anna's *dawdyhaus* burnt down in the middle of the night. Thank the Lord they're okay. It started as a chimney fire and it spread fast. I told them they could live in your house until we can get their new place."

Jeb let out a sigh of relief. "Of course. How long before the house is built?"

Roman grunted. "*Daed,* it's so cold out. We cut ice

already and it's not even January. I think when we get a thaw, we can build, but until then it's all up in the air."

"How high in the air?" Jeb asked.

"Joseph Miller thinks he needs to add on to his house to keep an eye on his parents. Ezekiel used some scraps of kiln dried wood to feed the fire and you just don't do that."

Jeb covered the receiver and moaned. "*Ach, nee.* You say you already told Ezekiel and Anna they could live in our house?"

"*Jah,* I did, *Daed.* Sorry if I overstepped. It was a frightful fire and Anna got into a panic and I said she could live at your place. She always loved it. Perked her right up. When the Millers add on, I can look in on your place along with Jonas and Denny."

Denny. His adopted man-boy turned Amish. "How is Denny? Keeping up in the rocker shop?"

"*Jah,* he is. And he goes over to help his father-in-law quite a bit. No change whatsoever with Michael's vision."

Hearing from back home put a lump in Jeb's throat. "I'll miss having Christmas with our *Gmay,*" he said, looking over at Daniel, "but sure am glad to be catching up with family out here in Ohio. *Ach,* and we met your uncle."

"*Daed,* isn't he shunned."

"It meant a lot to your *mamm.* We're going back and trying to find out just what happened to his faith." He scratched his chin. "Maybe it's

Providence that's making Ezekiel and Anna stay in our house for a while, so we'll have more time out here. Now, Fannie will take it hard. I fear the whole knitting circle will spin out of control. You tell them that we are not moving here but need to be here longer than expected. They need to learn to get along without their so-called Granny."

Roman laughed. "You're right. What's *mamm* doing to brighten up all of Holmes County?"

"A knitting circle, or a crochet, or whatever you call it. I was not all for it, but she thrives on it. Hey Roman, I know we need to cut this short and can write, but you know Freeman is out here, right? Well, I think he's sweet on Rachel and visa-versa."

"*Daed,* you've turned into *Mamm*. Matchmaking?" He bellowed out a laugh. "Are you reading her Jane Austen books now, too."

"Already read them, and they didn't prompt me to ask Freeman out. I prayed about it in the…fishing cabin."

"Don't rub that I'm not there fishing with you. Say, why haven't you ever made a shelter out there near your pond?"

Jeb smiled. "I'd live in it. Well, I'll write soon, and you do the same. Love you, son."

"Love you, too, *Daed. Mach's gut.*"

"*Mach's gut.*"

~*~

After the dinner dishes were washed and dried,

Freeman was eager to skate in the moonlight with Rachel. He'd never met a girl like her. She knew her mind but wasn't overbearing. There was a real genuineness about her. A goodness that shone through her chestnut colored eyes. He'd only known her for such a short time, but it seemed like the Lord dropped a special kind of love into his heart for this woman.

He felt a tinge of guilt that he'd asked the Byler men to practice the simple caning tonight, so they'd be ready for more advanced techniques. But, he did it so he could be alone with Rachel. When Rachel asked her little sisters to come with them, they complained about the cold and said they were learning to crochet with their *oma*.

So, it was only the two of them that walked along the back path that led to a pond on her aunt and uncle's land. The moonlight made the snow on the trees glisten. A barn owl hooted. "Such a peaceful night," he said.

Rachel agreed. "I've walked back here many a time. Sometimes to hear the quiet. Once we walk a bit down into the valley, you can't hear the traffic."

"Valley? I don't see a valley," Freeman said, confused.

"You're walking downhill." She snickered. "I've been to Smicksburg and I know that it's flat here in comparison, but we've always called it the valley."

Her voice seemed to pinch when she said valley. "You don't like valleys?" he asked.

When they reached the pond, Rachel took a seat on the bench to put on her skates. "Well, valleys in the Bible are hard places, *jah*?"

"The valley of the shadow of death sounds pretty hard," Freeman said, sitting next to her, sticking his feet into his skates. "Don't mean to be *nebby*, but are you in some kind of valley?"

"*Nebby*? What's that?"

"*Ach,* it means nosey. It's slang in our parts."

Rachel leaned back on the bench. "You're not being nosey. And you're not in my *Gmay* so I guess you're safe to talk to."

He turned to her, concerned. "People only talk like that when they're ready to jump the fence. Rachel, I hope I'm wrong."

She was quiet for a spell. Freeman rubbed his gloved hands together, creating heat. "Maybe we should get moving. Mighty cold to sit still." He peered out over the lake and couldn't see the other side. "Rachel, has someone tested the ice? Is it frozen but *gut*?"

Rachel said she ran back this afternoon to ask her uncle and he checked it. Solid ice of five inches due to the extreme cold. Freeman was convinced, but he skated the perimeter to check for slush. Everything was solid as marble.

"I'm surprised such a big lake can freeze up like this," he said.

Rachel laughed. "It's small. I can skate across it on one leg, and I'm not that great of a skater."

"Let me see you do it," Freeman challenged in jest, and Rachel took the bait. She lifted her hands above her head and gracefully spun around. He'd never seen anything like this.

"Why do you put your arms up? For balance?"

"Ballet. I took ballet during *Rumspringa*. I love it."

Freeman had done his own exploring of the English world and what it had to offer before he joined church. "I rode my buddy's motorcycle. Got addicted to the speed for a while."

"Addicted?" Rachel asked. "How long did you drive it?"

"*Ach,* six months. The thrill wore off, like everything else. After my two-year running around, I had enough. I could see that what the world had to offer didn't measure up to plain life. Everything was too fast, not just bikes. People talked too fast and too much, they live their lives too fast, like an emergency. *Nee*, I like it slow. It's more in pace with nature."

Rachel glided back to him, ever so graceful. "I still take ballet, but my parents don't know. There's a studio near the hotel I clean, and I find it so relaxing. My posture improved, too. Are you shocked?"

Freeman put his hands behind his back and skated a few times around the pond. Upon returning, he said. "*Jah,* I am surprised. By your age, you should know your mind. Didn't you start *Rumspringa* when sixteen or is it older out here?"

"Sixteen," Rachel informed. "The more I'm on it. I see how confined I am."

"How so?" Freeman dared ask.

"Too many rules. Why do I have to wear this apron all the time? I feel so self-conscious when working in the hotel. People gawk."

Freeman stared at Rachel, the moonlight giving her a heavenly glow. "You look pretty in your Amish dress. Aprons are worn for modesty, *jah*?"

Rachel tried to hide a smile. "You have to admit English girls are more fashionable."

"Not at all," Freeman was quick to say. "I like the prayer *kapps* the most. My *daed* told me it was romantic waiting to see my *mamm's* hair until their wedding day. It's the way it should be."

Rachel grew very quiet and skated back to the bench. Freeman couldn't tell, but it appeared tears were running down her cheeks. He sat next to her and saw for sure that they were. "I didn't mean to upset you."

"I'm so *ferhoodled*," she cried out, the frosty air whirling from her lips. "I am on the fence, but don't want to jump."

Freeman took her hand. "Then don't."

They sat listening to the night sounds, while peace enveloped them. Freeman felt it so natural to be holding this beautiful woman's hand. It was like they were the only people on the planet. Is this how Adam and Eve felt?

But the stillness was pierced by someone calling for Rachel, and she jumped. "I need to go," she blurted.

Confused, as they'd just arrived, he started to untie his skates; Freeman thought he'd given her *brieder* too much work to possibly do in two days, to have this special time with Rachel.

Footsteps chomping snow grew louder and the silhouette of a man appeared. "Benjamin, I gave you too much work for you to be done already," Freeman said, trying not to sound irritated.

"Amish-Boy, I'm not Benjamin. Rachel, we need to talk."

The voice was too gruff, and he feared for Rachel's safety. Did she know this man? Was he a bad influence in the outside world? He grabbed Rachel by the elbow. "You don't have to go."

"I do," she said, her voice strained.

It was clear Rachel was under this man's control. But who was he? And what gave him the right to come on private property like he owned it? He was helpless to see Rachel walk off with this man, but what could he do? She said she had to. How strange.

~*~

"How long?" Granny asked, a catch in her voice. "Why our house? Anna could live with her own kin, for Pete's sake." Trying to control herself, she felt defeated. *Nee*, her dander was indeed up. "Why didn't Roman ask us first?"

Jeb pulled her close, snuggling in bed under three quilts. "Love, nothing could calm Anna down. The whole town feels at home at our place and Roman blurted out an offer before thinking. Anna perked up when Roman mentioned our house."

Granny cocked her head, staring at Jeb. "How long?"

"Well, the ground's frozen. Real cold snap. So, a foundation would be hard to dig."

"How long?"

"We may be here until your birthday. Wouldn't you like to celebrate your birthday here with the *kinner*?"

She wanted to scream out no. She closed her eyes, trying to think of all the scriptures on self-control, contentment and trusting for God's timing. All she envisioned was her knitting circle back home. They'd be starting up the winter circle after Christmas. What book would they read as they knit? Would they decide to do embroidery again? Would Suzy and Marge banter over knitting verses crochet? And then Fannie's face became crystal clear. Fannie feared Granny would move to Ohio and this extended stay would panic her.

"Jeb, Fannie will take this hard." She wrung her

hands and stared at the oil lamp. Bea! Her dog!

"Jeb, we have to go home. What about Bea?"

He kissed her cheek. "Calm down, love. Roman's taking *gut* care of her."

Granny felt like a child, but she wanted to cry. She needed her dog! Could she be brought out by a van coming this way? Voices shouting outside diverted her attention. What on earth?

Jeb ran as fast as he could to the window. Peeking out, he squinted. "Looks like Rachel with an Englisher. Should I go out?"

So, Rachel and her English beau were quarreling. She didn't want to interfere with Rachel's romance, but was now hopeful that Freeman had made Rachel lose interest. Rachel was plainer than she realized, Granny pondered.

"I'm going out there!" Jeb snapped. "That man is mighty mad, and I think Rachel's crying."

"Jeb, stay put. If we can hear them, certainly Daniel can. Let him go out. Sometimes the secrets we're keeping for our *grosskinner* are for the parents. They need to step it up."

Jeb nodded. "You're right. Should I wake up Daniel? What if he can't hear. Such a sound sleeper."

"I don't know, Jeb. You decide."

Jeb ran to get his wool robe and wrapped himself up in it, asking her to pray as he ran from the room, not stopping to put on his slippers.

~*~

Jeb near skated in his bare feet outside, not taking the time to even put on boots. "Young man!" he shouted as he neared the couple. No, not the couple, but Rachel, Freeman and an Englisher. Freeman had a cloth to his nose, calling the Englisher a coward.

"What is going on out here?" Jeb boomed.

Rachel was crying and struggled to get out, "My fiancé hit Freeman."

Jeb wanted to put up his dukes but reminded himself he was a pacifist. "Rachel, this so-called man is your fiancé?"

"Yes, I am, sir, and this Amish man was flirting with her." He glowered at Freeman.

"He's my *opa*, Jared," Rachel said.

Jared flung his arms in the air. "And an *opa* is?"

"This *opa* is spitting mad," Jeb said evenly. "Now, I want you to leave this property now. I'll be telling Rachel's *Daed*...which means 'dad', and he'll be having words, I'm sure. Now get your *ferhoodled* body off this property."

Rachel began to sob, but she didn't contradict Jeb's demand. Jared stomped off, flinging back insults. Jeb opened his arms and Rachel flew into them. "Let's get *yinz* inside. Freeman, we need to tend to your nose."

The three went inside and Rachel put on the tea kettle. "I'm so sorry, *Opa*. Sorry about your nose,

Freeman."

Jeb waved Rachel's comments away. "It's not your fault. Jealousy's the root of hatred." He barely touched Freeman's swollen nose when he cried out in pain."

Sarah rushed into the kitchen, followed by Granny. "What happened?"

"Rachel can tell *yinz*. I think Freeman has a broken nose. Lean forward Freeman."

Sarah's brows knit together. "Did he fall?"

"Fell on someone's fist," Jeb roared, temper high. "Now, I need a medical person. Do *yinz* have one nearby?"

Granny lay Jeb's slippers by his feet and he slid them in. "*Danki*, love."

"I'll call 9-1-1 from the shop phone," Rachel said.

Jeb could tell Rachel was postponing the inevitable. Telling her parents about an English beau. Ex-beau, he hoped.

~*~

Dearest Fannie,

I'm sure you've heard about Anna wanting to live in my house for a spell. Well, Roman should have asked us first, to be sure, but I suppose it calmed Anna down. I don't know what God's purpose is in my extended stay here in Holmes County, but I want you to know that any rumors of us moving here aren't true. How could I leave my house with a wraparound porch with all those climbing roses? And my sheep! And my little women at knitting circle.

I tear right up just writing this. I've been to Lehman's and bought you something that will be delivered right to your doorstep. Can you believe that? I didn't even have to bring it home. You may not receive it before Christmas, it being the 20th already, but look for a medium sized box.

If I could have my little dog boxed up, I'd have her shipped here priority mail. Not only does she warm my feet, but she calms me. And I've needed calming since we've arrived. Keep praying for Rachel. As you know Freeman Yoder is here and I think Jeb made a match. Only thing is, Rachel is engaged to an Englisher who I thought was a good Christian man, but his character the other night wasn't becoming of a Christ follower. I suppose I shouldn't judge. We all have feet of clay.

Well, I'm glad to hear that Ruth has hosted most of the knitting circle meetings. Do you remember how timid she was, being in such a bad marriage? She barely spoke when we all first started to meet but look at her now. And Luke got so much help, I say praise be that he's a very gut husband.

Well, dear friend, write when you have time. Back to baking with Ruby and May. We're making a massive gingerbread house. It's a joy to get to know my grosskinner out here in Ohio, but I do miss Jenny, Millie and Tillie. Write and tell me how they are.

Much love,

Granny

She set the pen down on her desk, hearing her name sung out by May. Was she rested up yet? *Jah,* she was. She felt a load come off her, knowing that Fannie and her girls back home would be praying for her. She missed Smicksburg something awful and was still a bit sore at Roman for being so presumptuous to let someone live in her house, even if it calmed a soul.

She slipped runaway gray hair back into her prayer *kapp* and descended the steps. Halfway down she met Rachel, who wanted to talk. May rushed up behind Rachel, calling her a 'Granny Hog', always taking up their dear *grossmammi's* time. Granny said it would be quick, throwing Rachel a hint that she had to get back to baking. So, they proceeded back into Granny and Jeb's bedroom and once the door was shut, Rachel let out a loud groan.

"*Oma*, I want you to know something important. I know you told me to wait, but I'm marrying Jared the day after Christmas. No big wedding, no veil, no big castle, we're going to the Justice of the Peace."

Granny crossed her arms, adrenaline running. "Rachel, you're being impulsive, and we know haste is never right. You're not thinking clearly."

"Jared gave me an ultimatum. He's starting his job in New York in January and he wants me to be with him."

Freeman's bloody broken nose flashed before her. "He's violent, Rachel. How could you?"

"Violent? *Nee*, he was jealous is all." Rachel said. "He still can't believe he hit Freeman and is mighty sorry."

"So, he's showing signs of repentance. He'll

apologize to Freeman? Pay for the medical bill, as little as it is?"

Rachel pulled out the desk chair and slowly took a seat. "Well, *nee*. He said Freeman provoked him. Jared said it was a sign of his love for me that made him get so mad. If he wasn't so jealous, he wouldn't love me, *jah*?"

"Two wrongs don't make a right," Granny said, wiping her brow.

"What two wrongs?" Rachel asked.

"Being violent towards Freeman and justifying the sin of jealousy. Remember what your *opa* said about hatred is the root of jealousy. So, hatred, too. And we're told not to hate. Rachel, let me be blunt. I forbid you to marry Jared."

With eyes as round as owls, Rachel stared. Granny's pulse quickened. Did she just say that? She'd never been so brazen, but she knew Jared didn't love Rachel to be so impatient and pushy. Giving Rachel an ultimatum when Christmas was in a few days? Go to the justice of the peace? Not even a church wedding?

Rachel sat stone-faced. Granny threw her arms around her. "Honey, you know I love you, but I can't give my blessing to this union with Jared, but it's your parent's place to decide. And with such a rush, I'm telling your parents as soon as they get back."

Rachel began to quake, and Granny tried to soothe her. "*Oma*, you want me to stay Amish, don't you? Live a life of inconvenience, still hanging wash out on the line. Well, I've had enough of it. Jared said I'd want for nothing. *Nothing!* I see that my *daed's* a near workaholic and *Mamm* suffers. I don't want to live like that."

There was a knock on the door, and Ruby popped her head in. "*Oma*...Rachel, why are you crying?"

"I hate my life," Rachel snapped.

Ruby's pretty face was etched with concern. "It was bad that your ex-boyfriend hit Freeman. Wish I was older, and he loved me."

"*Ach,* Ruby, don't be silly. Freeman doesn't love me."

"*Jah,* he does. I heard him admit it."

Rachel grimaced. "Go on with you, Ruby. You did not."

"I did, too. He talks out loud to God outside at night. He takes night walks and talks to God."

Granny winced. "Don't tell me you go out and follow him."

Instantly, Ruby's face was red as beets. "Well, one time. But I wasn't following him. I was out walking myself and I heard him talking to God. That's when I followed him because I heard him say Rachel's name. He told God he'd never felt so strong about someone. He said he felt like he was supposed to.... cherish Rachel." She cupped her cheeks. "Rachel, you'd be a fool not to love someone like Freeman.

He's perfect!"

Footsteps could be heard, and Sarah entered the room. "I'm back." She took a glance at everyone and sighed. "What's wrong? Is Rachel bossing Ruby again?"

"*Nee*, *Mamm*, I am not. I came in here to talk in private with *Oma*. Ruby barged in."

Granny cleared her throat. "Sarah, I need to talk to you and Daniel right quick."

"*Oma*, don't," Rachel begged.

Granny gave her a knowing look. "I have to."

Chapter 8

Jeb tugged his fishing pole, thinking he had a nibble, but found once again his hook had scooped up pond scum. Well, it was being in the great outdoors that lured him outside, not fishing, really. Over the past few days, Daniel had taken him to a birding seminar, a symposium of sorts, organized by the Amish. He took a mental note that Deborah would like to attend, not organize, such an adventure in Smicksburg when they got home. He was sure she'd have shoeboxes filled for children living in poverty, for sure and certain. *Lord, bless my wife today as she bakes with Ruby and May.*

He noticed that Daniel and Sarah had returned from their buggy ride, snuggled together like two mourning doves. He was witnessing a miracle, he pondered. They were fighting like cats and dogs only weeks ago but nurturing their relationship had put a skip in both of their steps.

He rubbed his hands together, baited his hook, and let it plop into the fishing hole. Maybe this time he'd catch a bass. Jeb thought back to this own fishing hole. *Jah,* he missed it. His fish called to him, as he always said. *These fish in Ohio run away.* The sound of wheels on gravel made him groan. This pond so near the driveway scares the fish! When he looked up to see a red car and then Jared's face, he pulled up his hook and went into the cabin to build a fire. Yes, he'd hide from that man lest he lose his temper again. Running outside like a madman in his bare feet left him only with the sniffles and embarrassment. What did his *grosskinner* think of him?

He threw a log into the woodstove and settled in for a C.S. Lewis read. He thought of Jonas back home, their little reading group, and hoped his MS wasn't ailing him in such cold weather. He crossed his legs and opened his book, when someone rapped on the door. He glanced out the window to see the red car parked nearby. *Lord, I feel like a fool, hiding in here, but I don't trust my temper around that upstart whippersnapper.*

Another rap and Jared calling, "Mr. Weaver, are you in there?" made Jeb cringe. Well, he couldn't hide like King David in a cave, for Pete's sake. He yelled out for Jared to come in and the young man cautiously entered the one room cabin.

"Can we talk?" he asked.

Jeb wondered if Jared ate some humble pie

because he was…meek? Well, anyone can act. "What's on your mind?"

Jared took off his black knit hat and wrung it in his hands. "My behavior the other night was unjustifiable, but I'm asking for forgiveness."

Jeb was so shocked he started to have a coughing fit. Jared asked if he needed water, but Jeb shook his head. When he could talk, he told him he was startled. "Wasn't expecting you to ask for forgiveness."

"Because I'm not Amish?" Jared asked softly, taking the chair next to Jeb. "I'm a Christian, if you can believe it. I've felt convicted of my behavior for days. I talked to my pastor over at The Refuge Church and he gave me sound advice."

Jeb could only gape in disbelief. This was a totally different man. "Go on."

"Well, you see, I'm a lawyer and work mostly with divorces. It's stressful since I see families being ripped apart." Jared pursed his lips. "I represent parents trying to keep their kids and sometimes it doesn't work out. Well, I got a job offer in New York City to get out of being a divorce lawyer and ever since I've been a wreck. After I hit that Amish guy, I knew I'd lost it."

"*Jah,* you did. Lost respect of many in this household, for sure."

Jared appeared confused, but then added that he knew he came to the end of his rope. "My pastor showed me lots of scripture, and one surprised me."

He pulled out a small Bible from his coat pocket and pulled out the ribbon marker.

"Better to be poor and honest than to be dishonest and a fool. Enthusiasm without knowledge is no good; haste makes mistakes. People ruin their lives by their own foolishness and then are angry at the Lord." He closed the book. "That's Proverbs 19:1-3. My pastor said that other translations say haste is a sin."

"Meaning we miss the mark, *jah*?"

"Yes," Jared said. "I've been sinning in that way. And I've been so angry with God because I'm running from him. You see, I went into law to help the poor and disadvantaged, but all I saw in New York was dollar signs. Big ones. I've seen poverty and injustice in the inner city, and so I'm going to take a job in Cleveland making a fraction of what I make now." He chewed his bottom lip, pausing as if to gain courage. "And I hastily proposed to Rachel and need to call things off. You see, in the Word it says that enthusiasm without knowledge is not good, right? I'm real enthusiastic about Rachel until we talk about big issues. She's plain through and through. Lots of Amish people aren't as committed and I thought I could change her. It wasn't right."

Respect for this young man rose in Jeb's heart. "It takes a real man to see his faults and turn from them. Now this old fool needs to apologize for hastily running outside in his bare feet like a loon in a rage."

Jared extended his hand and Jeb shook it. "Pray for Rachel. I never wanted to hurt her."

Jeb tapped his book. "Pain is God's megaphone to rouse a deaf world."

"*The Problem of Pain* by C.S. Lewis, right?"

Jeb held up the book. "*Jah*. Lewis wrote this when his wife died of cancer. Can't imagine anything more painful."

Jared's brows furrowed. "Is your wife okay?"

Jeb could see why Rachel would care for such a thoughtful man. "Well, we're getting up in age and the time for us to part will come someday, but we're healthy as horses right now."

"Rachel said many times she wanted a marriage like her grandparents in Pennsylvania."

"*Ach,* Deborah's a saint to put up with me," Jeb said with a wink, and to his surprise he extended his arms and embraced Jared. "God bless you, young man."

~*~

Freeman rose to stretch his back and inspect the simple weave pattern on the chair seat. Simple, just how Rachel liked it. His heart was heavy after she told him of her plan to marry Jared. Why this girl made such an impression on his heart was a mystery, but maybe it was to open his heart up to other women. After taking countless girls on buggy rides, he'd all but given up. Maybe he needed to give Jane another chance? Maybe visit his friends out in Lancaster and cast a bigger net. He could not ignore his desire to settle down and have a family. 'Delight yourself in the Lord, and he will give you the desires of your heart,' the Bible said. Maybe he had his nose to the ground, minding the things of the earth too much?

He shook his head, trying to clear his thoughts, but oh how his nose still ached, and he winced. Freeman caught a glance of a red car parked by the fishing cabin. "*Ach,* Lord, help me," he prayed. He supposed Rachel was going to finally introduce Jared to the family in a more peaceable fashion. Getting marriage advice, no doubt. The Weaver's marriage was one to emulate.

Feeling suddenly restless, he got the shop broom and started to sweep and pray to his God out loud, as was his custom.

"Lord, why I care so much for Rachel is a mystery. Am I back on the pottery wheel, being painfully molded into something I should be? Something I lack? Patience? Confidence? Hope?"

The story of Gideon putting out a fleece before the Lord to see if God was with him when he came out of hiding and attack the Midianites came to mind. Put a fleece before God? Ask for a sign. The oddest, most ridiculous notion came to his mind, and he chided himself for being so silly. Stupid, really. But what did he have to lose?

"Lord, if Rachel is for me, I want Jared to tell me I'm better suited. That he sees how plain she really is and that I'm a better match."

He blushed at his own foolishness. This so-called fleece would never happen, and he had to give Rachel up. Jane Coblenz did encourage him in his passion for woodworking. She was still single, too, putting off marriage to help her widowed *mamm* raise her nine younger siblings. Now, that was admirable, he pondered. Mighty sacrificial woman Jane was, so why hadn't he taken her for a third buggy ride? Was he afraid of commitment?

He wanted to shake his head again, but still felt pressure along his nose bridge. So, he shifted his jaw and told himself he needed to grow up. If he wanted a wife and family, he needed to stop being so doubleminded. Yes, he would go home and talk to Jane. Not propose right off, but get to know her better, even though they played together as children. He needed to see Jane as a grown woman.

Feeling suddenly fatigued, he went to the chair he just finished for Rachel as a Christmas present. Someone needed to try it out. See if the caning was loose or taut. *Jah,* it was perfect. He tipped his black wool hat over his eyes to catch forty winks. He'd had a restless night thinking of Rachel.

After five minutes, he couldn't sleep, so he made a mental list of things to buy at Lehman's before he went back home for Christmas. His *mamm* needed a new apple peeler and loved popcorn so much, she'd love a new Whirley Pop. His *daed* would appreciate any new tools.

A gush of wind whirled into the shop as the door opened. He nudged his hat up to see Jared staring at him. He covered his nose. Not again! "Hello, Jared. What brings you in here? Need to buy something…for Rachel?" His voice was shaking like a scared little girl and he was so ashamed, but his nose!

Jared pulled up a wood chair. "I need to apologize to you. I've never hit a man before, but jealousy put me in a bad rage. A rage that scared me." He extended his hand and Freeman took it, shaking with a firm grip.

"I forgive you. Jealousy's a mighty powerful force, *jah*?"

"Yes, it is." Jared said. "I talked to my pastor about it. A long talk. I'll spare you the details, but I'll be moving to Cleveland for a new job and I need to let Rachel go. She's plain and I'm not. I'd try to change her, and she'd try the same." Gloom spread across his face. "I care for Rachel and I want her happy. And tell me if I'm speaking out of turn, not really knowing you, but I feel you'd be a better match. I think she cares about you but didn't want to lose me. I think I knew the night of my…fist meeting your nose." He forced a smile. "I'm really sorry for lashing out and I'll pay any medical bills. Did I break your nose?"

Freeman was so stunned he just brushed it off, saying it was not a problem. Jared stood, shook his hand again, and then he said he'd be talking to Rachel now. When the door closed and he was sure Jared was out of earshot, he threw his black hat in the air and yelled out a whoop. He spun around, holding his aching nose, and refraining himself from jumping. He'd just asked God for this very thing! As a sign. Jared told him he'd be a better match for Rachel. "Praise be!" he yelled.

~*~

With Christmas fast approaching, Granny needed to invite her brother to the school Christmas program on Christmas Eve. And she wanted to do it in person to gage his reaction. A reaction told her much.

So, when the hired driver deposited her at her brother's door, she shot up a prayer. Kimberly answered the door and asked for Granny's bonnet and cape. She was glad she'd worn her black shawl Ella and Ruth made her since it was quite a *nippy* day. She took a seat in the living room and was surprised that her brother seemed eager to see her. "Hello, Debbie. I'm glad you stopped by. I was afraid you'd go back without a visit."

Noah's face had more color; he must have been in shock when he first saw her.

"Where's Jeb?" motioning to a tall leather chair as he took the green stuffed chair that appeared to have vines crawling on it.

"Jeb's helping Daniel finish Christmas orders. My sons always had a way with wood, like you did."

Noah gripped the armrests and licked his lips. "I've made lots of the furniture in this house. Always wanted to learn upholstery to make a chair like this, but sewing machines…"

"Would make you miss *Mamm* and *Grossmammi?*" Granny asked. "I still do."

Noah cleared his throat. "I don't want to be disagreeable, but I fear my childhood memories aren't fond like yours. Let's just leave it at that."

Granny knew Noah and her *daed* butted horns more that anyone in the household. "*Daed* loved us, you know."

"Could have fooled me. Well, he had a soft spot for you, Debbie, his favorite, but I was the black sheep, not manly enough."

Granny was taken back by Noah's openness. "Sometimes it helps to talk about it. When we're little children, we see through little children's eyes. Now that we're old, we see how hard life can be."

Noah pulled a pipe and matches out of a carved box on the round table next to him. He lit it and made a smoke ring. "He called me a sissy too many times."

Granny gasped. "What?"

"It's true. Under his breath he called me a pansy or plain old sissy because I didn't like seeing animals killed. Don't worry. I got myself all figured out with lots of therapy. My natural bend is towards art, poetry and what some men like *daed* considered nonsense."

Granny knew Noah was more tenderhearted than her other brothers. And she'd read his poetry and she always thought he was as good as Robert Frost. Well, he wrote about nature, so maybe that was why she was drawn to Frost. "Noah, I could talk to you easier than any sibling."

Noah brightened. "Same for me. I'm not an unhappy man. I feel like I've lived a good life. Memories of childhood come back, talking to me."

"Don't you miss the Amish, deep down, Noah? You were devout in church."

He took another puff. "I got shunned. Nope, don't miss any of it."

"*Jah,* I know. But you left after baptism. You broke a vow. Why'd you do it? Get an education and sell the farm. You never did like farming, but *Daed* left it to you."

Noah's eyes grew round. "I lived in that house, taking care of our parents in their *dawdyhaus* for ten years, alone, but when they passed, I moved on. I was in my thirties and knew I couldn't stand to farm another day. Sold it all and went to college for several years. Debbie, the house was left to me. It's the Amish way. You don't have hard feelings, do you?"

Granny clenched her hands together. "*Nee*, not really. But, why did you sell to Walmart?"

"I needed the money to pay for college and make a living. I have no debt. One thing I learned from the Amish is to be frugal."

Granny had misjudged her brother. The only thing that had played like a ticker tape in her mind was 'he sold the family farm to Walmart' but she never asked him why. Was it because of the shunning? He'd have no financial safety net if he left. "Noah, you deserved to do what you did," she said with conviction. "You cared for our parents and I should have come out more. I've misjudged you, thinking you were led away from the Amish by greed, but I was wrong. I'm asking your forgiveness."

Noah's chin quivered as he shut his eyes tight. Rivulets of tears streamed down his cheeks. Granny ran to him, leaning her head against his. "I'm so sorry, Noah. But I had to obey the shunning."

Noah wept until Granny believed he was dried up. She was heartsick that this favorite brother of hers never got to explain himself. Anger arose in her when she remembered how harsh Noah's shunning was, all because of Walmart. If he'd sold to a farmer, she believed talking to him would have been allowed. But decades had passed, and what could be done?

They spent the rest of the afternoon in his greenhouse attached to his porch while she considered things. Being invited to a large Amish event wouldn't be appropriate, but having a talk with the local bishop about lifting the speaking ban would.

When she left, they embraced and they both shed tears for all the years they'd missed, with a promise to make up for lost time. Granny would not spend Second Christmas with anyone but her brother.

~*~

The next day, Granny was glad to have the knitting circle over for a little party. Sydney and Melody had stopped by just to chat, and she was beginning to bond with these two women. Truth be told, she enjoyed their company more than Fern. How judgmental she'd been toward others, and Granny was glad Sarah recognized this in herself. The whole family atmosphere had changed ever since Daniel and Sarah were like two peas in a pod. The only thing that dimmed the light in the family was Rachel's deep sorrow over Jared letting her go. She walked around like a ragdoll and barely ate a speck. She rejected any comfort, saying she'd never smile again. *How shortsighted the younger folk are*, Granny thought.

She saw Sydney and Melody pull in the driveway and she nimbly ran to get two white pastry bags from the counter and met them at the door. "Merry Christmas!"

Sydney embraced her first. "Merry Christmas to you, Granny!" She said 'Granny' with delight. Peeking in the bag, her eyes bugged. "Granny! They're so cute!"

Melody hugged Granny and thanked her for the gift and Granny's heart sang as the girls inspected their boot cuffs. "You can wear them around your ankles, too."

Melody beamed. "Granny, these are so special because the Amish aren't allowed to wear things like this."

"You're not Amish, *jah*? And I do think they're cute and clever. It looks like women are wearing long stockings when it's just a little cuff sticking out of their boots."

Sydney scrutinized the boot cuffs. "Your stitches are perfect. I could sell these at my salon. Do you want to make some for me to sell?"

Granny wondered if Sydney needed more money. "*Jah,* I can donate some."

Sydney laughed a boom. "I mean on consignment. I'd give you all the so-called commission though. These things will sell like hotcakes."

Granny sighed. "If you don't mind, I'd rather not. Sarah has offered to help me with my long-lost quilting skills. I got so sick of quilting, but Sarah has some more challenging patterns I'd like to try."

"She needs to open a shop," Sydney said with conviction. "Amish quilts are a fortune. Poor Daniel wouldn't have to work so hard if Sarah made an income."

Granny smiled. "Sarah's thought of that. Now, Melody, have you and Kenny been able to do much together lately?"

The women walked into the living room while Melody told that she'd seen some improvement. "He took me out to see a movie and it was so strange because it was about a family who adopted some kids. He asked me what I thought, and I told him the movie was good, but he didn't mean that. He meant the idea of taking in foster children. When he met Jeb, I think he put a bug in his ear about your adopted son."

"Denny!" Granny quipped, trying to hide her pride for Jeb, mentoring that rough around the edges Kenny. "We miss Denny but will have to bear it. Jeb and I need to be here longer since someone's living in my house."

Sydney took out her yarn and needles and with fingers flying, blinked in disbelief. "Why is someone at your place?"

"Because of a fire. Anna wouldn't calm down until my son told her she could stay at my house. She loves my kitchen. *Gut* baker."

Sarah joined the group, informing them that her *mamm* and Leah said they were down with colds.

"They don't want us sick on Christmas Day."

"I can't believe Christmas is after tomorrow," Melody said. "I know it comes every year, but it always catches me off guard, and I don't even have children to buy for. Well, at least yet." She turned to Sydney. "Are you done buying for your big family?"

Without looking up, Sydney said she gave them gift cards and a new Christmas ornament for the tree. She gasped and looked up. "I'm sorry. I know the Amish think a Christmas tree is…not right?"

Sarah laughed. "We don't judge, Sydney. We have our own customs. And we don't have Christmas on one day, but twelve. Ever hear of the Twelve Days of Christmas song?"

Sydney set down her needles. "You celebrate for twelve days? I'd die! Too much cooking."

"*Ach, nee*," Granny informed. "We have First Christmas on Christmas Day. Second Christmas the next day for more family and friends. We visit over twelve days until Old Christmas, January sixth. Now, not every day is a big meal and all, but people do visit and drop off gifts."

"The Amish buy Christmas presents?" Melody asked, shocked.

"I just gave you a present," Granny pointed out. "Not the large scale buying the Englishers do."

Sarah murmured under her breath. "Ridiculous."

"I heard that," Sydney mused. "You must see more of us Englishers since Daniel has a shop."

"That we do," Sarah said with a chuckle. "Daniel and I talked about me having a quilting shop."

Sydney clasped her hands. "That's what I was thinking. Helping Daniel make a living."

Sarah visibly shuddered. "Daniel said he wanted me to do it for my enjoyment. We make ends meet."

Sydney snickered. "Sarah. I didn't mean it like that. All you do with your kids is work, for sure. It's just that your quilts are the best I've seen in all of Holmes County."

Sarah flushed. "Really?"

"Yes. I think they deserve to be seen."

The enthusiasm in Sydney's voice was contagious. "I agree, Sarah," Granny said. "That room full of quilts needs a door put on, a walkway made, and Daniel needs to add to his sign, 'Rockers and Quilts.' It would give Jeb something to do since we're staying until February."

"I think you need to move here," Sydney quipped. "You can have more modern conveniences. I still can't believe you cook with a woodstove."

"*Ach,* it tastes better. We're allowed to have gas stoves if we have our own gas well, like many do, being on the Marcellus Shale, but I don't like gas. It's not natural."

"Wind is," Sarah put in. "Solar panels and a windmill are all you need to run a gas-powered stove and fridge."

Sydney leaned forward as if telling a secret. "There are people living off the grid and I wish I was one of them. Utilities are sky high and like Granny said, it's more natural. When it gets dark out, we should be going to sleep, don't you think?"

"At five o'clock in winter?" Melody asked. "

"You know what I mean," Sydney said. "I see the Amish up at the crack of dawn literally and they go to bed early, right?" she asked, waiting for Granny to answer.

"Most Amish get up quite early. It's our way, you know. I know of some Amish night owls who take walks at night. With houses full of *kinner*, it's a quiet time."

"Amen to that!" Sydney hooted. "But I'll be sad when all my birds fly the coop. I'll have to adopt or something."

Granny deeply admired Sydney. She hoped that Sydney's big heart would rub off on Fern and Leah, but they'd been avoiding knitting circle for the past two weeks. Last week they were too busy. Granny knew there was a strain between Sarah and her family, but she didn't seem to mind.

"Where's Rachel?" Sydney asked.

Granny looked to Sarah to explain and she told them of her breakup with Jared, and how Rachel had been moody and hard to live with.

"She's depressed," Melody said. "Feels rejected."

Sydney groaned. "No man is worth losing your mind over. He was a loser to let Rachel go. She's so sweet."

"He's English and said he did it for Rachel's sake," Sarah said. "She's plain and he respects that."

Sydney belted out, "Really? That was probably hard for him. I've seen it over and over living here in Holmes County. The stories I hear at my salon. For an Englisher to call off a wedding because he can see that down the road it wouldn't work is mighty impressive. He's mature for sure."

Sarah tilted her head. "I like Jared and I hope he's happy up in Cleveland."

Cold air blasted the room as Daniel opened the front door. Granny heard a bark. One just like Bea's. Little toenails tapping on wood floors grew near and soon Bea was on Granny's lap. "Bea! How'd you get here!" She hugged her sweet Bea with all her might. "Daniel, did you get her for me?"

"*Nee*, you have visitors."

Fannie and Janice ran into the room ringing out a Merry Christmas and explaining that Janice drove the church van to bring Bea out. She also brought a van full of women out to shop at Lehman's. Granny took in the sight of her dear friends. Fannie was clinging to her, cheeks wet with tears. Janice's lovely smile was accentuated by her ebony skin. What a lovely sight. After many thanks, Granny gazed into Bea's large chocolate eyes..

Chapter 9

Granny feasted her eyes on Fannie and Janice, having missed them immensely. "I can't believe you're here. You must meet the whole family and stay for supper."

Janice's brows arched. "I met Daniel on the way in. Spitting image of Roman. But snow's coming and I promised Jerry I'd drop Bea off and head on home." She pulled her wallet from her massive black and white checkered purse and jingled it. "But he did give me money to spend at Lehman's. I want an ice cream maker like yours. Do you know Jerry sold some rare books on eBay to get the money?"

With glistening eyes, Granny was radiant. "Very *gut* of him. Tell him I miss him and all the girls at Forget-Me-Not Manor." She slipped an arm through Fannie's. "And how is Melvin?"

"Busy with Christmas orders. The store is swamped with customers, but nothing like it is out here in Holmes County."

Granny motioned for Sarah to join the group after she saw Sydney and Melody out. She noticed Rachel was in the kitchen and motioned to her to come meet her friends. Reluctantly, Rachel obeyed. "This is Daniel's wife, Sarah, and her *dochder*, Rachel. We just got done with knitting circle."

Fannie gasped. "*Ach, nee.* When you start a circle, you get attached and you'll stay."

"*Nee*, I will not. Smicksburg is my home. My roses will be coming back to life in spring and I plan to be there to see and smell them."

Fannie turned to Rachel. "What do you think of Freeman? I had my eye on him in elementary school. He was nice as a kid and hasn't changed a bit."

Sarah wrapped an arm around Rachel. "Our girl is sad because of a broken engagement."

Fannie pat her heart. "My Melvin was dumped before he had eyes for me. Nothing against Lizzy now, of course, but she wasn't too nice to my husband. Melvin said he appreciates things in me more because of what his relationship with Lizzy lacked."

"Aunt Lizzy broke up with your husband?" Rachel asked.

Fannie let out nervous laughter. "*Ach,* Lizzy is your aunt now. She was a blessing to poor Roman after his wife passed." She leaned forward. "Do you know Jeb tried to hook up your uncle and me? Imagine that. I could be your aunt and we're nearly the same age."

Janice chuckled. "There's lots of romance that

comes out of our knitting circles. Granny's matched up several couples."

Granny knew that Jeb was trying to match Rachel with Freeman, and it looked promising, the way the two looked at each other.

Just then, Freeman jogged into the room, Ruby following. "Janice. Fannie. Can I catch a ride back home with *yinz*? I need to get back for Christmas."

"Sure," Janice said. "Lots of room in the church van. You pack up your stuff while we head on over to Lehman's."

Rachel fumbled over her words as she said good-bye to Janice and Fannie, declining an offer to go shopping. She darted out of the room as if being chased by a bull. An awkward silence filled the room. And then Ruby started to whimper and then burst into sobs, high tailing it outside. Freeman followed Ruby.

Granny felt limp as an over cooked noodle. "What's going on?"

Janice winked. "Freeman's leaving. Did the whole family get attached?"

Sarah sighed. "I was hoping he'd stay, but he needs to be with his family on Christmas. We'll miss him. Are most Amish young men in Smicksburg like him?" she asked Granny.

"Well, you find a bad apple in every bunch, but there's lots of Amish men like him; I've met some fine young men here in Millersburg."

"Well, Rachel's turned all of them away, having her secret engagement with Jared."

Fannie tapped her cheek with her index finger playfully. "Maybe Rachel needs to come out to Smicksburg for a visit when Granny comes home?"

Granny smiled. "Maybe."

~*~

Rachel could not stop crying. Confusion reigned in her mind. Jared breaking things off came as a relief because he was becoming someone she didn't admire anymore. His threat to marry or be dumped sent her into a whirlwind of emotion and in her haste, she almost married someone who admitted he was going to try to change her. Mold her into a modern English woman.

All along, she suppressed the growing feelings for Freeman. But he was leaving to go back home. *Ach,* she knew he cared for her, but she couldn't just blurt out she felt the same when she'd announced not long ago that she'd be getting married by Christmas. *Ferhoodled! He must think I'm ferhoodled!*

She paced across the bedroom floor, trying to think of a reason why Freeman needed to come back. Sydney almost accomplished her mission to have her *mamm* open a quilt shop. Did Freeman need to come out and help build the addition? She rolled her eyes. Of course not.

She went to the window to see the chunky snow covering everything like a popcorn stitched crochet blanket. Maybe the roads would be too slick for Janice to drive? Someone knocked on her door. One of her sisters needed help doing something again.

"Come in," she sputtered.

Ruby stampeded in, took Rachel's hands, and jumped. "Guess what!"

"You didn't burn your last batch of cookies?"

Grinning, Ruby tugged at one of Rachel's prayer *kapp* strings. "*Nee*, silly." She clapped her hands. "Freeman is staying so he can see me in the school program. He said specifically to *see me!*"

Rachel couldn't help but smile. "Not to see May?"

Ruby swooned and faked a dramatic faint on the bed. "Rachel, I'm so glad you don't like him. He's so perfect."

"He's too old for you," Rachel informed. "You're only sixteen?"

"Time for *Rumspringa* and courting!" She spun around. "And I like older men," Ruby said, straightening. "I'm not a little girl anymore."

As Rachel's mouth grew dry, she sat on the bed next to her sister. "Ruby, is this the first boy you've liked?"

"*Jah,* and the last. No one can ever come close to Freeman."

Putting a hand to her mouth, Rachel composed herself. "So, no other guy from our *Gmay* has ever gotten your attention? How about Noah Klein. I see how he looks at you."

Turning to Rachel, Ruby rested her head on one elbow. "He never looks at me." Instantly Ruby's countenance fell. "I'm not that pretty."

Rachel took Ruby's hand. "Honey, you're very pretty. Prettier than me, that's for sure, with those big fawn-like eyes. And anyone who catches you is a blessed man. But, remember, inner beauty is the most important thing." Rachel pressed her hands on her heart. "What we store up in here." As she said this, she knew she'd neglected this very thing. Working at the hotel had made her cross paths with too many televisions and she compared herself and her so-called dull life to the movie stars.

"*Danki*, Rachel. I'm glad you're not marrying Jared. He'd take you from us. But, promise me one thing."

"What's that?"

"Stay clear of Freeman?"

Rachel cared for Freeman in such a short time, but here was her sister declaring her 'first love' for a man. Rachel had to consider that her relationship with her sister was more important than Freeman. He wasn't her husband and most likely wouldn't be.

"Promise?" Ruby asked, a catch in her voice.

"*Jah,* sure. Until you like someone else,"

"I never will!"

Rachel braced herself and asked Ruby if she wanted to play Old Maid tonight. For some reason, that game would comfort her.

~*~

The night of the annual Christmas program, Rachel had to swallow a lump the size of the Grand Canyon. As she watched the little ones recite their poems, she wondered if she'd ever have a little one of her own. She'd mentioned this fear to Granny, who appeared unconcerned. *Lots of fish in the sea,* she'd said. And she reminded Rachel she was quite young for such hopelessness. Granny also helped her piece together all the emotions she'd rumbled through over the past weeks. Marrying Jared or else and then abruptly breaking off their engagement. But, oddly enough, Rachel felt true to herself and deep down, peaceful.

Jared had swept her off her bare feet the night they snuck down for a walk around the pond. With his red car tucked away in the forest to the east, they'd stayed up until four without realizing it. What an interesting man Jared was, and his world seemed to be less cumbersome than the Amish. He was a gentleman, not even stealing a kiss or peck on her cheek that night. Jared genuinely seemed to want to get to know her. All was going so well, until her grandparents came. They helped set her parents' marriage back on the right course and Rachel saw in her family what she wanted: a happy Amish family.

She and her *mamm* had clashed over the smallest

of issues, but the truth was, she was defensive. At times, she wanted to scream at her *mamm* for being so critical of her dear *daed*. But with recent talks with her *mamm*, she discovered she'd been lonely and discouraged. *Mamm* didn't feel attractive anymore. Aging had played tricks with her mind that she was wrinkled and not very appealing. So-called dating her husband again had changed her. And now with the help of the knitting circle, Sydney was helping her write a business model for her new quilt shop to open in spring.

Maybe it was the women in the circle that helped her bear the blow of Jared's breakup. Sydney had two husbands walk out on her. Melody was so unhappily married, but things were changing, so she'd said. Her Aunt Leah and her *Mammi Fern* had secure homes due to what Granny called fences. She smiled at the thought. Up late knitting with Granny, she'd explained how she'd had an old bull that scared the living daylights out of some of the boys in town. When the fence was up, they weren't afraid, but when Old Bull got out, they ran up a tree, screaming like girls, even though he was too tired to charge anyone.

So, Granny said fences, or lack thereof, can make one feel ill at ease. Insecure. At times, with no moral compass. Sydney called these fences boundaries. Sydney had strict rules she abided by, like the Amish. How immature Rachel felt when she discovered that everyone who's a grown adult with responsibilities must have not only boundaries, but priorities.

Well, hers came to the forefront when Jared jerked her into thinking about life in New York City. When he apologized for trying to change her, she knew he'd put in words all that she couldn't. They had both wanted to change each other.

Granny felt her forehead. "No fever. Rachel, you look ill."

Rachel did feel heart sick about many things. "*Jah,* I suppose."

"Do you want to go on back to the house?"

Tears pricked her eyes. This *grossmammi* had love oozing from her pours. "*Jah,* I'd like to go home."

Granny whispered to Jeb, who nodded, looked up at her with his big turquoise eyes full of concern, and nodded. As they made their way to the back of the schoolhouse, Freeman fell in pace with them, and once outside, announced that he wanted to go back to the farm.

The sky was inky black, making the stars vivid. The hoot of a screech owl pierced the night. Freeman took each by the elbows, asking them to watch for icy patches.

Something dawned on Rachel. "Freeman," she ventured. "Ruby will be upset if you don't watch her program. She set up the whole thing, being the teacher."

Freeman shivered. "I don't feel right. Getting to bed early should help."

As usual, Granny pampered Freeman the whole way home, a short five-minute ride, but by the time they got into the house, Granny had the tea kettle on, peppermint tea and herbal remedies on the counter, lickety-split.

"I sure hope you're not catching that flu going around," Granny said, putting a hand to Freeman's forehead. "*Ach,* you're burning up. Freeman, you get in bed. I'll bring up garlic tea."

"Garlic tea?" Freeman looked like he bit into a lemon. "Can I have another potion?"

"They're not potions, but real foods that prevent disease and cure. I think I'll take some garlic tea myself. An old woman like me needs to be careful."

Rachel embraced Granny. "*Jah,* we need to take *gut* care of you. Go on up to bed and I'll bring up the tea to you both."

"Aren't you sick?" Freeman asked Rachel.

Granny pat her heart. "Heart sick. Most painful ailment."

Embarrassed, Rachel dared look at Freeman. Their eyes locked. No words were said, but they both knew that him leaving to go back home was hard on them both. She was fond of him and may never see him again, but how fickle she would seem to accept any attention right after her engagement was broken off? He'd feel like a rebound. Did Freeman feel the same caution? *Ach,* everything would look better in the morning.

~*~

The next morning was Christmas Day, and Granny sprang out of bed, memories of Christmases shared with Noah running through her mind. Tomorrow, they'd reminisce all day long.

When Jeb let out a woeful groan, Granny thought it peculiar. "Is Bea bothering you, love? Keep you up with all her wiggling around?"

"My head," he whimpered like a child. "Something's wrong."

Granny soon found that Jeb had a temperature. She went to the wash basin and put cool wash cloths on his forehead. "I'll get Daniel. We need to get you to the doctor."

"Christmas," Jeb said. "No doc."

It was Christmas of all things. Well, that's why she admired nurses and doctors who worked in hospitals. "We'll get you to the ER."

"*Nee*. Just need sleep."

"Old man, you're going and that's that. Let me make arrangements." She flew out the door and bumped into Sarah. "Sarah, Jeb's sick."

"So is half the family. I'm calling Melody to see if she or Sydney can fetch our Amish herbal man."

Granny wished Reed Byler was nearby. "We have one of those in Smicksburg."

Sarah linked arms with Granny. "Come downstairs and have a Christmas breakfast. You'll need your strength."

"I need to get Jeb to the hospital," Granny sputtered. "Or take his temperature but quick."

Going down the stairs, Sarah said Rachel and Benjamin were up and about, with no sign of sickness.

"What about Freeman?" Granny asked, turning to go back upstairs. "Did he leave? He was so sick."

"He's in bed with a fever. Rachel will take Jeb's temperature and you'll have coffee. I don't think you're awake yet."

"Just nervous. I don't like it when Jeb's sick. He rarely is and he's…old."

"We'll keep an eye on him."

Granny felt like crying. Christmas day with a house full of sick loved ones? How could Jeb appreciate his present when so sick? And all the things she got for everyone. All crocheted or knit with love. And then it dawned on her that everything she made in secret were cozy comfort presents. Lap blankets, hot water bottle covers, and a doll for May. She felt instant relief. This family she loved so dearly would have gifts they needed right now.

~*~

Pouring hot chicken broth into soup mugs, Rachel wished Doc Martin would come right quick. She'd just took ice off her *grossdaddi* while Freeman's teeth were chattering. She remembered reading that the chills helped lower a temperature, so was she doing the right thing by taking Freeman something hot? Feeling inadequate, she hoped Doc Martin would soon arrive. Surely neither Sydney nor Melody wouldn't mind driving him to help on Christmas morning.

She mounted the steps, tray in hand, and breathed in deeply, feeling rather fatigued herself. She had a low-grade fever, but she wasn't going to let on to anyone. Her family needed her.

She paused as she rounded the corner to Freeman's room. Somehow, she knew she was plain, deep in her soul. How many times had her *mamm* tended to the family while sick, and everyone felt such comfort? She envisioned having a brood of her own and yes, they would have to be raised plain to suit her. Rachel was grateful Jared could foresee this friction in their marriage and let her go. For not only his good, but hers. And it pained him. She finally was absorbing it all and believed him. *God bless Jared. Lead him to someone who will fit him like a glove.*

Freeman was sitting up in bed, blowing air into his hands as if outside and freezing. "This soup will warm you up."

"Jane? What are you doing here?"

Startled, Rachel made Freeman look at her. "What's my name?"

He squinted. "Lily! Go get *Mamm*. My head's

exploding."

He was obviously delirious! "Freeman, you're not at home, but in Ohio."

He gripped his head as tears ran down his cheeks. "Get *Mamm* or *Daed*!" he shouted, and then fell back, stiff as a board and shook.

Rachel screamed as she believed she was witnessing a seizure. Her instincts told her to call down the hall for Granny and try to hold Freeman. She lay beside him, holding his rigid body, praying for God to do something. *Lord, help this dear man!* Tears pricked Rachel's eyes, yet she prayed more, and then she recited Psalm twenty-three to him. Halfway through, he ceased jerking and no signs of life were evident.

"*Mamm*!" she screamed. "Come quick!" She pat Freeman's cheek as she whimpered. "Freeman, come back to us!"

Someone pulled her back and she soon saw Doc Martin. "*Ach,* I'm so glad you're here!"

Sydney rushed into the room, along with her *mamm.* She darted to her *mamm* and cried like a *boppli.* "I think he's dead."

Doc Martin told everyone to be silent. After a quick assessment, he told them all to help him get Freeman into the car. They needed to go to the Emergency Room, and but quick.

~*~

Rachel insisted on going with them, while her *mamm* stayed home to care for the sick. Dear *Mamm*!

Why did she have to be so stubborn, no prideful, to not see all the good in her *mamm*?

Freeman was propped up between her and Sydney. "*Danki* for coming. You're like the March girls who left their Christmas breakfast to care for the Hummels."

Sydney snapped her fingers. "*Little Women*. I love that book. It's no trouble, Rachel. When you have kids, you learn to be up at all hours."

"But it is Christmas, and I'm thankful for you. That we met."

Sydney forced a smile. "Me, too. Freeman had a seizure. Does he have epilepsy?"

While Melody was driving, Doc Martin turned to them. "Meningitis is going around. From what Rachel described, he shows many symptoms of catching it."

"Catching it?" Sydney asked. "It's viral?"

Doc Martin's light blue eyes tried to portray confidence. "Well, sometimes a high fever can cause a seizure. I'm a self-taught medical man."

Freeman stirred and groggily opened his eyes. So lethargic, he strained to look at Rachel. "*Danki*."

Doc Martin gasped. "Do you know where you are? Who we are?"

Freeman was silent. The sleet beat against the window and it was hard to make out what he was trying to say, but Rachel heard him say her name.

She hugged him, weeping. *Danki* Lord was all she could say.

~*~

Sydney made a second trip to the hospital, this time driving Jeb with Granny at his side. Granny thanked Sydney profusely for sacrificing her Christmas to help her family. "Of course, I'd help," Sydney reassured repeatedly. Granny recalled some criticism she'd received at church; being too cozy with the English, especially ones that weren't Mennonite or in other Anabaptist groups. Granny rolled her eyes at the thought. If Jesus walked the earth, she reckoned He'd love spending the day with Sydney. Not a hypocritical bone in her body, no play acting or mask wearing, but a transparent woman. A woman flawed, like us all.

It unsettled Granny that she was getting so attached to Sydney and Melody. The circle of friends was oddly growing to include Kenny, Melody's husband and Sydney's grown children. Sydney was inviting clients to knitting circle, even printed out a poster to hang in her salon. But she'd be leaving. Would Sarah take over the knitting circle? Fern and Leah had yet to bond with the women. On the contrary, they were missing too many meetings to even be considered members.

Granny covered her mouth as she peered out the car window. Was Fern's husband home yet? Surely, he was home for Christmas. She mentally checked off that a pie dropped off at Fern's and a nice visit was in order. There were secrets growing in the farmhouse behind them, and like mold, it needed exposed to the sunlight.

Sydney cheerfully drove up to the hospital ER, telling Granny to call when she was needed again, and to give her an update on Jeb and, well, the whole family down with the flu or virus of some sort. A tall man entering the ER quickly ran to help Jeb in the door, as Jeb was catching his breath, leaning on Granny. "*Danki*," he was able to say.

In the waiting room, Granny couldn't help but admire the many paintings of Amish scenes. The one with Amish children chasing a pig amused her, bringing back memories of her five rambunctious boys. What a happy childhood they had tucked into their pockets, something to pull from as they aged. She was ever so happy with Rachel's resolve to live plain, out in the country, on a farm. She would have wilted living in the city.

Jeb's name was called, the paperwork done, and he was soon in an examination room. Stark white walls, yet with a little picture of an Amish girl. An Amish child that looked so like herself when a *kinner*. How peculiar.

Groaning while holding his head, Jeb asked if the lights could be turned off. "My eyes," he said. "Too bright."

The young doctor said she'd be quick, asking Jeb

many questions. She pinched the back of his hand, pulled down his eyes, and shook her head. "This hospital is filling up, but we have a few more beds left."

"You're admitting him?" Granny asked in dismay.

The doctor nodded while writing on her clipboard. "He's dehydrated. He'll need IV fluids and we'll need to keep an eye on him." She stopped, appearing puzzled. "Your name is Weaver? And you're Amish? Don't hear that surname much in Ohio."

"*Ach,* we're from Pennsylvania. My son lives here. I was born and raised here. I was a Byler, but that's a common name, too."

While a nurse got Jeb into a wheelchair, the doctor glanced over at the picture of the little Amish girl. "We have lots of paintings done by a Byler. Donates regularly. Nice man."

The intercom drowned out their conversation when the doctor was paged. She excused herself, rushing from the room. Granny edged her way over to the painting. She squinted to see the initials 'N.B' in the corner. Tears welled in Granny's eyes. She knew Noah dabbled in paint on *Rumspringa*. Did he paint this? Did he paint all the Amish pictures? If so, why did he paint the Amish?

Granny shook her head. She was tired and needed to tend to Jeb.

~*~

Rachel never left Freeman's side. She knew

women were to take care of women, and she should get word to Benjamin, but she gave it little thought. Freeman needed to be watched in case he had signs of having another seizure. But he seemed much better, even up reading the Bible the Gideons placed in the room. Should she go?

"Have you ever felt like Jonah? Running from God?" he asked her.

"*Jah*. Many times."

"When dating Jared?" he asked, rather boldly.

Rachel rested her chin on her hand. "Well, I ignored my true self until I felt like I was suffocating. I wouldn't say that was running from God, though."

"So, you didn't want to be Amish first and then met Jared? He didn't try to pull you away from the People?"

Rachel nodded. "I didn't like plain life. Wanted the conveniences I see at the hotel. Granny coming out helped me see *what-was-what.* She almost left the Amish because of wanting a clothes dryer," Rachel quipped.

Freeman smiled. "Most everyone in our *Gmay* wants a marriage like your *groosseldre.* It's talked about a lot at Singings."

"You still go to Singings?" Rachel asked. "I feel like I'm too old."

Freeman's face flushed. "Well, it's how you get to

know someone to court. Rachel, you're not an old *maidel.* You should go."

As they talked, Rachel could see Freeman felt much, much better. He was on some drip IV drugs though, and she wondered if they loosened his tongue. "Maybe I will go. Maybe in the spring." Her throat tightened, and she croaked out, "So, you'll go in Smicksburg?" She knocked at her chest. "Excuse me. Sounds like I swallowed a frog."

"Maybe I'll go to a Singing out here," he said with a glint in his eyes.

Was this the medication? He was so confused. "You're going back to Smicksburg, *jah*? How can you come to Singings out here?"

"I can pay a driver."

Rachel's nerves were now frayed, and she began to laugh. "But why? You live in Smicksburg."

Without flinching, Freeman said, "Because you're here."

Should she call for the nurse? His meds were too potent. "Freeman, you're not yourself."

"I've never been better," he said. "Need to get out of here so I can go home for Christmas and then come back."

"You're being silly. Who ever heard of a man going three hours away to attend an Amish youth gathering?"

"My *daed* did it. When he met my *mamm*, he…decided to get to know her better and he and his buddies hired a driver and traveled from Cherry

Creek, New York to Smicksburg. We have smaller settlements, and we visit each other more often. Out here in Holmes County, it may seem foolish."

Despite the room being cool, Rachel was on fire. *Ach,* she hoped she wasn't blushing so profusely that her cheeks were like beets. "So, you want to meet Amish from other settlements. You and your friends?"

Again, he said with all sincerity that he was coming out to visit her. Rachel ran from the room to get a nurse. Surely Freeman had a fever or something.

Chapter 10

Granny dozed off when Jeb was peacefully asleep, a ball of yarn in hand. She dreamt that Rachel was calling for help. When Jeb yelled out, 'Rachel, you okay?' Granny was startled from her dream. "Jeb, you rest. I'll take care of...Rachel."

Darting out of the room, Granny saw a very pale Rachel running to the nurse's station. She was telling them Freeman's medicine was making him say nonsense. Running up to Rachel, Granny slipped an arm around her. "Honey girl, are you okay?"

The nurse on duty held up a finger, talking discretely into the phone. Rachel was so flustered and lacking confidence, not like her nature. "Rachel, another seizure?"

"*Nee*, he's just talking nonsense."

"Such as?" Granny prodded.

"Well, that he's going to come back here to Ohio to attend Singings."

Granny muffled a laugh. "Well, lots more eligible Amish women out here. More Amish in Holmes

County now than Lancaster County, you know."

Rachel took Granny's hand, leading her to a bench. "Granny, he said he's coming out to see me!"

"Praise be!" Granny cried out. "I was wrong. Jeb is a *gut* matchmaker. Now, Rachel, we can see you're fond of Freeman, but I know how stubborn you are. You're a bit like me. If you care for Freeman, it's okay that you just had a broken engagement. I've seen it time and time again. The closer to the wedding date, reality sets in and couples split up."

"Granny, he's not serious. He's on drugs."

The nurse came around the desk. "Who's on drugs?"

"Freeman Yoder in room 777. He's talking crazy-like."

The nurse wasted no time in running into his room. She started small talk with Freeman. The weather, his food, was he upset being in the hospital on Christmas, and Freeman answered with perfect clarity. The nurse spun around to face Rachel. "I see nothing wrong."

"Then he has a fever or something," Rachel said.

The nurse held a hand gadget up to Freeman's temple and soon got a reading. "No temperature. What are you concerned about? What did Freeman say?"

Rachel fidgeted with the ends of her prayer *kapp*

strings. "*Ach,* just stuff hard to believe."

"Like he has superpowers?"

"*Nee.* I'm sorry. I think I'm still rattled about his seizure this morning."

Granny could see clearly that Rachel cared for Freeman, but maybe she didn't even realize it yet.

A man decked with a Christmas tree tie that lit up entered the room. "How's our patient?"

"He's doing much better," said the nurse.

He extended his hand to Rachel and then Granny. "I'm Doctor Hatmaker. He squeezed the lower tip of his tie and it chimed out a song. "Kids don't want to be in the hospital today, so I wear this to cheer them up."

"That's so nice of you," Granny said. "I think my husband would get a kick out of it. He's in 773."

"I'll be sure to visit." He turned to Rachel. "Now, Freeman's test results are in. No meningitis. His fever must have spiked so quickly his body went into shock. You say he had a seizure?"

"Well, Doc Martin, our Amish medical man said he thought it was a seizure, but he's not a real medical man."

"I know him. Good guy. Has your husband ever had a high fever before that made him lose consciousness?"

"You can talk to me," Freeman suggested. "I'm as right as rain. *Nee*, I've never lost consciousness. How high was my fever?"

The doctor looked at Rachel for an answer. She

stuttered out that she didn't know. Over 104 degrees, she believed.

"Well, let's keep him a few more hours for observation and then you folks can go home to enjoy your Christmas. He'll get an MRI to make sure everything's okay."

"What does that mean?" Rachel asked.

"Oh, an MRI is short for Magnetic Resonance Imaging—"

"I know that," Rachel interrupted, but why is he getting one?"

"Routine procedure after a seizure," he said.

Rachel looked panicked, and Granny took her hand.

"Most likely your husband, Jeb, has the same thing as Freeman. It's a nasty virus going around. Freeman tested negative for strep throat and flu, so it's that virus. Hospital is full because of it."

Doctor Hatmaker's eyes lingered on Granny. "Have I met you before?"

Granny was thinking this man looked familiar. "I grew up in Millersburg, but moved way back in 1963 to Smicksburg, Pennsylvania."

"What was your maiden name?" he asked.

"Byler. My folks had the farm where the new Walmart sits."

He snapped his fingers. "Noah Byler's little sister?"

Confused but touched, Granny nodded.

"We love Noah. We have a wing dedicated to him. It's Noah's Ark themed for children. He made a generous donation and it was the least we could do. And all his pictures make the patients feel more at ease."

Granny could barely breathe. Was she getting this virus? She crossed the room to plunk herself in the recliner. "Noah gave you money? And all the paintings, too. I can't believe it. *Ach,* I feel so awful."

"Why, Granny?" Rachel asked, kneeling at Granny's feet.

"Because for too many years I thought he was a greedy man for selling our farm to Walmart. He had every right, since he inherited it, but I had ill feelings."

Doctor Hatmaker made his tie ring out a Christmas tune and said he'd come back later, saying he wanted to talk to the real 'Little Debbie' that Noah talked so much about.

Granny felt nausea wash over her. Was she in shock now? Or, was she ill?

~*~

In a few hours, Sarah returned to the hospital, with the aid of Sydney, with several men and women from the church district willing to help. Of course, Granny didn't want to leave Jeb, but was achy from head to toe. Why her arms felt so heavy, she did not know. But, word had it, this virus was bad, and she needed to get home and sip on garlic tea.

So, Sydney took Freeman, Rachel and Granny home, even offering to stay. Granny cupped Sydney's pretty cheeks. "You're so sweet. *Danki*, but you've done enough today. Go on home to your *kinner*."

Tears welled in Sydney's eyes. "I'm so glad I met you. I never knew my real grandma."

Throwing her arms around her, the deep love of God ran through Granny's veins for this woman. "I'm so glad we met. You've become dear to me. Maybe a little too much."

Swiping a runaway tear, Sydney made fun of herself for being such a baby. "You're afraid of getting too close because you want to stay in Holmes County?"

Granny had never admitted this, but it was true. As much as Rachel was resisting her feelings for Freeman, she was resisting her feelings toward Holmes County. She was now grateful that Anna was living in her house, even cooking on her Pioneer Princess Stove. "*Jah,* Sydney. I suppose. I have a *bruder* that's shunned I hope to have dinner with tomorrow, but I fear we need to postpone. Wouldn't want him to catch this bug."

Sydney stood there with her mouth unhinged. "Wow. And I thought my family was messed up.

You have a brother who's shunned? Wait, you can't eat with him. I know some things about the Amish."

"I know. No eating with shunned Amish. We'd sit at different tables," Granny said with a wink. "When I go over, he has little fold out tables, and we nibble on little sandwiches. And then his cook makes scones! *Ach,* I need the recipe."

Sydney tilted her head. "What's your brother's name?"

"Noah Byler."

Sydney held on to the countertop. "Noah Byler? I call

him the Mayor of Holmes County. He knows everybody."

"Is he the mayor?" Granny asked, putting a hand to her mouth.

"No, but he may as well be. He's your brother? Oh, get out!"

Feeling tired, Granny headed to the stove. Filling the tea kettle with water, she set it on the gas stove. "I thought he was a recluse, truth be told. Doctor Hatmaker said he painted most of the Amish pictures in the hospital. It baffles me why he left if he paints about plain folk."

Sydney sat at the kitchen table. "Maybe he misses his plain roots deep down. Or, he's remembering his happy times being Amish. That's a pathway to forgiveness, you know. Be grateful for what you have, and it nips bitterness right in the bud."

"Is that right?" Granny asked. "You seem to talk from experience."

"I do," Sydney said. "I used to be so angry with the family I was born into, two husbands up and leaving, so I decided there's lots of people in the world who need pampering. So, I treat every client as a gift from God, and I'm grateful for them. Now, I have so many truly wonderful people in my life, there is no room for feeling sorry for myself."

Granny reached for Sydney's hand. "You're inspiring. Promise me that when I go back to Smicksburg you'll write."

Sydney let out her infectious laugh. "I have out of state customers. How about you get all your Amish girlfriends together and I do a group haircut."

Granny held on to her prayer *kapp*. "We don't cut our hair."

"I know," Sydney joked. "How about I come bring Rachel out to see Freeman?"

Sydney's comical brows wiggling to beat the band made Granny giggle. "You see it, too?"

"I'm not blind. They love each other, but they're just too…"

"Stubborn. It runs in the family."

"You're so easygoing, not stubborn. Now, Sarah seemed a bit uptight when we first came here for knitting, but she's loosened up. If Rachel's stubborn, it comes from her other side."

The whistle blew and Granny rose to make tea, but Sydney insisted on doing it. "I want a clove of garlic in a mug of hot water with some honey. It's all out."

"That I can do. Used to be a waitress while in high school."

Ach, was there a sound more soothing than tea being made, even if it was garlic tea. "Sydney, is Fern's husband home for Christmas?"

"Well, Sarah told me today how disappointed she was that her *daed* was still in Florida. But I suppose he has horrible arthritis and can't take the cold. Fern should be down there with him. If I had a husband as nice as Matthew, I'd be right by his side. Fern is… I can't say the word."

Sydney set the tea on the table. "Test it to see if you like it."

"I won't like it, but it's *gut* for me. Now, tell me about Fern. Do you think she's lonely?"

Sydney made peppermint tea and sat across from Granny. "I don't mean to be unkind, but Fern's been a real trial to me. You know she doesn't come to knitting circle because I'm a 'painted lady', right?"

"Meaning you wear makeup?" Granny asked.

"Yes, and I've had two husbands. Never mind I raised five kids without their help, and they left me for young chicks. No, Fern looks at me like she looks at Melody."

This sank Granny's heart. "How does she look at

yinz?"

"Like we're contaminated. Like we're not holy enough for her."

This is what Granny feared. Fern was driving people away, possibly her husband, because of a critical spirit. Sarah barely visited, and when she did, she had fences, or boundaries. Daniel came first and she'd listen to no more bad mouthing of her husband.

"Sydney, have you ever read *Emma* by Jane Austen?"

"A zillion times! Why?"

Granny scratched her chin. "Well, remember when Mrs. Elton moved to town and put everyone down? Looked down at their country ways?"

Sydney nodded with anticipation.

"Emma had a party for her, *jah*? She tried to help her."

Sydney sighed audibly. "But it didn't work."

Granny raised a finger. "*Ach,* but she tried. And doesn't the Bible say to overcome evil with good?"

Sydney's eyes bugged. "You think Fern is evil?"

"*Nee,* but our feelings about her are, don't you think? What if she's really a hurting woman?"

Sydney threw her arms in the air. "Touchdown! I love how you think!"

"*Danki,*" Granny said. "Let's think on this. I'm headed up to bed."

Sydney hugged Granny. "Do you want me to stop by your brother's house and let him know you're sick?"

What a thoughtful young lady. "*Jah,* if you could. Tell him I miss him, and we need to postpone Second Christmas."

~*~

The next afternoon, Granny held Bea close, the warmth of the tiny dog reducing her chills and comforting her soul. Everything ached, so when Doc Martin came to ask about her symptoms, she said it was a full-body flu. If she hadn't sipped on garlic tea, she knew it would be worse.

Jeb was home this morning and informed that Sydney got word to Noah to stay clear of the virus-ridden Weaver household. Sydney was indeed a messenger pigeon. "Bless that girl", Granny croaked out.

"What girl?" a familiar voice asked. She struggled to sit up, and though the room was dim due to the blinds being down, she could see a man. A bearded man? "Are you from our *Gmay*?"

"It's Kenny. Melody asked me to keep an eye on you while she made the rounds."

"What rounds?" Granny asked, holding the quilt up to her chin, shivering.

"Just about everyone in your family is sick. Melody checked on Leah and Fern. They're okay. Leah was out making a snowman… with her kids. Melody stayed for hot chocolate, but Sydney's here with some of her friends."

Granny heard pain in his voice when he mentioned kids. How could she open up this conversation? An idea popped into her head. "Can you get my stationery in the desk drawer. Plain white, no flowers."

He seemed confused but obeyed.

"I hope Lehman's delivered Denny, our adopted son, his Whirley-Pop on time for Christmas."

"Melody told me about this son. Is he trouble at times? I don't want Melody stressed out if we adopt."

"We've had our ups and downs, but we love him and he's so appreciative."

"So you recommend adopting an older child? One that needs a good home?"

"*Ach*, there's tiny ones who need homes. Many Amish take in foster kinner and they eventually adopt. Everyone's different."

Kenny seemed to be pondering her words, so she wrote a quick note to Denny.

My dear son,

A Christmas without you is hard. Did you get your popcorn machine? I hope you and Becca like it. My handwriting is a bit shaky. I caught a virus. Do not worry. I'll be fine. I'll write tomorrow or the next day.

All my love,

Granny

This minor task wore her out. "Kenny, my head hurts. Can't the room be any darker?"

"Sure. I can hang blankets over the shades. That works like black-out curtains."

"*Ach,* please. You know, I'm so sick, I'm delirious. I smell flowers."

After Kenny secured blankets on the three windows, he sat a large vase filled with roses on her nightstand. "From your brother." Kenny read the card.

"Little Debbie, I hope you feel better. We'll celebrate Second Christmas sometime soon. Love, Noah."

Little Debbie. Love. It was as if life was breathed into her heart. Comfort eased her. "*Danki*, Kenny."

"Sydney will be in to check on you, but do you need anything now?"

Such a nice man. What a great foster father he would be, and maybe he'd adopt like they did Denny. "You're a *wunderbar* man, Kenny. I just need rest."

~*~

Over the next week, everyone was up and about, but only the minimal number of chores were done. Granny knit one row of a baby blanket, and her arms ached so, she had to quit. So, she decided to watch the birds at the many feeders Daniel had hung around the massive maple tree in the front yard.

When the downy woodpecker beat its beak against the tree, she wondered if it ever got a headache. *Ach, I'm so ferhoodled! Of course not.* She noticed for the first time that blue jays indeed had gray feathers. The only blue in them was light playing off their feathers. She wanted to record this in her bird journal but felt motionless.

Soon six pairs of mourning doves landed to peck at the seeds on the ground. She mused that Ruth said mourning doves mourned because they mated for life. How many times had she credited their knitting circle for helping her through a tough marriage and receiving beauty for ashes? Ruth and Luke were two peas in a pod, Luke now doing bird counting with her.

A pair of cardinals danced around each other, the male showing off his vibrant red hues. Granny never ceased to marvel that God made the female birds less colorful, so they'd camouflage into the background, keeping prey away from their nests.

Granny's eyelids were heavy, so when the Baptist Church van pulled up, she thought she was dreaming. She pulled her shawl tight and let her head rest against the rocker back. When an arctic blast blew over her, she wished she had the energy to get a quilt. But soon, one was upon her. She opened her eyes to see Denny. "My boy!"

Jeb shuffled across the massive living room with open arms. "My boy!"

Denny made his sweet boyish grin. "I came as

soon as I could. You're sick?"

Granny dabbed the corner of her eyes. "Denny, if it was serious, we'd call for you."

He knelt by her. "Don't cry."

She hugged him around the neck soundly. "I'm not crying. My eyes are watering."

"That means she's crying happy tears," Jeb informed.

"*Jah,* I'm so glad to see our son, Jeb. Denny, you need to meet your *bruder,* Daniel."

Daniel joined them, offering Denny his hand. "So, you're my little *bruder.* Big age gap, *jah*?"

Of course, Daniel had children older than Denny. Soon everyone was being introduced, and only May wasn't shocked that he was supposed to be called Uncle Denny. Rachel and Benjamin appeared bewildered, but said it was nice to meet their uncle.

Denny, as lighthearted as ever, made a joke of the whole thing. "Just call me Denny. It's too weird for me to have older nieces and nephews." He slapped Benjamin on the back. "You look my age. I'm eighteen, almost nineteen."

"*Jah,* we're still teenagers," Benjamin said. "Is it true though that you're married?"

Denny comically beat his chest. "Whatever I did to deserve Becca, I'll never know. Sweetest, prettiest girl in all of Smicksburg…but she is putting on the pounds lately." He winked at Jeb, as if they were in on a secret.

Rachel chimed in. "You should never talk about a

woman's weight."

While they bantered, Granny examined Jeb's eyes. They were turquoise, which meant he was in deep thought. Becca putting on weight? "Denny, will you be a *daed*?"

He bobbed his head. "*Jah*. So, you'll be an *oma* again!"

This was too much emotion, and this time Granny burst into tears. Her boy, who was taken by the state of Pennsylvania for abuse, who feared of being a bad *daed* like his father, was so happy to be a father. His fears were being eaten away by love. His father-in-law was the epitome of a loving husband and father. Praise be.

Denny held her until the tears ran dry. "Honey, you'll be the best *daed*."

"*Jah,* I know. Not being proud, you know. I won't be my *daed*. I want to be like Jeb, Roman and Michael."

Daniel overheard. "Be like my *bruder,* Roman? He's as stubborn as a mule."

Denny cocked his head back as if punched. "He's my partner and super patient. Good father and husband." Denny's eyes darkened. "I can only hope to be more like him."

Jeb slapped Denny's back. "Daniel's teasing. All us Weavers have a stubborn streak. It's our sweet wives that mellow us out."

Daniel put an arm around Sarah's waist. "Amen to that."

Denny caught on and laughed. "Becca's the better part of me, for sure."

Freeman, who'd been holing himself up in his bedroom appeared. "Denny, what are you doing here?"

"Checking on my folks. Hey, man, when are you coming home? I think Jane misses you. Always asking Becca if you're moving out here or something."

All eyes were now on Freeman. He calmly said, "Not to live, but I plan to visit…a lot." He shot a quick glance at Rachel, and everyone seemed to understand, except Denny. Jeb's eyes landed on Granny, as if to say, 'I told you so.'

Denny winced. "Why would you come out here a lot? Did you make some business contacts?"

Freeman plunged his hands into his pockets and told Denny he'd explain later.

Granny searched the room for Janice or Suzy. "Who drove you out here? Do not tell me you drove," she asked Denny, knowing giving up his car to be Amish was the hardest feat.

"Janice dropped me off. It was painful listening to all those Amish women yack about quilting patterns and recipes for three hours. Freeman, there's room for you to go back with me. Are you up for it?"

Rachel stepped forward. "He's contagious with a virus. Everyone in the van would get sick."

Denny covered his mouth. "Am I contagious now?"

"I'd wear a bandana over your mouth on the way back, unless you can stay for a while," Granny asked, hope in her voice.

"Let me see. Freeman and I will need cotton balls for our aching ears due to women gossiping, and bandanas for our mouths. What a sight we'd make." He kissed Granny's prayer *kapp*. "I wish I could stay, but Michael needs me."

"No change in his sight?" Jeb asked.

Denny paused, collecting himself. "He hides how bad his vision is. Becca and I think he's losing more…" He inhaled deeply and turned to Jeb. "I wish Becca wouldn't try so hard to be strong. I wish she'd stop saying her teeth hurt."

"Has she seen a dentist?" Sarah asked.

Jeb put a hand up. "We men in Smicksburg have a book club. We read a lot of C.S. Lewis. He said, it is easier to say, 'My tooth is aching' than to say, 'My heart is broken.' Is that what you mean, son?"

Denny bit his lower lip and nodded. "*Jah,* so I need to get back to Becca."

Rachel let out a gasp. "You're such a *gut* husband, for a teenager!"

Jeb's chest expanded in pride. "He's a Weaver. Of course, he's a *gut* husband."

Everyone laughed, but Granny noticed Rachel

and Freeman's eyes latch. Praise be.

Chapter 11

Rachel followed Freeman back to his room. "Why are you hiding up here?"

"I'm not hiding. Just preparing myself to say *mach's gut.*" He took out his suitcase. "Guess I need to pack up my tools."

He didn't make eye contact and Rachel was starting to feel rejected. "Who's Jane?"

"She's a girl I took on a buggy ride a few times. All of Smicksburg expects us to get married."

Wind rattled the windowpanes. "Then why did you lead me on?"

"What?"

"You heard me. You have a girl who thinks you'll marry her back home."

"We're not engaged."

Rachel tapped her foot. "Did you make promises to this Jane girl? Like you'd only be in Holmes County for a week or so?"

He shrugged. "I can't remember."

"So, when you get back home, I should take your promise to return with a grain of salt." She clenched her fists and held back tears with all her willpower…and succeeded.

Oddly, Freeman took her hand and asked if she'd help him pack his tools. She said no, but he begged. There was something in his body language that told Rachel he really cared about her, despite trying to suppress all her growing emotions for this man.

She agreed, and they headed to the workshop, once inside, he took her hand and led her to the ladder back chair, caned in a simple weave. "Merry Christmas, my plain girl."

Rachel held on to the armrests and then began running her hand over the smooth surface. She stood up and yes, it was simplicity itself. Her heart beat out of her chest, and call it impulsiveness or a reaction, she threw her arms around Freeman's neck. "*Danki*. Don't go." She bit back tears, but her body shook.

He held her tight. "I said I'll be back, and I mean it. Rachel, I plan to win you. You still love Jared, but in time…"

Rachel wanted to shout out that she loved *him* now but knew a tiny piece of her heart still belonged to Jared. "Do you promise you'll come out?" She lowered herself and cupped his face in her hands. "Promise?"

The door blew open and in stepped Ruby. Freeman and Rachel backed away. Ruby fled the workshop, calling Rachel a liar.

"What's that all about?" Freeman asked.

Rachel lowered her head. "Ruby thinks she's in love with you. She made me promise to stay away."

He tapped Rachel's nose. "Well, now you have an assignment after I leave. Take Ruby to Singings and steer lots of men her way."

Rachel looked up demurely. "I will. You do the same for that Jane girl. She…scares me."

Freeman hugged Rachel. "I'm going to miss you."

Rachel looked up with puckered lips. But he did not kiss her. Embarrassed, she backed away.

He snickered. "If I kiss you, I'll never go back to Smicksburg. And, Rachel, when we do kiss, I want it to be with all your heart, *jah*? No Jared on your mind."

Her heart swelled with admiration for Freeman's character.

~*~

Granny and Jeb were overwhelmed saying good-bye to their boy, so they retired to their bedroom for some quiet time. But it wasn't long before there was a knock on the door. Benjamin cracked the door open. "Can I come in?"

"*Jah*," Jeb said with an obligatory smile.

Benjamin near skipped in. "I talked to Denny. I can't believe he's married."

"It was the right time," Jeb said. "What's up, Benjamin?"

Benjamin straddled a wooden chair and Granny put her yarn down. Obviously, their grandson needed to talk to them both.

"You two know I'm courting someone and want to get married. Denny's a bit younger than me, so I think it's time I told my parents."

"Benjamin, you don't want to be a rebound to a woman widowed for a year."

"I'm not. We really love each other."

Granny twisted up her lips. "A woman doesn't get over a husband in a year."

"*Jah,*" Jeb agreed. "That's why we Amish think it wise to remarry after two years. I thought we agreed that you wait at least another year."

"Heather wants a wedding on…*Ach,* you'll think she's carnal." He wiped his brow. "Okay, she wants to get married on Valentine's Day."

"That is *ferhoodled,*" Jeb boomed.

"*Ach,* I think that's so romantic," Granny cooed. "And it's my birthday, too. I always felt special that I was born that day." She poked Jeb. "What's wrong with them marrying in February."

Jeb's chin jutted. "It's your birthday."

"And?"

Jeb raised his hands in surrender. "I love to spoil you on that day."

Granny knew her heart was turning to putty. "I know. And I have every birthday card you've ever given me."

Jeb slid closer to Granny. "I had something real special planned for this year."

Granny could see Benjamin was getting mighty

uncomfortable. "Benjamin, it's not that it's my birthday, but you need to wait a year. Marriage is for life and I can tell you'd make a *gut* husband, but let Heather know her heart."

"She's twenty-three. I think she knows her mind."

"Heart, not mind," Granny corrected. "Most women think they know their minds, but it's the heart that counts. It rises ever so slowly. Give it time."

Benjamin pursed his lips. "Well, the Bible says that out of the abundance of the heart, the mouth speaks, *jah*? She says she loves me and wants to get married on Valentine's Day."

"Give it time," Granny repeated. "I wonder if she misses romance on Valentine's Day. Memories of her husband rising up?"

It was if a lightbulb went off in Benjamin's brain. "Maybe. I never thought of that. It's not even wedding season. Truth is, my *daed's* going to make me a full partner now that *Mamm* is opening a quilt shop. I'd have enough money to wed in February, Christmas sales were out of the roof."

This made an alarm ring in Granny. "And Heather knows of your success?"

"*Jah,* I brag too much about how much we made. Heather made up a budget and thinks we can make ends meet."

"Hold your horses," Jeb said sternly. "You know

I speak plain-like. Does this girl love you or the security of a nice income?"

Uncharacteristically of Benjamin, he kicked over the chair. "What? Don't you think a woman can love me just for being me?"

Granny held her chest. "Benjamin, your reaction tells me everything."

"What?" barked Benjamin.

"That the truth hurts and your *opa* hit it on the nail."

Daniel rushed into the room. "Someone hurt?"

"Your son's pride," Jeb growled. "Now, pick up that chair and apologize to your *oma*. And one last thing. You are definitely not as mature as Denny."

~*~

Granny ventured out to see her *bruder* on a mild January day, no chance of the virus being contagious. After three weeks of dealing with fatigue, she was her spry self. Sydney dropped her off at Noah's doorstep, and the two embraced.

"Make sure you ask him," Sydney said firmly.

She knew Sydney's heart was so full of compassion, she might be just imagining things. "*Jah*, of course."

"I'll wait until you're inside, just in case he's in bed."

"Go on with you," Granny quipped. "It's your imagination."

Sydney tapped the steering will with her enormous ring. "I'm waiting."

Granny rang the doorbell, and no one came for a spell.

She pressed the button again and the maid opened the door, telling her Noah wasn't up for company today. She looked past Granny and waved to Sydney. "See you next week?"

"Got you on my books."

Kimberly smiled. "She's my beautician." She put a hand on Granny's shoulder. "You better go back home. Like I said, Noah's not up for visitors today."

Jeb's persnickety speech popped out of her. "I'm his sister, so I'll be coming in." Granny walked past Kimberly, despite the protest. "Where is he?"

"He's in his room."

"Which staircase should I use?"

"Mrs. Byler, I have strict orders not to let anyone in."

"Noah Byler is my *bruder*, but my name's Weaver. Deborah Weaver and I'm seeing my *bruder*."

A quick knock on the door and Sydney stuck her head in. "Sorry, Kimberly, but I told her."

"What?" Kimberly asked, appearing confused.

"That you're really a nurse. And the kind you are."

Kimberly fumbled for words. "Well, I do all kinds of in-home care."

Granny took a seat in one of the leather Queen Anne chairs. "Speak plainly, Kimberly. Be truthful." Her chin quivered as she got out these words.

"What ails Noah?"

Sydney took a seat close to Granny. "Remember at the hospital when the doctor said there was a new wing built? It's a cancer wing."

"Cancer?" Granny pressed her hands to her heart. "I don't understand."

Sydney looked to Kimberly as if to get the okay to continue, and Kimberly gave it. "It's high time she knew."

"Well, you see," Sydney started. "Noah's been getting his hair cut at my place for the past five years. Ever since he came back from Slovenia…or Croatia? Well, he was a traveler, but his health declined." She squeezed Granny's hand. "He came back to his roots to spend…the rest of his life. He never let on about his battle with cancer but slipped once when he said he was seeing a doctor I know is an oncologist."

"But if he had cancer five years ago, he must be in remission?" Granny could not absorb this. "He could have died five years ago, you mean?"

Sydney's eyes flooded with tears. "He's been fighting it. Has good days and bad. On good days, he opens up this place for parties."

"Weddings," Granny corrected. "He said weddings took place here."

"I was there when he said it," Kimberly admitted. "We've had two weddings, but the place is opened for children with cancer. He puts on a big party. Lots of cake and ice cream."

Granny tightened her grip on Sydney's hand. "He always loved making homemade ice cream growing up."

"He has people make it," Kimberly said, her voice filled with emotion. "The whole truth is that behind the property is a building with several dairy cows. Doesn't look like your typical barn to blend in with the estate. He has kids milk cows, we pasteurize it, and then get to cranking."

Memories of Noah cranking their ice cream makers, eyes alight, made her realize he did have fond memories of being raised plain. He was no farmer, yet he wanted children to milk cows. When she collected herself, she asked, "Do the *kinner* like milking cows?"

Kimberly nodded. "After Noah demonstrates. He tells them stories of growing up on a farm and how much work is entailed. He said he wasn't cut out for it, but many are, and it teaches them discipline."

"*Jah,* it does," was all Granny could get out. "What kind of cancer?"

Kimberly rattled of a long name and Granny knew her mind could not take anymore. She needed to be with Jeb, because when she felt that the sun rays shining through the windows appeared to mock her, she knew only her dear husband could say the words to make the world seem right.

Sydney hugged Granny. "It's a form of leukemia.

He's fighting it, Granny. Has real good days, but today is not one."

"*Danki.* I need to see Jeb."

~*~

Granny cried for three days, and Jeb was surprised on the fourth that she got up early, pinned her hair up, situated her prayer *kapp*, and said she was fine. She would not wallow in sorrow, but needed to talk to Noah, everything else was hear-say. But then Granny's chin quivered, and she rolled her eyes as if impatient with herself. So, Jeb suggested he make the visit. Her tears may upset Noah, Jeb reasoned, since he had that Byler blood flowing through him that didn't take kind to pity. This was his way of reminding his wife that she needed room to be human.

So, Jeb called Noah from the workshop phone and he agreed to see him at lunch. He then called Sydney for a ride and in no time, he was on Noah's doorstep, ringing the doorbell. The so-called maid, who Jeb knew was a nurse, ushered him in, and Noah greeted him with an outstretched hand. Jeb shook it.

"Where's Little Debbie?" Noah chirped.

Jeb never was one for twisting the truth, so he paused. "Noah, let's sit down for a chat."

"Do you want anything for lunch?" Noah asked. "Debbie and I eat off of trays, so we don't eat at the same table, me being shunned and all."

"*Ach,* it's not that. Just want to ask you something."

Noah was in good spirits and chuckled. "Jeb, you never could mince words, always so direct. Do you want coffee or tea? Cold outside."

Jeb nodded and made his way into the large living room, picking the luxurious leather recliner. *Ach,* how he wished he could stretch out on it and close his eyes. Avoid this conversation.

Noah sat across from him in a red plaid chair, resting his feet on a small matching ottoman. "Is Debbie okay?"

Jeb twisted up his lips. "Well, she's sad. Word got around town that you aren't well."

"Fit as a fiddle," Noah said, his tone flat.

"So, the rumors going around that you have cancer aren't true?"

Noah gasped. "Oh, that. Jeb, I've been dealing with it for so long, I forget somedays. It's like taking care of an allergy."

Jeb frowned. "An allergy? Well, that doesn't make sense."

"Well, people get seasonal allergy shots and others never know when hay fever is going to affect them. That's what my cancer is like. It's a form of leukemia."

"Blood cancer?" Jeb asked.

Noah grimaced. "I don't like the 'C' word. I had a

real brush with that long ago and it nearly killed me."

Jeb shuddered. "You had cancer before?"

Sorrow filled Noah's light blue eyes. "There's so much you and Debbie don't know."

"I have time to listen," Jeb said tenderly.

"Well," Noah started, "before my shunning, I was engaged to Mary Miller and I've never loved another woman since. But I had signs of not being well. Jeb, you're a man so I can tell you this. My prostate was enlarged, and I was diagnosed with what they thought was prostatitis. An infection, and that's all. But it scared me. Some literature said I could be impotent."

Noah paused, studying Jeb. "You understand?"

"*Jah,* of course. You feared you couldn't have *kinner.*"

"Yes, and I couldn't do that to Mary. But I knew I did the right thing when the real diagnosis came in. Prostate cancer. I had to have surgery. Jeb, I didn't feel like a man, and I ran away. Marriage and family are the heart of the Amish life. I could never be a father, and I'd have to live here and see Mary childless or married to another. I hid it all. Hid it from my parents, if you can believe it. I said I was having surgery for an infection and everything was going to be okay."

Jeb was plum shocked. Not only was Noah's revelation a shock, but he was going on with such detail, the poor man obviously needed to tell someone about this for a very long time. "So, you say your parents didn't know?"

"No one did."

"How'd you pay for the surgery?"

Noah was turning pale. "I started to lie for the first time. I sold my best horse, a real champion, and then the land that I bought for Mary and me to build a house. Even took out a loan. I got over my head in debt, truth be told, and used credit cards. So, when my parents passed, I sold the farm to Walmart and was able to pay it all back and I put lots aside for further treatment."

Jeb wondered how gullible the ministers and bishop must have been to have one of their own slip through, not intervening. "No one caught on?"

"Well, when anyone asked, I said I was on heavy medicine."

Jeb decided to drop it, not hounding Noah for details. "How old were you when you left?"

"Late thirties. I never felt more alone after the shunning. Jeb, I could not tell them such a private matter. The whole *Gmay* would find out."

"You could have told the bishop you had cancer, not having to give all the details."

Noah cocked an eyebrow. "Nothing's a secret among the Amish. And the medical bills kept coming in, and I couldn't burden the people to pay."

"It's why we live in community…"

"Jeb, I was mad. Grieving, I suppose. I've served God my whole life for what? To be treated like he hates me. I didn't want anything to do with God, so keeping true to my baptismal vows was impossible. So, I ran away."

Jeb's heart was filled with sorrow. Out of all of Deborah's brothers, Noah was the kindest. "I wish you could have told me."

"How would things be different? And I didn't want Debbie to know."

Jeb cracked his knuckles. "That cancer was long ago. Is it connected to this leukemia?"

"Well, once you have prostate cancer, other cancers can come later. I'm blessed that I lived many years cancer free and only need to keep an eye on this type of leukemia. I have good days and bad, but it's manageable."

He said 'blessed', and Jeb sat erect, praying for courage. "So, you've been blessed to be here, nothing worse plaguing you. Do you see God's blessing, or are you saying blessing like 'God bless you' after a sneeze?"

Noah's Adam's apple bobbed. "I'm not sure. Deep down I know there's a God, but I find it hard not to be bitter."

Jeb looked around at all the paintings. So, traveling and getting all the money in the world left him bitter. "Noah, only God fills the heart. There's still time. Why not come back to the People? You don't have to go into detail, but let us help you find your way."

Noah's brow furrowed. "I don't want to dress plain and I have this big house they wouldn't approve of. There's a home church someone invited me to and I'm thinking of going."

Jeb winked. "Home church like the Amish, *jah*?"

Noah gave a slight smile. "I suppose." He leaned over. "Jeb, now that I've told you everything, I feel bold enough to ask. Do you know anything of Mary Miller? I believe you met her once."

Jeb guffawed. "Mary Miller? I know a hundred Mary Millers. Do you want me to ask Deborah? She writes those circle letters and hears from Amish from across America."

"Yes, ask her…"

"I understand. Deborah will know what to do."

Noah raised a hand. "I only want to give her closure. Confess why I broke our engagement and all."

The nurse came in with a tray of tea and cookies. "Sorry I'm so late. That stove is finicky. I'll call the repair man."

"*Danki*, Jeb said. "Nothing like hot tea on such a cold day."

~*~

The next night, Rachel and Ruby went to the Singing at Aunt Leah's house. This was Ruby's first ever Singing, having turned sixteen, and her cheeks glowed red, not from the cold, but anticipation. Ruby was sure she'd be asked to take a moonlit drive; Rachel would reject any offers and have a quick walk home.

They were invited for dinner to have supper with her grandparents and Rachel was surprised how her grandfather looked so sheepish about not being home for Christmas, like a dog with its tail between its legs. Her grandma shot up from the table and collected plates that still had food on them, announcing that dessert was ready. Her grandfather threw his napkin on his plate, saying he had a headache and was going to his room.

Ruby, never one to hide her emotions, flew at *Mammi Fern* and hugged her. "What's wrong?"

Fern stiff upper lip bent a bit, patting Ruby's back. "Nothing you can fix. Now, you two go help your Aunt Leah get ready for the Singing."

Ruby pouted. "But I love your apple pie. You can say I half made it since I helped you put up all those apples."

Rachel realized how much closer Ruby was to *Mammi Fern*, and she had a tight knit bond with *Oma* from Smicksburg due to constant letter writing. Visions of living by her flitted through her mind, but she reined them in. Freeman hadn't written since he left last week. A letter took two days to arrive, so he was back in Smicksburg, most likely being encouraged to pay attention to Jane.

Ruby cut three pieces of apple pie, hot from the

oven, and *Mammi Fern* scooped vanilla ice cream onto each plate.

"We always have food to cheer us, *jah*?" *Mammi Fern* tried to say with a cheery voice that fell flat. She dug into her pie and drummed her fingers on the table. "*Jah,* when your husband wants to up and move to Pinecraft, Florida, food is a blessing."

Rachel almost choked on her pie. "Move?"

"*Jah,* he and his *bruder* can ride those big tricycles down there, says everything's so close and Mennonites mix with the Amish so much they're called Amish Mennonites, or something like that."

Ruby leaned her head on her grandmother's shoulder. "You'd never leave, would you?"

Rachel wanted to remind them all that Matthew had arthritis and was in pain in cold weather, but everyone knew this. Surely her grandmother knew this. "How can we make things happier for him here? Has he seen a doctor for his arthritis?" Rachel asked.

Fern hunkered down over her pie. "*Nee.* He thinks they're all quacks."

"He's tried before," Ruby said. "Didn't that one medicine help him?"

"They won't prescribe that pain medicine anymore," *Mammi Fern* said. "People got addicted to it, I hear."

Rachel knew of other Amish that moved south

due to health concerns. Did she dare ask? "*Mammi Fern*, we'd miss you, but why don't you and *Grossdaddi* live in Florida like other snowbirds. Live in Pinecraft for winter."

Ruby nodded in approval. "*Gut* idea. Why don't you go down with him?"

Fern crossed her arms. "Christmas! How could I be away from family for Christmas!"

Rachel was touched and annoyed right about now. She was so fond of her *grossdaddi* and it was selfish of her grandmother to not put him first, all because of Christmas. But, she was touched because Fern's soft side came through, making them realize just how attached their grandmother was to her family.

Aunt Leah raced through the door to the kitchen. "I burnt three dozen cookies, *Mamm!* Do you have any extra for the Singing?"

"*Ach,* you know I do," Fern said. "What else am I supposed to do over here but bake and eat."

Aunt Leah slowly closed her eyes, as if praying for strength. "Things will get better. We'll talk, but I need something to serve the kids."

Fern gingerly rose to pull a large plastic container below a kitchen cabinet. "Made these yesterday. Best take them or they'll be gone by tomorrow." She patted her growing middle. "I need to do something else. Maybe I'll crochet tonight."

Rachel ran to kiss her grandmother's cheek. "I'll visit after Singing."

"You'll be out riding with someone." She touched Rachel's face. "Someone will catch you someday."

Aunt Leah seconded that motion. "Hard to believe Ruby can go to a Singing. And what a nice mild winter night with a full moon."

Rachel was thankful for the full moon so she could easily walk home, maybe linger at the pond, and reminisce about skating with Freeman.

Chapter 12

It was like Rachel suspected. Ruby was asked to go riding with Tall Billy and she walked to the pond, bathed in moonlight. What a glorious night, but oh so lonely. She sat on the bench and smelt the crisp air. Something about winter, the snow, the melting and thawing water, seemed to cleanse the earth.

She hugged herself. Was she right in turning Micah Coblenz down for a buggy ride? How could she when Freeman was always in her heart? She found it shocking that she no longer thought of Jared since she met Freeman. She assumed it would take years to get over a broken engagement, but she was no longer hurt. To the contrary, she felt eager to get on with her life. Settle down and have a family.

A barn owl let out its haunting hoot and she closed her eyes to take in night sounds. The pond rippled and there was a gentle bending of the maple tree branches. Next month, they'd be tapping the trees for maple syrup.

The owl hooted four times. That was odd. It usually did its usual three note song. She looked around, searching the trees. The moonlight reflected off the pond, giving more light.

The owl hooted six times. Now, she was spooked. It wasn't coming from the trees, but behind her. Frightened that someone was playing a joke on her, she clenched the seat of the bench.

"Rachel?" a voice said softly.

Rachel turned to see Freeman. "*Ach,* you scared me." She couldn't help but laugh. "Why not just come up to me and talk? Why all the hooting?"

"I didn't know if it was you or Ruby." He took her hand. "Benjamin said I could use his buggy. Can we take a ride?"

Tears pricked her eyes. "You came, just like you said."

"Got in too late for the Singing."

They walked hand in hand to the horse stable. "How did you know there was a Singing tonight? And where?"

"Jeb called Roman and I got the message."

Rachel laughed. "My *opa!* Did he give you the idea of scaring me out of my wits?"

Freeman led the buggy out of the stable and they were soon on the road. "Didn't want to see Ruby, since she likes me."

"She's out with Tall Billy. He's liked her since first grade. It's his first Singing, too. Ruby seemed mighty happy he asked for a buggy ride, but then again, girls not asked always feel awkward."

Freeman took her hand and pulled up the buggy robe. "Did you feel awkward, walking home all alone?"

Rachel laughed. "Someone asked me to take a ride, but I said *nee*."

He squeezed her hand. "Why?"

Rachel nudged him. "Fishing for a compliment, Freeman Yoder?"

He seemed confused. "Why would I do that?"

"*Ach,* I'm sorry." She felt heat rise to her forehead, and Rachel was glad the moonlight didn't show how profusely she was blushing. "Well, I said no, because…"

"Because?"

Rachel cleared her throat. "I wanted to ride with you. Didn't want to lead Micah on."

Freeman turned onto a country road with no traffic. "Rachel, I've missed you."

She leaned her head on Freeman's shoulder. "Me, too. I was afraid you'd forget me. Was afraid you'd be out riding with Jane. Courting Jane."

He wrapped his arm around her and tilted her chin. "Rachel, I've never loved Jane. Never loved anyone before I met you. I realize that now." He kissed her cheek. "Will you be my girl? Be mine forever?"

Rachel turned away. "Are you asking me to marry you?"

He released her. "Maybe I misunderstood. You're

not ready yet. You need time to get over Jared."

Rachel was too full of emotion to talk. Could she say yes to a marriage proposal after being so hasty to say yes to Jared? She could hold her emotions in check no longer and flung her arms around Freeman. "I do love you, but I'm so afraid. When Jared and I got engaged, we started to quarrel."

He held her head to his chest. "*Ach,* Rachel, I understand. We can wait. I won't pressure you. We'll have a nice courtship."

This was so contrary to Jared. "What?"

"I don't want to rush you. You need to be all mine when we wed with no Jared left in your heart."

Rachel tapped her heart. "He's gone already."

Freeman looked at her doubtfully. "Really?"

"I've only thought of you since you left," she blurted out, and then covered her mouth. A giggle escaped. "*Jah,* Freeman, I love you. I don't think I ever loved anyone before."

Freeman pulled to the side of the road, and Rachel thought he was going to kiss her. But he jumped out of the buggy, ran into the field and threw his hat into the air, shouting for joy. And then he rushed to the buggy, saying he had to get that out of his system, and kissed her affectionately.

~*~

The next morning while feeding the soaking, clean clothes through the wringer washer, Rachel couldn't keep from smiling. How would she keep her engagement a secret, as was the Amish way? When she finally finished, she ran upstairs to get Ruby since it was her turn to hang up the clothes in the basement to dry. Passing through the kitchen, she met her *opa*'s eyes, and he wiggled his eyebrows, his eyes twinkling.

"Ruby, I'm done," she told her sister.

Ruby wiped her eyes. "I'm so tired. Why is wash day on Monday when Singings are on Sunday night?" She arched and stretched her arms above her head. "Had a *gut* time."

From her tone, Ruby seemed smitten with Tall Billy. When the kitchen was clear except for her *opa*, she asked him where Freeman was. She'd been up since four o'clock to get a head start on the laundry to spend time with him.

"He caught a ride back to Smicksburg this morning."

Rachel was filling her plate with pancakes, but suddenly lost her appetite. "When?"

"*Ach,* early. He has a job to get back to, you know." Jeb winked. "I wonder why he came out." His lips narrowed to a thread thin line.

Rachel wondered why he didn't say good-bye.

"I'm a messenger pigeon. He told me to tell you he'd never leave if he saw you. Love can make us do strange things."

"Like what?" Rachel asked, sitting opposite from him.

"Well, not be able to keep our mind on task.

When I started to love your *oma*, I felt like half my brain was gone. I wrote her poetry, was late for work, and couldn't even read. My mind was always on her. It took time to come down to my normal self. That's when I proposed."

Rachel wasn't sure if Freeman told her *opa* they spoke of marriage, and this was a hint that they needed to slow down. "How long did it take?"

"Well, I met your *oma* in the summer and we wed the following spring."

Rachel poked her pancake. "How long before you got engaged?"

Jeb looked up, concentrating. "Well, we got engaged around Christmas. So, from summer to Christmas. *Nee,* wait. We butt horns like sheep until…November, if I recall. So, it was only a month for me to get my bearings to propose." He wiped his brow. "Seemed longer."

"So, you got engaged in a month after courting?"

Jeb put up a hand. "It doesn't mean you have to be so hasty. We tested our love until spring."

Rachel didn't have a problem waiting until spring. "When the right man comes along, I'll be patient and 'test our love' like you say."

"*Gut.* Will you be moving to Smicksburg?" Jeb asked.

Rachel laughed. "Now why would I do that?"

Jeb chuckled. "You'll miss us when we go home,

jah?" His eyes poured forth such tender love and understanding, Rachel knew without a doubt he knew about her engagement.

"*Danki* for asking Freeman out, *Opa*. He really is the best Amish man I've ever known."

Jeb's eyes watered. "Just wanted you to be as happy as I am." He tugged on his gray beard. "Rachel, can you do something with your *oma* today? She's still a little down about her *bruder's* cancer diagnosis."

"I'd be happy to." She wiggled her eyebrows. "And I have some news to tell her."

~*~

Granny sat in the rocker by the window, the clear azure sky not hindered by clouds, flooded the room with sun beams. She opened her Bible to Psalms. The book of comfort that never failed her. Janice told her that the girls at Forget-Me-Not Manor were told to stop and recite Psalm Twenty-Three several times a day and really ponder on it. So, she closed her eyes and whispered:

The Lord is my shepherd;
I shall not want.
He makes me to lie down in green pastures;
He leads me beside the still waters.
He restores my soul;
He leads me in the paths of righteousness
For His name's sake.

Yea, though I walk through the valley of the shadow of death,
I will fear no evil;
For You are with me;
Your rod and Your staff, they comfort me.

You prepare a table before me in the presence of my enemies;
You anoint my head with oil;
My cup runs over.
Surely goodness and mercy shall follow me
All the days of my life;
And I will dwell in the house of the Lord forever.

The image of Jeb putting oil on a sheep's bruise for healing came to mind. Oil aided in healing. Would she be so bold to ask the Lord to send his healing balm on Noah and heal him? Give her more time with him? Have him reconcile with the Amish church, which she believed deep down he longed to do? And if he found devout Mary Miller, she'd be sure to lead him back into the fold.

"Deborah Weaver, you need to stop trying to fix everything. The Lord is your shepherd. Let Him lead," she reminded herself. But she would ask Noah about Mary when the time was right.

Her door squeaked open and she assumed it was Jeb, but it was Rachel. But Rachel always knocked.

Surely, she and Freeman were in love. "Come in."

Rachel near skipped into the room and kissed her *oma* on the cheek. "Got the wash done and wondered if you wanted to do something today."

Baking pies came to mind, along with Fern. "Rachel, let's make pies with your other *oma*."

"What? You don't want to go to Lehman's? Walmart?"

"*Nee*. I have all I need."

"We have knitting circle here on Wednesday. I think we need to make hats for premature *bopplin*. So, we need yarn."

Granny relished time with the dear girl. Did she need some one-on-one time with her?

"*Oma*, I have to work two days this week at the hotel. I want you all to myself, plus I have such *gut* news!" She spun around. "I tell you everything." She took her *oma's* hands. "I'm engaged to Freeman."

Granny wanted to be overjoyed, but this was so sudden. "He is a loveable man, but so soon?"

"We won't wed until spring, or even November. We plan to test our love."

Now Granny could rejoice. "Jeb and I did just that, but I knew he was the one when he asked me to be his wife."

Rachel squealed. "Me, too. He's so kind. Freeman said he wants to marry me when Jared is not in my heart. I can say he's no longer there, but Freeman wants to make sure."

They embraced and Granny felt that they needed to do something special. "You decide what we do, Rachel. Let's celebrate."

Rachel's face split into a smile. "Go to the fabric shop so I can start on my wedding dress and then buy lots of yarn. Crocheting and knitting comfort me, and I miss Freeman already."

Granny knew she was going to have to congratulate Jeb on his successful matchmaking, and her heart leapt for joy.

~*~

Seeing his wife go to a fabric store lifted Jeb's heart. She was recovering from the blow of Noah's diagnosis. But Jeb felt he needed to let Daniel, being the head of this house, know they wanted to invite him over for dinner and help him. Deborah had an inkling Noah wanted to come back to the people after seeing all those paintings of Amish farms at the hospital. So, during a work break, Jeb asked the other boys to leave the shop, needing to have a word with their *daed.*

"You seem like your mind is on something mighty serious," Daniel said, sitting on the deep windowsill.

"It is," Jeb started. "It's your Uncle Noah. When's the last time you've seen him?"

"He's shunned, so unless we cross paths in town, I don't seek out a visit."

Jeb began pacing the shop, hands clenched behind

his back. "Well, your *mamm* and I found out he's been struggling. We visited a few times."

Daniel near sneered. "He's shunned."

"I'm the bishop of my district of your *mamm's Gmay*. Being out here for a long stay made her want to make contact. We found out a lot about him. He's been fighting cancer off and on for years but didn't want to burden the *Gmay* with all the medical expenses."

Daniel's eyes grew tender. "It's why we live as we do. Uncle Noah is too proud?"

Jeb raked his fingers through his hair. "It's mighty complicated and I don't know what I should be telling. I'm hoping we can have him over…for supper."

"He *is* shunned," Daniel reminded again.

"We can have two tables pushed together?"

Crossing his arms, Daniel let out an audible sigh. "We need to talk to Bishop Andy."

Jeb snapped his fingers. "*Jah and* lift the no talking ban. Too harsh."

"I agree. I'd like to have an uncle nearby. Another Weaver, not more Bylers."

Jeb studied his son's face. "Are you lonely out here. Miss Smicksburg?"

"*Jah,* I do."

Jeb sat in the ladder-back chair Freeman made for Rachel. "Ever wonder why this chair is here and not for sale?"

"*Jah,* Rachel said it's hers. Gift from Freeman?

When's the wedding?"

"Come again," Jeb said.

"*Daed,* I see how much Rachel talks to you and *Mamm.* Is she engaged?"

Jeb smiled. "Well, I can't say for sure, but let's just say you may have another reason to visit Smicksburg in the future."

Daniel lifted his hands in victory. "You did it. You got Rachel to stay in the church by asking Freeman out. *Danki* so much!" He embraced Jeb and slapped his back. "I'm so relieved."

Jeb remembered Daniel jumping up on him for a piggyback ride and emotions flooded him. How could he say good-bye in February? How he'd missed this son.

~*~

After their shopping spree, Granny asked Rachel to drive the buggy back to Leah's farm. She needed to encourage Leah and Fern to come to knitting circle. So, when they were ushered into Leah's mammoth living room, they were surprised to see Fern reading her Bible by the large front window, tears streaming down her plump cheeks.

"Nothing like the Word of God to touch our souls," Granny said, going over to Fern and placing a hand on her shoulder. "Maybe you can share what you're reading at knitting circle on Wednesday."

Fern's eyes threw fiery darts. "I'm trying to find a scripture to get back at Matthew."

Granny stepped back as if stung by a bee. "We don't use the Bible to fight."

Leah asked them to go over to the attached *dawdyhaus*, as the *kinner* didn't need to hear this debate. Rachel asked Leah if she needed help with the *kinner*, and Leah accepted with gratitude.

So, Granny followed Fern into her domain. Once in, Fern told Matthew to go upstairs, and that she had company.

Appalled by Fern's behavior, Granny gave Matthew a warm welcome. He was such a kind man and how he lived with Fern was a mystery. He meekly left the room and footsteps could be heard ascending the steps.

"Do you want some tea? Coffee?"

"Tea." The proverb about teakettles came to Granny's mind. "When I see a tea kettle, I always think of that Amish proverb, "Be like the tea kettle; when it's up to its neck in hot water, it sings.""

Fern harrumphed. "Deborah, I'm not a child."

Slowly taking a seat at the table, Granny wanted to say she wasn't either. Singing lifted the spirits. "Fern, what ails you? Can I help you?"

Again, tears drizzled down Fern's cheeks as she poured hot water into a teacup. "You like peppermint, *jah*?"

"Whatever you have is fine."

Fern put a little basket filled with an assortment of teabags on the table. "Take your pick." She then stepped into her living room, and in minutes came back with a Tupperware container. "I keep cookies out of the kitchen, so I don't eat them."

Granny didn't understand Fern's logic, but decided she must mean out of sight, out of mind. "So, you spent lots of time in your kitchen? Do you like to bake?"

Fern composed herself, trying to keep her hand steady while putting a plate of cookies on the table. "*Jah,* baking calms me and it gives me purpose. All the *grosskinner* next door love my cookies. I don't bake too much for Sarah anymore…"

Knowing Sarah loved her *mamm* but needed to set a boundary, prompted Granny to share about her *grosskinner* next door. "My Roman has a new wife, you know. And Lizzie felt like I'd be first in Jenny, Millie and Tillie's affections. So, I backed off. Sometimes people need room to grow."

Another harrumph. "Well, things must be done differently in Smicksburg."

Granny cut to the chase. "Fern, I'll ask again. What ails you?"

Wiping tears, Fern pointed up. "My husband. He wants to move to Florida, of all things."

"It helps his arthritis?" Granny asked.

"His *bruder* moved to Florida and now of course, Matthew wants to, too."

Granny cringed at such degrading words. It was as if Fern thought her husband had no mind of his own. And if Jeb had such pain, she'd go to the moon with him. She stayed here longer, knowing deep down he missed Daniel and the family.

"Did I ever tell you how fretful I was until I started having the knitting circle a few years back? So many problems the women were going through were beyond my help, so I started what I call 'casting off prayers'. You know when you're done knitting and you release the needle from the garment, it comes off. It's the casting off part of knitting. One day, as I was fretting and casting off, I thought of the scripture that says, 'Cast your care on the Lord, for he cares for you.' The part 'he cares for you' hit me between the eyes. God cares. Over the years, I've learned to give things to God to work out. Cast my cares on Him."

"Prayer doesn't solve everything, Deborah," Fern interrupted.

"When I truly stop fretting and give my cares to God, I live for today. I don't have a day filled with worry, but it's open to see whatever God has for me."

Fern leaned her elbows on the table. "So, I just tell God to get Matthew to see he's following his *bruder*?"

Granny inwardly rolled her eyes. Poor Matthew. "*Nee*, you go to God in prayer. Thank him for all his benefits. Be grateful. Praise him with song. I sing the hymn 'In the Garden' quite a bit. And then when the soul is calmed a bit, tell the Lord that you don't have the ability to control your life or the life of others, and give it all to him. Ask God to have His way."

She pondered whether she should tell Fern what she was fretting over as an example. *Jah,* she would. "Now, Jeb's been having a *gut* time here in Millersburg. He misses Daniel and the *kinner* something awful, but not his duties as bishop back home. When he talks about staying longer than February, my heart sinks like a big rock in a pond. But I've decided not to fret. I give it to God, pray, and ask the Lord to either change Jeb's heart or mine."

Fern slapped her chest. "You'd leave Smicksburg?"

Granny's throat constricted. "I'm thinking…hoping…maybe it's for a season, not forever."

Fern's face softened enough to let her wrinkled brow near disappear. "Seasons. Rachel wanted us to only go in winter, but we'd miss out on Christmas here with our family."

Granny reached for Fern's hands. "Isn't Matthew worth it?"

She nodded. "I do love that old man."

Granny stifled a laugh. She called Jeb 'Old Man' in jest all the time. Maybe Fern was a kindred spirit after-all. "Come to knitting circle on Wednesday."

Fern raised her nose. "I don't like those worldly women you invited. That Sydney has been divorced twice!"

Granny had to push up her dropped jaw. "Mary Magdalene was a prostitute before she followed Jesus."

"Well, that Melody flirted with Daniel a bit too much. Saw it with my own eyes, even though Sarah seemed blind to it."

Granny wasn't up for a debate. She rose to make her departure, but paused, needing to set the record straight. "Melody was in a very unhappy marriage, but Kenny is coming along. Now, Rachel and I need to get back home to help with supper. See you Wednesday."

She rushed from the room ignoring more critical comments flung at her by Fern. Granny knew Sydney and Melody could knock off Fern's rough edges…or at least some of them.

~*~

Rachel ran into the kitchen to help her *mamm*, already at work making mashed potatoes. "I hope I have lots of *kinner* close together like Aunt Leah. *Ach,* I had so much fun with the cousins." She shifted closer to her *mamm*. "*Oma's* not so down about her *bruder's* cancer after a nice day out."

"I'm glad to hear it," Sarah said. "How is Aunt Leah?"

Rachel tapped her middle. "Tired and emotional, being in the family way. *Oma* talked to her though, and she said she'd be coming to knitting circle."

Sarah didn't know how Daniel would take it that *she* was in the family way. A new *boppli* while trying to run a quilt shop? Impossible. But she needed to tell someone. Leah? *Nee*, Granny. Ever since the midwife confirmed her suspicions, she longed to have her new *boppli* be held and rocked by her dear mother-in-law. Maybe Granny would stay longer, even move out to Ohio. "Rachel, where is your *oma*?"

"I'm coming," Granny said. "Wanted to read my letter from Fannie before I helped in the kitchen. She's so afraid of change, but Lord knows life's full of it."

"What's she afraid of?" Rachel asked.

"Me moving here permanently," Granny said.

"*Ach,* I almost forgot," Sarah said. "You have a few letters on your dresser to read," she told Rachel, hoping she'd rush out of the room to allow her some privacy with Granny. That's just what Rachel did, and Sarah heard her whisper with joy, "Freeman." Sarah paused to thank God for the young man who was turning her daughter's heart back to her plain roots.

"You're smiling, Sarah. What are you thinking?" Granny asked, opening the pickled beets.

"Many things. But, there's one that I want to tell you first." She inhaled deeply. "I'm pregnant. Do you think Daniel will be happy?"

Granny rushed to embrace Sarah. "Praise be. Another Weaver to rock and cuddle. *Ach,* Daniel will be so pleased."

"But he's already budgeting in the money to build my quilt shop. We do need some extra money and-"

"Fiddlesticks," Granny quipped. "A *boppli* is priceless, a true gift from God. Why worry about money?"

Sarah blustered out nervous laughter. "Well, I think we'll have a wedding to pay for soon."

"And we'll all pull together," Granny said, taking Sarah's hands. "We're here for you."

Sarah looked down at their intertwined hands. She was much stronger with this woman nearby, her own *mamm* sucking the essence of life out of her at times. "How long will you be here for me?" Sarah's chin quivered and then she let the tears flow. "I'm sorry. I'm so emotional, you know, being pregnant."

Granny squeezed Sarah's hands. "I do know. We all need support. I'll be out here when the *boppli* arrives."

Sarah pulled a handkerchief from her pocket. "I wish you lived here. It's hard trying to see the bright side when someone's always pulling the shades down."

"Your *mamm*?"

Sarah's shoulder's shook. "*Jah.* Leah can't take it

anymore. Am I a sinner for not wanting to help my *mamm* in her old age?"

Granny led Sarah to a nearby chair, insisting she sit down. "Your *mamm* isn't so elderly she needs constant care. She's younger than I am. And between you and me, I have a feeling she'll be spending next winter in Florida with your *daed*."

Sarah gasped. "She told you that?"

"In so many words. We just had a long talk."

"You're a miracle worker, *Mamm*. How did you do it?"

Granny rose a brow. "Made her think of her husband instead of herself and told her I was in a similar predicament."

"What predicament?" Sarah asked, swiping a tear.

Granny bit her lower lip. "Jeb's tired. If we moved out here, he'd be released from his duties of being a bishop. And he misses Daniel. All of *yinz*."

Sarah felt her temples throb, her heart racing with anticipation. "You'd leave Smicksburg?"

Granny's eyes clouded. "We don't pray 'Thy will be done' unless we mean it. I pray it daily, so *Jah*, I'd move here. My *bruder* needs me, too."

Sarah squealed in delight.

Granny raised a finger. "Don't say anything to anyone. Nothing is settled, but one thing is for sure and certain. I'll be here to rock those twins you're carrying."

Sarah shot up. "Twins? I never said I was carrying twins!"

Granny covered her mouth in astonishment. "I don't know why I said that. Maybe it's because Roman has twin *dochders*...and you've had twins before. A slip of the tongue. With your quilt shop and new *boppli*, twins would be too much. But God's will be done, *jah*?"

"I can't have a quilt shop with a new *boppli*," Sarah protested.

"Our Sydney at knitting circle had a new *boppli* when her beauty parlor opened. And you may just have two *grossmammi* to help with the *boppli*."

Sarah slowly closed her eyes. "It feels so *gut* to be mothered. I love you so."

Chapter 13

Rachel ripped Freeman's letter open to read:

My dear Rachel,

How can I miss you so much when I just saw you? I took on extra work to pay for a driver but my daed took a nasty fall on the ice and broke his leg. He's got it in a cast and can't get around unless he's using crutches. He's so optimistic, though. He said January's the time to rest, like the land, and he has books stacked up a mile high to read to pass the time.

I need to take on his work in the shop plus barn chores and can't get away. I'm so sorry. I hope my buddy Jeremiah will fill in for me. I don't know how I could stay away from you for much longer, but I'm memorizing James 1:3-4:

The trying of your faith worketh patience. But let patience have her perfect work, that ye may be perfect and entire, wanting nothing.

Right before that it says to rejoice in trials. So, that's what I'm trying to do, but it's so hard. I miss you dear Rachel.

Freeman

Rachel reread it over and over, but "*want nothing*" kept shouting at her. Could Freeman want patience so much he wouldn't need her? Want her? And how could their love grow if she couldn't see him?

Would it be too bold for her to go back to Smicksburg with her grandparents next month? No one would suspect her true reason. *To see her Freeman.*

She read the letter again. Rachel did *not* like the tone. Why put in a Bible passage? That wasn't very romantic. Freeman suddenly seemed so far away. Too far away. Maybe the material she bought to make her wedding dress could be returned.

Her head spinning, she flung herself on her bed, glad Ruby wasn't around, and had privacy. She read the passage of scripture again. Let patience have its perfect work? What did that even mean?

Rachel wondered how she could fly into the house like a merry kite and be in the depths of despair within minutes. This was not steady character. Or, she didn't trust Freeman. He said he missed her. Did she believe him?

She rolled over and wanted to cry, but something deep within cried out, "No more!" No, she would not be an emotional wreck like she was when engaged to Jared. She would not have mood swings like *Mammi Fern. Nee,* she would be like Granny. She'd recondition her mind like Granny's friend, Fannie, who'd written encouraging letters.

She did trust Freeman. Love believed the best, hoped for the best. A firm resolve flared in Rachel to write to him more and believe that her incredible beau in Smicksburg meant what he said.

She glanced at the letter again. *My dearest Rachel…I*

miss you…I took on extra work…

"Grow up, Rachel," she said, getting up and straightening her prayer *kapp*. "It's time to grow up."

She searched her desk drawer for her best stationery and began a reassuring letter to Freeman.

~*~

Feeling rather chipper the next morning, Granny called Sydney to get a ride to Noah's. She'd put off this visit until she could talk heart-to-heart without gushing a river of tears. When she rang the doorbell that chimed a happy tune, she was surprised that Noah greeted her.

"I saw Sydney's car and knew it was you," he said, embracing her. He waved to Sydney and she gave him a thumbs up. "*Ach*, nicest girl in town in my book."

"You said '*Ach*.' Noah, do you still talk Penn Dutch slang?"

"Oops. I slipped. Maybe it's because I'm around you."

Granny knew Noah was always more carefree around her. What a special bond they shared while young. They sat for a spell, smiling, until Granny's tears started to well up. "You'll be fine, *jah*? Jeb told me."

"I'm glad to have good doctors. There's a lot of people worse off. What gets me is the children. I'm old, but they're so young to be thinking of or fearing death." He forced a laugh. "Us old geezers know our time is coming sooner than later."

Granny grinned. "Speak for yourself. I'm a year younger, you know." She scratched her chin, pondering if she should proceed with her plan.

"What's on your mind, Debbie? I see the wheels turning. Questions about my cancer?"

She brushed her palms against the fine leather. "I'd like to read more about it. If you could get me some information, I'd like that. But, you're right. Something is on my mind." She lifted two fingers. "We hop on bunny trails when we talk, and I need to remember these two things. First, Jeb and Daniel went to visit the bishop to see if he'd lift the no speaking ban from the shunning, and he was happy to do it."

Noah crossed his arms and legs, looking so relaxed. "So, that's why so many have stopped me at the mall or in passing, shaking my hand. I thought word got out about my cancer."

"Well, maybe it was both. And Noah, my *kinner* want to get to know you. Would you come over for dinner at Daniel and Sarah's sometime soon?"

"Would I have to sit at a different table, still being shunned?"

Granny winked. "I thought it all out. We'll use two tables pushed together with one tablecloth covering them both."

Noah clapped his hands with a hoot. "I like that. Sure, I'd like to come, but I have good and bad days, so it's hard to plan."

Granny's mouth grew dry. *Ach,* she hated this cancer her *bruder* fought. "Well, there's always lots of extra food on an Off-Sunday, so how about you come then? This Sunday?"

"I started to attend an Anglican church that my doctor goes to. Doing lots of good to the people of Nigeria. That's the kind of Christianity I like; not all talk."

Granny put up a hand. "The Amish and Mennonites have Christian Aid Ministries right here in Berlin. We all need to do our part." She proceeded to her next point before he had a chance to say anything degrading about the Amish. He obviously had a bone to pick. "I wrote back home to see if anyone in my neck of the woods knows a Mary Miller."

His eyebrows shot up in shock. "And?"

"And they're looking. So many Mary Millers. Doesn't her family live in these parts?"

"Not anymore," Noah said, hand on his throat. "Sure, would like to see her again."

"We'll keep trying. Wish her name wasn't so common."

"To see Mary again, to explain why I ran off like a child, would give me great peace of mind."

"I'm glad to hear it. I'll be like one of *Daed's* bloodhounds, keeping the scent."

Kimberly came in with tea sandwiches. Noah said eating from trays was convenient, since they couldn't push two of his heavy tables together.

Granny was so grateful that Noah would be coming over for Sunday dinner and that he was having a good day, along with the fact that he wanted to see Mary. The Mary Miller she remembered was Amish to her core, and Noah knew this. Noah longed for plain life for sure and certain.

~*~

Sarah put her feet up, happy to have her house to herself, enjoying complete silence. She eyed her swollen ankles. How much water retention would she have with this pregnancy? She was no spring chicken. Did she have the strength for a new *boppli*?

She inhaled the scent of peppermint as she sipped her tea. A plate of cookies on the coffee table made her mouth water. Cookies her *mamm* asked her to take off her hands. Poor *Mamm*. She was bored in the winter and baked a bit too much, and her figure showed it.

She heard a knock at the door but decided to ignore it. It was most likely their big old dog laying across the entryway, ever the guard dog.

But now she heard a knock no dog could make, since it came in a rhythm. How she wanted to ignore this intruder. It must be an Englisher, using the front door. An Englisher! She'd sold a quilt, and this was probably the owner wanting to pick it up.

She gingerly made her way to the door and opened it to see an Amish woman with a little toddler holding her hand. "Hello."

"Hi. You must be Ben's *mamm*. I'm Heather and this is Little James."

Ben's *mamm*? Her tone was too 'all knowing' about her young son. "Do you have something Benjamin needs to repair? You can go on down to the shop."

Heather glanced back at the car parked along the road. Heather waved and the driver drove off. "So, I just go into the shop while they're working? Is it safe for James?"

"If you hold him. We're hoping to open a shop for customers soon. I make quilts." Sarah felt so foolish babbling on, but what did this woman want with her son?

"Well, I guess it's *gut* for us to get acquainted. My driver will be back in an hour, after doing some errands." She smiled, showing perfect, dazzling white teeth. Her cherry lips were doll-like, and her green eyes matched her mint dress, making them ever so vivid.

"Do you want a cookie?" Sarah asked, dumbfounded.

Little James politely said he wanted one '*pwease*.' Heather reminded him not to spoil his dinner, so he could have one small cookie, not one of the gobs.

Sarah sipped her tea, fatigue washing over her.

Little James bit into his chocolate cookie, and then licked his lips. "Cookies at the wedding?" he asked.

Heather lit up. "We'll have lots of cookies at the wedding."

Baffled beyond belief, Sarah asked if they were attending a wedding soon. Little James pointed to his *mamm*. "Ben and Mama."

Sarah sat erect, now on full alert. "Your mama's getting married to a man named Ben?" Sarah asked, so nervous she almost started laughing.

Heather told her son to go play with the little dog by the woodstove, which he promptly did. "Mrs. Weaver, didn't Ben tell you?"

Sarah was too afraid to speak. She shook her head faster than a bird after a bath.

"Your son and I are getting married next wedding season."

Sarah wanted to say this lady had the wrong address to someone named Ben. Who was it? "*Ach,* you're courting Ben Zook? He lives a mile down the road. Easy mistake."

Heather's eyes dimmed. "*Nee*, I'm talking about Ben Weaver and I know this is his house. Mrs. Weaver, I'm sorry Ben never told you. We do court in secret, being Amish, but I urged Ben to tell you he's marrying a widow who has a son. I want Little James to be welcomed into the family. He's already lost his *daed*. I suppose Ben didn't think it was important."

Hurt was etched into Heather's face, but Sarah

didn't want to carry on such a serious conversation without Daniel. She did have questions though. "You've been a widow for over two years, since you're not wearing black?"

"It's just been a year. Ben's never seen me in this color: mint's my favorite."

"And how old are you?" Sarah asked, hoping not to sound annoyed.

"I'm twenty-three."

Sarah rubbed her temples. "Ben is mature for his age, but I don't know if he's mature enough to be a *daed.* I mean, *boppli's* are hard work. Lots of work!"

"Ben's not a *boppli* anymore. And he's very fond of James."

"How long have you been seeing my son?" Sarah blurted out in exasperation.

Heather jerked at Sarah's harsh tone. She asked her son to come to her and asked if she could use the phone in the shop to call her driver. Heather gave no explanation and Sarah feared she was being harsh and judgmental like her *mamm.* "Heather, wait. I'm tired. I'm in shock, is all. Can my husband and I talk to you and Benjamin? I don't mean to be so...prickly."

Heather neared Sarah and hugged her. "Life can surprise us at times, *jah*?" She held Sarah at arm's length and her green eyes penetrated Sarah's soul. "One day you have a husband who's gone. A husband who you liked since first grade. I never thought I'd remarry ever, but talking with Ben, his patient ways, drew all the sorrow out of me. Mrs. Weaver, you raised your son to be a very *gut* man."

Man. Ben was a man. Sarah began to relax a bit and offered Heather some tea.

~*~

Wednesday rolled around, and Granny, Sarah and Rachel were busy making cookies in the kitchen. Granny saw the light had gone out of Rachel's eyes a few days back, but she hadn't opened up about any troubles. Best not borrow trouble, she reminded herself.

As they put piping hot snickerdoodle cookies and chocolate gobs on the coffee table, Fern came in with a plastic tote. "I made these cookies for the *kinner*. I'm on a diet."

Rachel stifled a laugh, but Fern caught it. "When I was young, I was as thin as you. Wait until you get my age." She darted a gaze to Granny. "Well, some of us keep it off better, I suppose."

Knowing Fern's weight was a health risk, she simply said, "Jeb and I move around as much as possible. A *gut* walk after a big meal is common in Italy."

All eyes quizzically landed on her.

"I have a friend, Angelina, who immigrated from Italy. She's the one who got me walking more."

Fern harrumphed. "So cozy with the English."

Perturbed, Granny said, "She's not English. I told

you Angelina is from Italy."

Fern grimaced. "You know my meaning."

Granny couldn't believe how contrary Fern could be. "*Jah,* I know your meaning, and I have Trusted English Friends. We Amish allow for that."

A knock at the door let them know Sydney had arrived. Granny gave Fern a knowing look that she best not say anything degrading to her friend. Sydney entered with two women, possibly in their late twenties, or early thirties. "Hi all. I hope you don't mind if I invited Charlotte and Juliet." She turned to Fern. "They want to learn how to knit so badly, and I know you're good at it."

Granny thought the girls stunningly beautiful, but they wore heavy eye makeup, and Charlotte's black hair was streaked with red. Would Fern be able to hold her tongue?

Juliet piped in. "I'm so glad to be here. I just love the Amish and all their ways. Everything is so peaceful."

Sydney put an arm around Juliet. "Isn't she a doll. Charlotte is her older sister."

"Only by two years," Charlotte quipped.

"I thought you were twins," Rachel said. "You look so much alike."

The sisters looked at each other and in unison said, "Thank you!"

Sarah invited them in, taking their coats, and

asked them to take a seat around the coffee table full of cookies. "Does anyone want some tea?"

Rounds of '*Jah*'s' and 'Yes's' echoed around the room.

"Where is Melody?" Granny asked Sydney.

Sydney raised her hands in praise. "She and Kenny are meeting some potential foster kids who need permanent homes."

"They're going to be like, '*Instant Family*.'" Charlotte said. "That movie got my husband and me thinking."

"Thinking about what?" Granny questioned, as she picked up the little hat that she was crocheting for premature babies over at the hospital.

Charlotte said without a twinge of sadness, "I can't have children, but I'm content to be the best aunt to my nieces and nephews. But, now that Melody is looking into foster parenting, it's got my husband and I thinking."

Sydney bellowed a laugh. "They all have hair appointments at the same time, and we talk until after hours. These girls are gems. Now, girls, you go sit by Fern." She covered her mouth "We just babbled on and on and didn't let everyone introduce themselves."

They quickly got acquainted, and Sydney went on to say that Charlotte and Juliet needed to go sit on each side of Fern so she could teach them how to knit. When she added, "She won't bite. Just growls at me," Fern's face became red as beets.

"I don't growl at you, Sydney."

"On the inside you do," Sydney said. "I know I'm a challenge, but that's okay. How boring would life be if we were all the same."

Rachel offered Charlotte and Juliet a smile. "We Amish dress the same, but believe me, we're all so different."

Fern clucked her tongue. "We all have *Gelassenheit,* Rachel."

"*Gelasen*-what?" Juliet asked with a giggle.

Granny was quick to intervene. "*Gelassenheit* in a nutshell means humility. Contentment with what you have. Yielding to each other in community."

Juliet patted her heart. "We have that in our church, don't we Charlotte?"

Charlotte's eyes watered and looked as if she was about to cry. Sydney stood up, clapped her hands, saying "Chop, chop, time to sit and knit. Leave our troubles outside."

Granny said, "Amen," knowing that these two new members had burdens that needed carrying, even though they were like two songbirds tweeting on a spring day. Maybe they would bump off some of Fern's rough edges.

Having her *bruder* on her mind, Granny decided to break the silence with the announcement of the bishop's decision. "My *bruder*, Noah, is coming over for dinner on Sunday, and I'm so pleased."

"We'll get to know our great-uncle," Rachel gushed. "I've seen him in town, but since the bishop has lifted the no speaking part of the ban, which was ridiculously harsh, we can now be family, like we should have been."

Sarah beamed. "I'm looking forward to him coming."

Fern had Charlotte and Juliet hovering over, hanging on her every word on how to cast on. But she paused to ask, "Is he going to sit at the same table?"

Rachel looked over at Granny as if asking permission, and Granny nodded in approval. "We're going to have two tables pushed together and use one tablecloth. Granny's friend from Italy does it all the time, since they have big families."

Fern rolled her eyes in obvious disapproval, but when Charlotte got frustrated at how hard it was to weave the yarn between her fingers, Fern went back to her tutoring…looking mighty comfortable with these dear sisters.

Rachel seemed to brighten as well. Whatever ailed her flew out the window while at circle, at least most of the time. Their eyes met, and Rachel changed seats to sit next to Granny. "I've been meaning to talk to you. Freeman's *daed* broke his leg and he can't come out to visit." She leaned closer to Granny and murmured. "But I'm going to be like you, and not my other *grossmammi*. I see real love in your marriage, and I know love is patient and kind."

Granny put a finger to her lips. "Someone may overhear."

"With that January wind rattling the windows, I doubt it," she said. "It'll be February this weekend, and that means Valentine's Day will be soon…and your birthday, of course."

Sarah overheard. "We need to celebrate Granny's birthday somehow." She went to her calendar on the wall. "I'll bake a cake."

Cheers rang out, even Fern clapped her hands.

"Does everyone call you Granny?" Charlotte asked.

"Well, *jah*. Most of the folks back home do. I'm only visiting."

"Where are you from?" Juliet asked.

"Smicksburg, Pennsylvania." She lovingly let her eyes rest on Sarah. "I'm here for a long visit. And, you never know which way the wind blows, so I may be here until spring. My husband is getting much needed rest and my *bruder* and I are bonding again. Can you believe after decades of not seeing each other, we feel like no time has lapsed?" Granny tried to hide her grief over Noah's medical issues. "I pray we both have *gut* health to enjoy each other for many years."

Juliet looked up, rather pensive. "I thank God every day for my husband's good health. He's had problems, but we've turned over every stone medically, and he's doing quite well."

Sydney tried to fan away tears. "Juliet is so strong."

"I am not," Juliet corrected. "I'd be a mess if I didn't have a relationship with God."

Fern put an arm around Juliet. "What's wrong with your husband?"

"He had brain cancer three years ago and even though the tumor was removed, it can come back. His scans are clear though, thank God. And I really mean, thank God. My husband is the best thing that's ever happened to me."

"How old is he now?" Fern asked, compassion gushing from her.

"Twenty-eight. If he makes it to his forties, I'll be happy. The boys will be grown and will better understand."

Granny suddenly felt uneasy. Here was Juliet hoping her husband would live to forty. If she was young and Jeb had cancer, would she sink into self-pity and depression, or be like this vibrant young woman whose faith was evident?

Back home in Smicksburg, the knitting circle gave a space to rub shoulders and help each other grow. What would she learn from these two sisters? Charlotte not able to have children would be devastating, but like her sister, she seemed quite content. What was their secret? What could she learn from them? And as she sat and crocheted, she fancied herself living in Millersburg for a longer period of time. *Lord, are you changing my heart?*

~*~

The sunrays beaming across the polished oak floors smiled at Granny. A sunny day in midwinter was a delight, and double so when she would sit again with her *bruder* around a table…or two… for a meal. The whole house was buzzing with anticipation of getting to know the long-lost uncle. Praise be the no-speaking ban was lifted. Granny smoothed the tablecloth over the spot where the two tables met. How silly, but it was a rule to not sit at the same table with shunned ex-Amish, along with no exchanging money or services. Within Granny rose that twenty-some year-old young woman, struggling with compliance with rules, but her dear husband had helped her see that some order had to be followed to live in community.

As Sarah basted the roast, Rachel mashed potatoes, Ruby and May iced the cake. The scents mingled together creating a 'welcome home' scent, and Granny wanted to raise her hands and say, 'Praise the Lord', like her Baptist friends back home.

However, Fern arrived with a container of cookies, cheeks red. Sarah's brows furrowed, and Rachel's mouth gaped. She was not invited.

"Well, this is a nice welcome on an Off-Sunday," Fern huffed.

"My *bruder's* coming over for dinner," Granny

said, hoping Fern knew this was a delicate situation. A private situation.

But, before Fern could respond, a black car drove up to the house, and Noah gingerly got out with a cane. *Ach,* Lord. Is he having a bad day? His nurse, Kimberly, helped him up the stairs and Granny met him with open arms. "*Ach, Bruder*, so *gut* to have you."

His mellow eyes seemed to take in Granny in a way that told her he was reminiscing about the many meals together while growing up. Meals missed in between. Lost time. He held up his cane. "Needed it today. Feeling a bit wobbly."

Granny touched his face. "You don't have to explain. We're so glad you're here."

All the women in the kitchen introduced themselves, hugging him, and overjoyed to have this reunion. However, Fern was eying the table, lifting the tablecloth to see the two tables pushed together. When her eyes met Noah's, daggers flew, but she withdrew into the living room, asking Granny for a word.

Granny obeyed and soon Fern was warning her to move the tables apart. "Shunned folks don't sit at the same table as Amish in *gut* standing."

"It's not the same table."

Fern plunged her fists into her ample hips. "The tables are touching."

Not able to restrain herself, Granny rolled her eyes, something she rarely did. "For Pete's sake,

Fern. What's wrong with you? Did you come over here to inspect us? Report to the bishop?"

Fumbling for words, Fern said no. But, since the ban was lifted on speaking to Noah, she had some 'valuable' information she waited decades to reveal. She withdrew from Granny and asked Noah if she could have a private talk with him. He eyed Granny with suspicion, and Granny said she'd be staying to hear whatever it is she wanted to say. Hopefully it didn't relate to his shunning.

They took seats around the coffee table and Fern, face so flushed and eyes so hawk-like, gave Granny such uneasiness, she reached over to hold Noah's hand. They'd face this together.

"Noah, you may recall Mary Miller was my best friend."

Noah nodded. "Yes. Have you kept in touch with her? I've never been able to find her."

Fern moaned. "She never married, you know. All because you broke her heart. *Ach,* believe me, others wanted to court her, but she said *nee*."

Noah's chin quivered. "It's private, but I am sorry to hear that. Is she…still alive?"

"Of course, she's alive. We're not fossils yet. Lives alone in a *dawdyhaus* behind her niece."

Granny watched Noah's reaction. That's where the proof was, in the reaction. His eyes shone. "How can I see her?"

"Buy a ticket to Lancaster County, I suppose. If she wants to see you, that is."

Granny knew there were hundreds of Mary Millers in Lancaster, and this solved the mystery as to why Noah couldn't find her. "We need her address." Granny said. It was not a question, but a reasonable demand.

"Well, I'll write and see if she wants…anything to do with the man who left her, even after he proposed."

Noah leaned his head back on the chair "Fern, I recall you being an outspoken woman. I see some things never change. You still wear me out."

Fern huffed. "Well, I speak my mind, if that's what you mean."

Noah rubbed his eyes, appearing to wilt. Granny told Fern it was time for her to go and pulled her up with all her might. "Noah tires easily." Anger akin to rage simmered in Granny. As she led Fern out on the porch, she growled like never before. "You know he's fighting cancer. How can you be so heartless?"

"He wasn't fighting cancer when he broke Mary's heart."

Granny stomped a foot. "*Jah,* he was. *Ach,* but it's not your business. Now, give me her address."

Fern looked humbled. She was a dog with her tail between her legs, hunched over. "So, he had cancer when he broke- "

"It's none of your business, Fern." Granny wanted to scream that it's Amish people like her that make others leave the faith, but she bit her tongue. The image of Charlotte and Juliet, their beautiful spirits, came to her and she had to trust the Lord above that the knitting circle girls would knock Fern's rough edges off. Yes, she did believe in miracles.

Chapter 14

Rachel asked Benjamin if they could have a brother-sister talk, a heart-to-heart, like they were accustomed to doing. This *bruder* of hers had wisdom beyond his years, but he also had the biggest heart, and she didn't want him taken in by Heather. Were her *mamm*'s concerns valid? Rachel was excited that her *mamm* asked her for advice about Benjamin. What a compliment. What a mother-daughter bond they enjoyed now. They'd both changed. And it was all because of her dear *oma* from Smicksburg.

Taking hot chocolate up to Rachel's bedroom, Benjamin made himself at home in the rocker while Rachel sat on the floor, near the vent where the heat rose from below. She crossed her ankles and began.

"Benjamin, I see Heather came over to visit you. Why would she do that?"

Benjamin laughed. "So, the cat's out of the bag, *jah*? *Mamm* told you about us?"

"*Jah,* she did. We're concerned. Are you ready to be a *daed*? And don't you want to be the first love of a younger Amish girl? So many flirt with you at

Singings, it's ridiculous."

"With me?" Benjamin chuckled. "I don't see it."

"Well, I do. So does Ruby since she's been going. Why not take some girls out on buggy rides and get to know a few?"

Benjamin, never one to get upset, but sticking firm to his convictions, acknowledged what she said with intensity. "I'm glad you're concerned. If you were marrying a widower, I'd think maybe he didn't love you, but just needed a *mamm* for his *kinner*. But, it's not like that with Heather."

"How do you know, Benjamin?" She held her head. "I had it in my mind that you'd marry a girl who knew she was getting the best man in town. You'd talk about plans to build a house, our *Gmay* would all pitch in to help you get settled, but Heather already has a place, doesn't she?"

Benjamin swung his foot onto his knee. "What we imagine doesn't always happen. When I helped Heather on her farm after being a widow, we never thought we'd begin to love each other. I think it was her son that was the common bond. Quite a little fellow."

Rachel sipped her cocoa. "Listen to yourself. You bonded over a little boy who just lost his *daed,* and you filled his shoes, *jah*? That's attractive to a widow. Are you sure you love Heather or the notion of rescuing her and the boy? Can she keep her farm without your help?"

Silence. Only the sound of laughter downstairs echoing around the walls. Benjamin leaned over, his head in his hands. "I don't think so."

Rachel felt as wise as her *oma.* "When I was dating Jared, I was disillusioned. I envisioned a life far different than what he wanted. It was a loving thing for him to break off our engagement. Benjamin, it's not wrong for you to not see Heather for a while and see if your love is real."

"Is that what you and Freeman are doing?" he asked.

"*Jah,* we are."

"And?" Benjamin prodded.

"I love him more and more. I'd move to Smicksburg for him, even though he said he'd move here for me. He's the right one for me, even if he can't visit for a while. We write and well, I feel like I'd let go of the best man ever if I wasn't patient enough to wait for God's perfect timing."

Benjamin forced a smile, but then his face contorted, and he bit back tears. "I really care about Heather, but…"

~*~

Late that night, Rachel couldn't sleep. She missed Freeman something fierce. So, she tip-toed out of the room, careful not to wake Ruby up, and quiet as a cat made her way down to the kitchen and lit the gas light over the table. She took out stationery that was always in the China closet, and wrote:

Dear Freeman,

I can't sleep. I miss you so much. But our love will be stronger, that I know for sure. My oma told me that metal gets stronger while in the fire, plus impurities are burned out. But it hurts. I want to share things with you and letter writing isn't the same.

Today, I had a talk with Benjamin. He knows he must break things off with the widow he's engaged to. His compassionate heart wanted to rescue a woman who will lose her farm without his help. He'd also be an instant daed to a little boy, and that appealed to him. I believe the little boy brought them close together, but it's not real love. I don't know if Heather realizes how lonely she is and desperate to keep her farm. Benjamin is an answer, not someone she loves.

Pray for Benjamin and promise me something. If you're having doubts about our relationship, let me know. I want real, true love, like my oma and opa from Smicksburg. Promise me, okay?

I don't know why I'm babbling on like this.

I miss you!

Rachel

~*~

Jeb, looking through binoculars, called Daniel over to look at the bald eagle that swooped down into the pond in the back field. "Take a look."

Daniel adjusted the focus. "That's a hawk."

"*Nee*, it's too big. It's a bald eagle. Their heads don't turn white until they're four years old."

Shaking his head, Daniel disagreed, pointing out

the red tail. "It's a red-tailed hawk. *Mamm* will know for sure. She's the real birder in the family." Daniel continued to look at the plethora of birds that visited the feeding stations across the yard. "If it's a hawk, it'll snatch some of the songbirds."

"*Since* it's an eagle, it'll do the same," Jeb said with an air of superiority, knowing he was right, and then burst into a chuckle. "I miss our bird squabbling days. Wish you didn't live so far away." Jeb let this slip and regretted it immediately. "But your home is here..."

"Yours could be, too." Daniel said in a hopeful tone. "What on earth? What is Fern doing?"

Jeb took the binoculars to see Fern walking briskly back and forth outside her house, obviously letting off steam. "She's upset about something, I guess."

"I feel sorry for Matthew. Fern drives him up a tree. Since Sarah said she doesn't want to get in the middle of things, along with Leah, it's forced them to work things out in their marriage."

Jeb put an arm around Daniel. "Like you and Sarah, *jah*?"

Daniel blushed like a schoolboy with a crush on a girl. "*Jah,* like my sweetheart girl and me. I'm so thankful for your advice."

"When are you breaking ground for her quilt shop? That Sydney knows how to get a business up and running, *jah*? I think she's *gut* for Sarah."

Daniel nodded in agreement. "Fern thinks Sydney's a Jezebel straight out of the Bible. But she's raved about the two new girls who came last week, even though they have streaked hair and heavy eye makeup."

"God looks at the heart, not judging by the outward appearance. Have you ever wondered if you could flip people inside out, like a pair of trousers, what you'd see?"

Daniel blinked in disbelief. "*Nee*, but it's a *gut* thought. Since you and *Mamm* have been here, I've accepted people more. I don't judge my customers for their tattoos, weird tee shirts with skeletons or blue hair." He laughed. "The colors men and women dye their hair nowadays is sometimes comical and I have to bite my lip so I won't laugh."

Jeb refilled his coffee cup. "Was it uncomfortable having your Uncle Noah over?"

"*Nee*, not at all. I like him. It's sad why he left the Amish though. The People would have paid for treatment. And *Mamm* told me all about Mary Miller."

Jeb sighed. "Noah was too proud, even though I like him a lot. You must humble yourself to ask for help, *jah*?"

"But, *Daed,* he couldn't have children after the operation. Or it was highly unlikely with all the chemo."

"You met Denny, our teenage son. Folks can always adopt."

Daniel fidgeted with his suspender straps. "*Daed,* you think humble people ask for help, but what if it's selfish?"

"What's on your mind, son?" Jeb knew by Daniel's sudden pensive mood that this was a weighty matter. "Go on. Spit it out."

After a long pause, he shook his head. "It's not fair."

"What isn't?" Jeb asked.

"Asking you and *Mamm* to move out here. Not for a visit, but permanently. *Yinz* would be *gut* for the *kinner* and the new *boppli.*"

Jeb held to the table and sat down. "New *boppli*?"

Daniel's brows shot up. "*Mamm* didn't tell you?"

"Nee. She's had a lot on her mind. Another Weaver in Holmes County? I like that name being spread out in these parts."

Jeb could read Daniel's face. He wanted kin out in Ohio he could relate to, not being close to his in-laws. Or was it that Deborah and himself really did make a difference. Well, Deborah he knew for sure, but since he'd arrived, all he did was help in the rocker shop and fish.

A scripture came to mind. Something about teaching God's ways to your children, talking to them, when you sit down, take a walk…when doing the little things in life. Deborah baking pies with so many young girls ended up in chatting about their problems. Maybe this extended visit allowed Daniel's family to open up naturally. No pressure to squeeze all their time together in two weeks.

"Son, I'll be praying about us moving here. There's always a bend in the road, like your *Mamm* says, but I fear she won't like it. She's mighty attached to Smicksburg."

Daniel agreed. "Maybe a year-long visit? Or six months? Either way, you'll want your privacy and we'd build a *dawdyhaus*."

He got up to hug Daniel. "You'd do that?"

"Sure would."

Jeb felt like he was the richest man in town. Noah was indeed the richest in worldly possessions, but not in the things that mattered. He shot up a prayer that Noah would find the happiness he enjoyed.

~*~

Granny regretted walking all the way back to Fern's house. Not only did her knees hurt, but she never expected such resistance from Fern to hand over Mary Miller's address.

"I want to write first to see if Mary is up to hearing such news," Fern said. "I don't give out other's addresses without their permission."

"Fiddlesticks," Granny snapped. "The Amish give out their addresses like recipes. We all write circle letters to strangers."

Matthew entered the room. "What's all this about?" he demanded to know.

Fern stepped back, not used to Matthew being so bold. "It's private."

"Well, I hear you shouting, and I don't want you being rude to a guest."

Fern flustered. "Go back and read *The Budget.*"

Matthew plopped himself at the kitchen table in defiance. "Deborah, what's all this about?"

Granny was so dumbfounded that Matthew was acting so out of character, she felt his forehead. "Matthew, are you okay?"

"Right as rain since I talked to the bishop. *Gut* advice on how to be the one who wears the trousers in a marriage." He turned to Fern. "Now, what's all this about?"

Fern narrowed her eyes to slits. "You didn't talk to the bishop. You talked to that *bruder* of yours! He's too domineering."

Granny groaned. She was saying once again that Matthew's brain was mush and he couldn't think for himself.

"Fern, I'm not beating around the bush anymore. I did talk to the bishop and he said a marriage that you feel like you're walking on eggshells needs help. He expects to see us both next week for some *gut* counsel." His eyes ablaze, he turned to Granny. "What do you want? I'm not deaf yet. Something about an address?"

Fern ran out the back door in a rage, slamming the door so hard, the plates in the China cabinet rattled. Granny started to go after Fern, but Matthew stopped her.

"She'll cool down. Let her pace outside a bit, stew

a bit, but she's fine. The bishop's advice hit the target. Now, what do you want from her?"

Feeling shaken, Granny wiped her brow. "I came for an address Fern said she'd give me but now refuses. Do you remember Mary Miller?"

"Sure do," Noah said. "Sweet woman. Why doesn't Fern want to give out Mary's address?"

"She wants to warn Mary about my *bruder*, Noah Byler, wanting to contact her."

Matthew let his head sink into his hands. "She tires herself out. She tries to do God's job. Mary Miller is a grown woman. Noah should write and let the chips fall where they may. It's time Fern stops trying to control everything." He shifted. "I'll be having this conversation with her. I'm sorry for putting you on the spot. My temper flared quite a bit, but..."

"She's worn your patience thin? Don't feel bad. I raised my voice, too. It's been quite some time that someone has fired me up so." She covered her mouth. "I shouldn't be saying this to you."

He swooshed at the air. "You aren't the first person. The bishop asked me what took so long. It's easy to just skedaddle than...confront. I'm not *gut* at it, but I know I have to." He wrung his hands. "She goes on and on about that hairdresser having had two divorces, but she doesn't know that I'd have left and divorced long ago if the Amish allowed it."

Granny wanted to put cotton in her ears. Matthew was like a breaking dam. One crack and then the dam soon breaks, gushing out water. "You can talk to Jeb if you want. He's helped many with marital problems."

Fern swung open the door and slammed it again, teacups rattling. She marched over to her address book, scribbled violently, and flung Mary Miller's address at Granny. Her icy eyes glared at her husband. "Are you happy now?"

Matthew rose and stood erect. "*Danki*. It's been a while since you *honored* a request."

"Command, you mean?"

Granny dismissed herself abruptly. Sore knees or not, she'd trudge back to the farmhouse to get away from this quarrelsome house. When would she stop trying to be like Angelina, her dear Italian pen pal who walked a mile a day? She wasn't made from the same stock.

When she stepped outside, a buggy was going past. She waved and Benjamin pulled over. "Need a ride?" he asked, rather forlorn.

Granny hopped into the buggy. From Benjamin's countenance, he was out of sorts. But she didn't ask what ailed him. She needed tea, her yarn, and some peace and quiet.

~*~

Sarah handed Rachel a letter, shock registering on her face.

"What is it, *Mamm*?"

"It's postmarked Cleveland. Are you writing to Jared?"

Grabbing the letter, Rachel surveyed the envelope. It was Jared's handwriting. "I've never written. It's probably a letter apologizing about breaking off our engagement and wanting to remain friends." What could she say, never expecting to hear from him again?

Seeing that her *mamm* was fretting, she opened the letter up right there, suggesting they take a break from *redding* up the house.

Sarah agreed and Rachel poured them each their second cup of coffee. Rachel soon heard Granny's voice and she invited her to join them. After three mugs were on the table, Rachel sat at the long oak table to read aloud:

Dear Rachel,

Cleveland is not what I expected. It's too cramped living in this tiny apartment. I miss the wide-open spaces in Holmes County. This has taken me by surprise. I never appreciated the peaceful setting I grew in. I miss Refuge Church. I miss you. Can we hit the rewind button and start our relationship with no secrets? Not try to change each other. I promise you I'd find a job not too far from your family and we'd visit often, if you'll have me back. I can't be Amish, but maybe Mennonite. The Mennonites that drive cars, that is.

Please write back if I still have a chance with you.

Love,
Jared

Rachel calmly set the letter down. "I won't be writing back."

Sarah flinched. "Rachel, really?"

"*Mamm*, I feel nothing. Someone's taken Jared's place."

Granny glowed. "Freeman?"

Rachel smiled. "You know it's Freeman, *Oma*. Who else? I know this family thinks I'm fickle, but I'm not."

Granny reached for Rachel's hands and squeezed them. "I don't think you're fickle. You were just confused for a spell. Your reaction to this letter makes something rock solid."

"What's that *Oma*?" Rachel asked, always eager to learn more from this wise woman.

Well," Granny started, "we can act in ways we know deep down isn't the truth. We deceive ourselves. I didn't know I loved Jeb until he got real sick. It was my reaction that told me what my heart refused to admit. Your reaction to Jared's letter is exciting." She glanced at Sarah. "It tells us we need to plan a wedding."

Rachel's heart knew this was the moment she'd dreamed of her whole life. Loving a man with no doubts, building a future together with an Amish man she respected. It was the Amish way so engrained in her since birth. And she loved it.

Sarah drank down her coffee without taking a breath. Eyes wide, she asked, "I suspected he proposed, but Rachel, are you sure? Absolutely sure? You haven't known Freeman long."

With a steadfast heart, Rachel said she had no doubts. Not a one. And as she said this, her longing to write to Freeman and tell him she'd marry him as soon as possible rose within. "How soon can we get a wedding arranged?"

Now Sarah was white as the snow outside. "Rachel, you've become very levelheaded. Why, Benjamin told your *daed* and me how you helped him see he needed to break things off with Heather. You've grown by leaps and bounds, but marriage now? Can't you wait a year or two? Where would you live? How would you make a living?"

Rachel looked to Granny, startled. "Freeman said he'd move to Holmes County for me, since living around my family means so much. Do you think he's serious?"

Granny nodded. "Freeman doesn't say things he doesn't mean."

Sarah massaged her temples. "Rachel, can you wait until November? During wedding season?"

Rachel tried to restrain herself but failed. "Lots of weddings take place in the winter."

Granny fidgeted with her prayer *kapp* ribbons. "You could move to Smicksburg and live at

Freeman's place. That's where his work is."

"I could," Rachel said, straightening. "I'd do anything for him. Where he is, that's where my home is."

Sarah burst into tears. Granny offered her a handkerchief and she grabbed it.

"Sarah, my Daniel moved out here for you, remember. You refused to live in Smicksburg, wanting to live near your family." Granny put her hand on Sarah's. "Now, I'm not faulting you, but just saying I know how you feel. We only have Roman living back home now. *Jah,* it's painful, but one thing in life that's guaranteed is change, I reckon."

Sarah gasped for air. "But Rachel and I were finally becoming…bosom friends."

Rachel had wanted this relationship with her *mamm* her whole life, and what a well-spring of life it was to hear such endearing words. She ran around the table and hugged her *mamm.* "We are bosom friends. That won't change."

"*Jah,* it will if you move far away."

"Montana is far," Granny interjected. "With all my heart I wish my sons would move closer. Ohio would be nice. Vans go back and forth from Smicksburg to Holmes County all the time. Sarah, you might like the adventure."

No change in Sarah as tears ran out like a faucet. Jeb and Daniel came into the room, wondering what all the commotion was about. When Daniel found out that Rachel might be moving to Smicksburg, his eyes clouded, and he pulled her to himself and held her tight.

Rachel's ecstasy in getting married to Freeman with no doubts lasted a short two-minutes. When her grandparents came in November, she knew she was a thorn in her parents' sides. Now, with the help of her *oma* and *opa*, she was a beloved daughter they couldn't part with. And she was ever so thankful…yet a tinge of sadness stirred in her heart. How she loved Holmes County.

~*~

Sydney stopped over with blueprints her new friend had drawn up for Sarah's quilt shop. "We'll have a window on the south side to let in lots of sunlight," Sydney gushed.

"Sunlight fades material," Sarah pointed out. "And…"

Granny set aside her knitting and joined them in the kitchen. "I like blueprints. Interesting. Makes a body wonder how they make those fancy cathedrals and whatnot We keep it simple."

Sydney gave Granny a side hug. "I have a few fancy things in mind. We'll have lattice window inserts. It'll look different than all the other quilt shops." She snapped her fingers. "We don't want Sarah to show quilts and have a potential customer not be able to come back to the right store to buy it. They may go into the other white clapboard

Amish style shops." She shifted the paper on the table. "Right here will be a big sign in a color that gets attention. Maybe red? I don't know."

Sarah licked her lips. "We don't want to be in competition with other quilt shops."

"That's what business is all about!" Sydney exclaimed, flabbergasted. "Don't tell me your shops have to all look the same, like your houses."

"You see Daniel's shop, *jah*? It's painted white clapboard and my shop will look the same."

Sydney was astonished. "Well, how can we make your customers remember where you are? There's so many Amish quilt shops, and they all look the same."

"I can use Daniel's sale's receipt book since the address is on there." Sarah proposed

"But it doesn't say quilt shop!" Sydney pointed out. "You need your own sign *and* business cards. Now, I'm going to start a website. I know how to use SEO, so when people Google, 'Amish Quilts in Holmes County', your shop will pop up first."

Granny didn't understand a word Sydney said, but did understand Sarah's look of dismay. *Ach,* she was pregnant and didn't want a quilt shop just now. Maybe in a few years. "Sydney, it's ever so *gut* of you to go to all this trouble, but Sarah's going to have to wait on opening a quilt shop. She's, ah, …pregnant."

Sydney blinked in disbelief. "Really?" Her mouth gaped. "But, you're…"

"I'm old," Sarah said with a laugh. "It's okay to say it."

"Well, your youngest is eight, right? A baby will tie you down." Sydney bit a nail. "But I worked when my kids were babies."

Granny hugged herself. "I love *bopplin.* They're all like little angels from above."

"Oh, I think so, too," Sydney stammered. "Sarah? You look like a deer in headlights."

Sarah's crimson cheeks grew more saturated. "I'm still a bit shocked. Of course, I'm happy. All *bopplin* are gifts," she said, chin shaking. And then she let the tears flow. "I can't have a quilt shop now. Not with a new *boppli.*"

Rachel meandered into the room and gasped when she saw her *mamm*'s tears. "What's wrong?"

"Nothing at all," Sydney said. "Your mom will have this baby, and everyone will pitch in and she'll have her quilt shop. Your mom needs this for herself. You have Rachel here to help you. She's old enough to be a mother herself."

At this, Sarah cried all the harder. Granny took Sydney aside while Rachel soothed her mother. "Sydney, Rachel's planning on marrying a man from my neck of the woods. She'll be moving to Smicksburg and Sarah's taking it hard."

Sydney's shoulders sagged. "That stinks."

"Her relationship with Rachel was just getting on sure footing and Sarah regrets lost time."

Shaking her head, Sydney let out an audible sigh. "Life never works out like we plan. Can this Freeman move out here?"

He helps his *daed* with the family business making furniture. Some mighty fancy."

"Well, there's lots of tourism in Holmes County and some stores can't keep up. Is it like that in Smicksburg?" Sydney asked.

Granny mulled this over. "*Nee*. Now that I've been here for two months, I see there's far more tourism." Holmes County was a bustle of activity, something she was finally getting used to, and liking it. Could the Yoders move out to these parts and be better off? *Lord, have your way.*

Chapter 15

Over the next few days, Granny felt a bit under the weather, so she knit quite a bit in her room. Jeb checked on her frequently, asking her if she had the winter blues. Her reply was always that she was tired. On the third day, Jeb massaged her shoulders and asked if she needed Vitamin D supplements for energy. Maybe head over to Walmart to get some things she needed? But, she shrugged, saying he could go with Daniel. Have some father-son time.

"Deborah, I can read you like a book. You're upset about something. What's wrong?"

"I'm tired," was all she could get out. She'd felt feverish at first, but was right as rain, only tired. Did she need some supplements?

"Okay, I'll tell you what I see," Jeb started. "You miss Smicksburg and just the thought of living here permanently is depressing you."

Granny's kitchen came to mind. Baking on her Pioneer Princess stove had been a delight. Having family and friends over to knit or bake…in her kitchen. Her kitchen! "Jeb, I miss having my own kitchen."

Jeb scratched his head nodding. "I miss us having our own place. Daniel said they'd build a *dawdyhaus*, and I appreciate it and all, but…"

"It's not Smicksburg? Miss your role in our *Gmay*?"

Jeb sat in the other rocker. "That I do not miss. I'm an old man, remember?" he asked with a wink.

Their long running joke of calling each other 'old man' and 'old woman' hadn't been used much since they'd arrived in Ohio. It was a term of endearment, one that always brought a smile to them both. "Well, Jeb, we're not spring chickens. Is there a bend in the road? I've been pondering that for days. Daniel wants us to stay and I see the need with Sarah having another *boppli*."

"They needed our help with the older ones. *Bopplin* cry, eat and coo a lot. Teenagers on *Rumspringa* are making big decisions. All they've been taught is tried by fire. Do you know May asked me the other day why she had to wear such weird clothes?"

"She's only eight. That's a *gut* question," Granny said.

"In my day, I knew when I was a wee one, we dressed different because we were set apart, not like the world." Jeb twiddled his thumbs. "*Kinner* these days…"

Granny set down her yarn. "Jeb, you were of the strictest Amish order, and you rarely saw anyone outside your *Gmay*, *jah*? Here in Holmes County, there's a dozen or more variety of Amish. And have you noticed that most have businesses, not farming anymore? We're not as isolated like we used to be."

Slouching, Jeb groaned. "*Kinner* are exposed too much here. Smicksburg's a simpler place." He hit the bent wood chair arm. "Do I sound too old? Things always look better in the past."

Granny reached for his hand. "I see the same thing. I almost fainted when some at *Gmay* said their *kinner* go to public school by their own choice. I never heard of such a thing, but Ivy Fisher went until she was in eighth grade and is a devout Amish young lady."

"She is…" Jeb agreed. "She's pretty, too. And Benjamin's age…"

Granny chuckled. "If folks back home knew you turned into a matchmaker like me, they'd get a *gut* laugh."

Jeb wiggled his bushy eyebrows. "You're right. Something's satisfying in seeing two young people find each other…with a little help."

Granny's heart lifted. She knew all of Jeb's escapades in getting Rachel and Freeman together. *Jah,* she could see Ivy and Benjamin together once Benjamin stopped moping over his breakup with Heather.

"Maybe we're needed here, and you know it. Is that what has you down?" Jeb asked, his question framed in a tone of pure love.

Appreciation for this dear man rose. "*Jah,* I suppose. But how long will we be needed here? Months more?"

"Daniel wants to break ground on a *dawdyhaus* when the ground thaws. He's not building that quilt shop, which puzzles me to no end."

"Sarah's talking about using the closed in porch off the back of the house. I think it's a *gut* solution since she can be near the *boppli.* Sydney's helping her see outside the box."

Jeb pulled a string of her yarn. "We need to do a casting off prayer?"

Granny nodded. "I've been doing just that for days. And you are the answer, old man."

"Me? What do you mean?"

"Well, I've been mulling over all that's transpired since we arrived for Thanksgiving, not able to pinpoint what unsettled me so. Talking to you has been *gut* therapy. An answer to prayer. We need to consider moving here…or not."

Jeb got up, scooped his wife in his arms, and kissed her soundly. "I love you, old woman."

She squeezed him tight. "And I love you, old man."

~*~

As February marched on, Rachel found her heart settling quite a bit. Letters from Freeman did indeed fill in the loss of his presence. She tucked his love letters into her hope chest, some days rereading them. She was learning to cherish this time at home since she'd be leaving once married.

Ruby bounced into their bedroom. "Rachel, can you keep a secret?"

"I hope so. But, don't tell me something too serious to keep a secret."

Ruby raised her hands and squealed. "Tall Billy asked me to court."

"Court? You mean dating, like the English call it. Courting is with the intention of marriage. You're too young."

"Am not." She fanned her red cheeks. "He's perfect and well set up in his family business."

Rachel cocked a brow. "You just turned sixteen. It'll be a long courtship."

"Or not." Ruby plunked herself on the braided rug. "You don't seem happy for me."

"*Ach,* I am. You've just started going to Singings and well, let lots of guys take you home."

Ruby winced. "That's what I told Tall Billy, but he said he wants to claim me for his own before someone else does."

Rachel was learning that love was patient, and this irritated her. "Love wants the best for others and is patient. Freeman taught me that. Don't let Tall Billy pressure you. Take your time and meet lots of young folk during your *Rumspringa.*" She gently folded Freeman's letter and put it in her pocket.

"He's like clockwork with his letter writing."

Ruby sat and slouched against the bed. "You were lucky to get Freeman. He really is the best Amish man alive. But…"

"But?"

"You'll be moving to Smicksburg and I'll die being the oldest girl in this house. Too many pairs of trousers to wash. But Granny will be here to help."

"Come again?" Rachel said. "You don't expect *Oma* to do so much work."

"*Ach, nee.* But she will be here and always eager to help. Never did see someone in their seventies with so much energy."

Rachel picked up her crochet project. "I suppose this vacation has done her *gut.* She's nice and rested up."

Ruby eyed her sister. "So, you haven't heard?"

Oma had been to herself, feeling under the weather. "I know. She's better and as *mamm* says, can run circles around all of us. Is she downstairs baking more pies for Uncle Noah?"

Ruby cleared her throat. "You know that *Daed* is trying to convince *Oma* and *Opa* to move here permanently."

"*Jah,* I know. But *Oma* will never leave Smicksburg. She's as attached to that town as a mother hen to her chicks. And you see all the letters she gets from out there. The town would fall apart without her wise advice and giving heart."

Ruby cleared her throat. "Well, her loving heart always puts *Opa* first, *jah*? And he likes it out here…"

Rachel froze. "Don't tell me she's going to move here permanently! I've begged her my whole life to do it, and I'll be leaving."

Ruby smoothed her apron and tucked a runaway stray hair under her prayer *kapp*. "Nothing is for sure, but I overheard *Daed* talking to *Opa*. Something about they'd be praying about it. *Opa*'s tired of his ministry duties."

A lump formed in Rachel's throat and she wanted to burst into tears. Her dream of going over to visit her *grosseldre* from Freeman's house was a dream. "All my life I prayed they'd move out here, and now it might happen, but I'll be gone. And I don't know a soul in Smicksburg."

"*Jah* you do," Ruby said. "Fannie was here and also Denny, *Oma* and *Opa's* adopted son."

Rachel tried hard to not think selfish thoughts, but this one she had to let fly. "How can they abandon their adopted son?"

Ruby ogled her. "He's a grown man."

"He's a teenager. And he'll be crushed."

"How do you know?" Ruby asked, incredulously.

"Because they're the sweetest people on the planet." Rachel sprang up. "I need to take a walk to the pond." She near ran from the room and down the stairs.

But at the bottom stood Granny, looking concerned. "Rachel, was the letter bad news?"

Rachel felt like she'd pop if she didn't walk off this unexpected burst of nervous energy. "*Nee*, not bad news." She looked into her *oma's* light blue eyes, a sea of tranquility. "Is it true you're not going back to Smicksburg?"

Granny held on to the handrail. "Rachel, nothing definite has been decided. You know how fond I am of my kitchen."

Rachel hugged her. "I knew it. Ruby didn't understand. You'd never leave Smicksburg."

Granny pat Rachel's face. "We never know which way the wind blows, and that's the way it is with God's calling."

"God's calling? What do you mean? Have you talked to the folks over at Christian Aid Ministries? Are you and *Opa* planning on getting involved in that ministry?"

Granny looked puzzled. "*Nee.* The calling to be a help to my family. That's always been my true calling, even though others say it's hospitality." She leaned in closer to Rachel. "Your *mamm* needs me here just a bit longer, being pregnant and all."

"But Ruby said *Daed* was building a *dawdyhaus*." Rachel held back tears as she watched her precious *oma* fumble for words.

"I look at it as a vacation house. When we visit, we can have our own place for a long stay. You know I need my own kitchen." She winked and cupped Rachel's cheeks. "But if I'm out here for a long vacation, let the Lord's will be done."

Rachel remembered her best friend saying nearly the same thing when she visited Indiana. She moved there permanently. She kissed her *oma* on the cheek and grabbed her winter shawl, outer bonnet, and headed to the pond.

~*~

Granny caught Jeb by the shirt sleeve. "I need to tell you something."

"Everything all right?"

"*Jah,*" she started, nudging him into the utility room. "Jeb, I was talking to Rachel, and I think I have a solution to our moving issue. You know how many Amish go to Pinecraft or stay with family for extended vacations? How about we look at the *dawdyhaus* like it's a vacation home?"

Pulling his beard, Jeb slowly nodded his head. "I see what you mean. It wouldn't upset folks back home if we came out for long vacations, but what about my ministerial duties? Do you think it's time I became a senior bishop?"

Granny had to be truthful. "You get mighty tired, but you're still capable. Look at Eli Hostetler, he's in his late eighties and still a bishop."

He clamped his large hands on her thin shoulders. "You want me to be a senior bishop, *jah*? Have more time to visit the boys scattering all over kingdom come and visit out here more." He bent to kiss her forehead. "We need two of you to run all the charity work in Smicksburg and here. It's you who's tired. I see it."

Shocked at this statement, her jaw unhinged. "I'm not tired."

"You stayed in your room for three days, Deborah. You're whooped."

When he called her Deborah, he meant business. She straightened. "Fretting too much wore me out, but since we talked, it helped. How about you write the ministers and see what they say, and we look at the *dawdyhaus* as a vacation home."

"I'll do that, love," he said tenderly and kissed her.

Just then the outside door opened, and Benjamin walked in. He stepped back, fumbling for words. "You still…"

Jeb laughed. "That old Amish proverb about kissing wearing out isn't true. You'll find out someday." He smirked. "What do you think of Ivy Fisher?"

Benjamin's natural blush line on his cheeks deepened. "Every guy wants to court her."

Jeb put an arm around Granny. "Seven times this woman said no to marriage proposals. Everyone wanted to marry her, but she picked a Weaver. Our stock is hardy and goes back to the strictest of the Old Order Amish." He winked. "That's how I got her. Ask Ivy to go for a buggy ride."

Granny could hear the confidence in Jeb's voice,

having matched Rachel with Freeman. How many times over the years had he teased her about being a matchmaker like Emma Woodhouse in her beloved Jane Austen book. She wanted to poke him, tell him to stop, but Benjamin's countenance changed…looking more confident…like Jeb.

"I think Ivy's the sweetest girl out in these parts. She might be coming over to help make pies with your *oma*." Jeb cued Granny to join him with his plan.

Benjamin was now beet red. "She's friends with my sisters."

"Never seen her visit." Granny rubbed Jeb's back. "I'll tell her to come over soon to bake. Maybe she can join our knitting circle. It's growing, you know."

Scurrying past them, Benjamin said he needed to tell his *daed* something. Jeb cocked an eyebrow. "He likes her."

"It's too soon after Heather. But we planted a seed, old man. Is your new hobby matchmaking?"

He gave a comical grin. "Never too late to teach old dogs new tricks." He turned to leave but spun back around. "Love, I forgot to tell you. Daniel and I are headed up to Lake Erie to ice fish next weekend, it being an Off-Sunday, no church and all. Slipped my mind. Do you care?"

Jeb's love for the great outdoors, especially when the fish called him, made him most attractive. Jeb was a real man. "You have a *gut* time, old man. I hope to spend time with my *bruder*."

~*~

The next day, the mail came like clockwork, and Ruby slid the pile on the table. "Here's some letters for you, *Oma*."

"*Danki*. I'll read them in my room. Still get teared up when my knitting girls tell me how much they miss me back home."

She quickly ascended the stairs and nestled herself in her rocker. Upon seeing a letter with the return address named Mary Miller, her heart skipped a beat. Ripping it open, she read:

Dear Deborah,

Thank you ever so much for your letter and writing to me. I'm surprised Fern gave it out since I'm shunned. Saying I lived in a dawdyhaus behind my niece was misleading. I live in a carriage house in the back of my niece. I'm not Amish any longer.

Many think I left Holmes County because of Noah breaking our engagement. That's partially true. But I had doubts about remaining Amish and when I made the decision, it was too hard living among the People. I moved in with my aunt whose Beachy Amish and wasn't shunned. When my family left the plain life, we were shunned out here. We wandered around to find a church and found one that led us into a loving relationship with Jesus Christ. We believe in salvation by grace and talking straight to God, not afraid to call Him friend.

You must think I'm sinful since many Amish believe if you

leave the Amish you'll go to hell. This just isn't true. My Bible tells me otherwise. I'm telling you this because I've lost track of many in Holmes County for decades and they may not know I'm shunned. Noah may not know. So, it's a heads up. Do you still want me to come out?

How is Noah? I'd love to see him. He was gone for so long that we lost touch. I'm in my sixties now, retired from being a nurse. I have lots of free time now to roam around as I please. And I'm not one bit afraid to drive in the snow like my niece.

Write back and let me know when I can see Noah. Wouldn't it be funny to surprise him on Valentine's Day? Not everyone has the humor I do, but Noah always loved it.

Write back and let me know your thoughts. Tell Fern I said hello and to write again soon. You know she writes to me in secret. Please don't tell anyone.

Sincerely,

Mary Miller

"She's as spunky as a teenage girl on *Rumspringa*," Granny said with a chuckle. She pondered the fact that Fern wrote to Mary all these years, and she knew about her shunning. Was Fern like a turtle, a hard exterior but soft and pliable inside? This friendship with Mary implied so.

She looked upon the other letters. One from Fannie. One from Ella. One from Ruth. Every time they wrote, she missed them more. How could she endure living here until spring when the earth would thaw enough to dig a foundation for Anna and Ezekiel's new place. Sometimes March came in like a lamb, not a lion, as the Almanac said. Sometimes early March was ever so mild.

With a deep sigh, she opened the letters, some five pages long. How could she keep up? A circle letter. *Jah,* she'd send it to Fannie, who could send it to each of her '*Little Women*' and then she could read them all, like a novelette.

Feeling full of emotion, she decided to sing parts of her favorite song, *His Eye is on the Sparrow:*

"Let not your heart be troubled," His tender word I hear,
And resting on His goodness, I lose my doubts and fears;
Though by the path He leadeth, but one step I may see;
His eye is on the sparrow, and I know He watches me;
His eye is on the sparrow, and I know He watches me.

Whenever I am tempted, whenever clouds arise,
When songs give place to sighing, when hope within me dies,
I draw the closer to Him, from care He sets me free;
His eye is on the sparrow, and I know He watches me;
His eye is on the sparrow, and I know He watches me.

Filling a bit lifted, Granny decided to go downstairs and watch the many birds at the feeders. This time to mull over the promise that God was watching over her every step, and give her wings.

~*~

Rachel emptied her hope chest, dreaming of her life with Freeman. The separation was indeed unbearable, but he was worth it. His letters came three times a week, some so tender Rachel's heart was melting. Literally. God was softening her heart regarding Him in ways she never realized she'd resisted. How many times had she read a Bible verse and rolled her eyes? Especially on submission in a marriage. But Freeman's love made her want to trust him. Was this why she'd never courted? Never been baptized?

She hugged her knees, pondering it all. In the English world, women were stronger than Amish women. Were they like Sydney? Having to be strong because their husbands didn't stick around? She thought of Melody and Kenny and how they were an opening lily every time she saw them.

Granny always said people spun together are stronger, like the wool she spins into yarn. Were people afraid to be spun together? Were they too independent? Was she, as an Amish woman, too independent? Afraid to be a part of a community she'd be accountable to?

Her heart burned with passion for Freeman. Until now, she didn't realize what was holding her back. She was afraid of losing control, but with Freeman by her side, she felt secure. He would be her refuge in a storm, and the desire to marry grew and grew.

She'd need baptismal instruction, but the classes had already started. *But, her opa was a bishop!* Would he teach her so she could kneel before the People in holy baptism, and marry Freeman sooner than later?

Let's not be hasty, Freeman had said, but then he wrote a page to say good-bye and how hard it was to be apart.

Granny knocked on the door and entered. "Need anything else for your hope chest?" she asked, admiring the China handed down from generations. "Who's the China from? *Mammi Fern* I suppose."

"*Jah*. It was a wedding present," Rachel said, holding up a delicate teacup, scattered with roses. "Pretty pattern."

Granny admired the platter. "Matthew bought this or inherited it?"

"He bought it." Rachel stifled a laugh. "He told me about *Mammi Fern* was as delicate as a rose, so he sold a horse to buy it. My *Mammi Fern* must have changed, *jah*? She's anything but delicate."

Granny sat on the bed. "Well, they seem to be struggling. We can all see that, but it didn't happen overnight."

Rachel was eager for marital wisdom. "How can Freeman and I make sure we don't end up like them?"

Granny asked for a Bible, and Rachel handed her the one on her nightstand. As Granny fingered the pages, she was reverent toward the Good Book. Listen to part of the Song of Solomon. Some think it shows God's love for the church, other the love between a husband and wife. I see it both ways:

My dove in the clefts of the rock,
In the hiding places of the mountainside,
Let me see your face.
Let me hear your voice;
for your voice is sweet, and your face is lovely.

Granny's brows furrowed. "That's how your *grosseldre* started out. But there's a word of caution in the next verse:

Catch for us the foxes,
the little foxes that plunder the vineyards;
for our vineyards are in blossom.

She gently closed the book. "Jeb and I use this verse to warn couples that it's the little foxes that spoil the vines. You see, Rachel. It's not the big tragedies in life that spoil our marriages, but the little things, the day in day out grumbling, not showing kindness, disrespect, and everything that...hardens our hearts towards each other."

Rachel recalled how her parents' marriage irked her over the past few years. "*Oma*, I see that my parents let the little foxes ruin some vines, but now they're different."

"*Jah,* for sure. They needed time to make those foxes scamper. Remember, Rachel, put Freeman first and take time to talk from the heart daily. That's how you catch the foxes."

Furrowing her brow, she thought hard of one of Freeman's faults. "*Oma*, Freeman is perfect. It's only me who has little foxes that will eat away at our love."

Granny let out a hoot. "Freeman is not perfect. *Ach,* Rachel. No one is. That's the beauty of marriage. We help each other when we fall short."

Rachel stared at the tiny roses on a saucer. "*Mammi Fern* doesn't think she falls short…could you talk to her about their foxes? I see how miserable they are, and it scares me."

"It scares you that you'll have a marriage like theirs?"

Rachel bowed her head. "Maybe. I don't know. I think it's because you and *Opa* are so happy and they're not. I want them to have what you have." She clenched her hands, begging. "Please?"

Granny said they'd make a visit, but it was their responsibility to clear out the little foxes. Rachel agreed, and realized by their talk she was harboring much fear. Was fear a little fox that needed routed out of the garden in her heart? Granny always gave her so much to contemplate

Chapter 16

Sarah could see Melody's car parked by the rocker shop, and her blood began to boil. Daniel was off-limits! They'd talked openly about it, and she trusted that Melody would make no further advances on her husband. She grabbed her cape in haste to confront this disloyal friend. What a fool she'd been for trusting an Englisher.

She hurried along the sidewalk, despite the ice. "Why didn't Daniel throw down some salt to thaw the ice?" she murmured. She kept up her rapid pace until Daniel raced out of the rocker shop.

"Honey, you could slip. You're pregnant."

Her eyes threw daggers. "I came to confront Melody."

Daniel turned her around, trying to embrace her as he led her back to the house. "She's buying two *kinner* sized rockers."

Sarah's heart thumped too hard to comprehend. "What?"

"They're doing *gut* in their foster parenting classes and are hoping to take in two little ones."

Melody ran out to them. "Sarah, are you okay?"

Sarah felt like such a fool. "I, ah, wanted to talk to Daniel about something, but…I just told him."

Melody threw Sarah a warm smile, letting her know she understood. "Kenny and I have gotten so close over the foster care program. It forced us to unearth buried issues. I know my man now in a way I'd never been able to. We're praying for two children, and as an act of faith, we're getting two rockers. We're also decorating two spare bedrooms. I'd love to have them Amish themed and was going to ask if I could look at your quilts when I was done ordering the rockers."

Daniel squeezed Sarah's shoulder. "How about you two go in and look at quilts, and then you both come out and pick out rockers."

They both nodded in consent, and Melody was soon joining Sarah in her back porch where the quilts were hung on wooden bars, thanks to Daniel and Jeb. Sarah was grateful the porch was organized, but it looked too much like a shop.

"This is gorgeous!" Melody sparked. "It's like the other Amish little quilt shops. How come I never saw it?"

Sarah shrugged. "We don't use it in winter."

Melody slid what appeared to be a minicomputer out of her big purse. "I'm going to interview you for my book. Now, a room this size could be used for hanging wash, right? You wouldn't need to go outside?"

Not being in a mood to answer questions about

the Amish, Sarah inwardly put on self-control, and tried to be pleasant. "We wash our clothes in the basement. There's a big drain and this room doesn't have one."

Melody tapped away on her gadget. "Now, Granny said they hang their clothes outside in Smicksburg. Is it a rule to hang laundry inside here in Ohio? But, wait. I saw laundry hung outside on the way over."

This gave Sarah a flicker of laughter. How tired she was carrying a *boppli* in her forties. "It's not in our *Ordnung* to hang our clothes in any which way, as long as we don't use a clothes dryer."

Melody didn't look up as she typed. "*Ordnung,* that means rules, right?"

Sarah's feet were growing frigid. "I need to start the noon meal. Can we talk another time? Daniel brings a kerosene heater in here when someone wants to look at quilts. How about after next knitting circle?" She motioned for Melody to go back inside.

"The noon meal. That puzzles me. Why do you have your big meal at noon?"

Now, Sarah pointing inside was a command and Melody obeyed. "Don't you eat lunch?"

Melody shifted her weight, appearing confused. "Of course. Why do you ask?"

"Because the Amish eat lunch, too, but we call it

the noon meal, or many do, not all. You see, many of our ways are the same as yours."

Melody looked defeated. "You're opposed to me writing about the Amish, aren't you?"

Sarah took a seat. "I guess I assume there's nothing so interesting about our way of life. It's mundane at times."

"You're wrong," Melody said. "When I come in an Amish home, it's so quiet and peaceful. The way rooms aren't cluttered makes me feel like I can breathe better. Maybe you're too familiar with the Amish ways to see just how special you are." She snapped her fingers. "And that's why you need a shop. Show people what I'm jealous of."

"Which is?" Sarah asked, truly wanting to know.

Eyes narrowed and lips thin, Melody went on. "I feel like we've been fed a big lie. All the ways TV, billboards, just every wear you look, it says we need to buy something to be happy. Well, Kenny and I fell for that lie and got into debt. And for what? Our marriage to almost fall apart?"

Sarah knew exactly what Melody meant, since her marriage had almost died on the vine, due to neglect. "I think many things can distract us from what's important."

"But the Amish have it so much easier!" Melody roared. "I'm sick of English ways."

Sarah could see this was not about Amish simplicity, but something deeper. "Melody, what ails you?"

At this, Melody flew into a rage. "You should see how many children are neglected. The stories we've heard from former foster kids who try to give us the 'big picture' of what we're getting into are appalling."

"And?" Sarah prodded.

"I'm afraid I'll be a bad mom and have to return these kids we met that need to be adopted." She burst into tears.

Sarah sprang up and held the woman she'd had evil thoughts of just minutes ago. "You'll do a good job. It's the overly confident people who fall on their faces."

Melody couldn't speak but rested in Sarah's arms. *Danki, Lord for the knitting circle and my dear in-laws who came to visit. They've made such a difference. How could I have been so blind in many ways to Outsider's troubles. Not just Outsiders, but my own People. My parents?*

~*~

Jeb had a skip in his step. He pinched Rachel's cheek before sitting down for breakfast. "It's ice fishing time up on Lake Erie, and you're coming."

Rachel found her *opa* comical, but this was over the top. "Me? Ice fish?"

"Women fish in Smicksburg. Haven't you ever gone ice fishing?"

When the breakfast of pancakes, eggs and sausage was on the table, Daniel near breathed in his meal. "The van comes soon, *Daed*." He winked at Rachel.

"You need to dress warm. Better get moving."

"What on earth do you two have up your sleeves?"

"Make yourself look presentable," Jeb added.

Benjamin let out an uncontrollable laugh. "How obvious can you get?"

Even Granny was laughing, and Rachel looked to her *mamm* for comfort or explanation.

Jeb went on about how he could tutor Rachel more on her baptismal classes if she went ice fishing. He told her they had all the supplies, so she should snap to it and get on long johns, a long wool skirt and get ready to go but fast.

Rachel rolled her eyes and shot up, mighty peeved, and rushed to the stairs when there was a knock on the front door.

"Get the door, Rachel," Jeb said with gusto.

She slowly walked to her *opa* and examined his eyes. They had that same snicker when he was trying to matchmake. She gasped and ran to open the door. There stood Freeman, a smile splitting his face. He pulled her out onto the porch for privacy, held her tight, and then planted the tenderest of kisses on her lips. "Freeman, it's so *gut* to see you. But, why didn't you write to let me prepare for your visit."

He knelt his forehead on hers. "It's Jeb's big surprise. Said you always wanted to go ice fishing on Lake Erie."

Rachel cocked her head back like a rooster. "Ice

fish? Me? I'd be too afraid."

"You're not afraid to ice skate on your pond. The lake is frozen for sure by now and we don't go out far at all."

"I d-don't know. I'm *ferhoodled.* How did you get away from caring for your *daed*?"

He winked. "Jeb sent me money to pay for my ride out and for someone to help my *daed.* He said it was an early Valentine's Day present." He scratched his chin. "He really likes Valentine's Day, *jah*?"

My opa is the best! Rachel wanted to scream. "That was nice of him. But I'd rather not go, unless to be with you. The wind off the lake makes it bitter cold."

He took her hand. "Then I'm not going either. I'll stay and visit my girl." He kissed her cheek.

She protested, but when he said there was no other place he'd rather be than with her, thinking and planning their future, she jumped on him, wrapping her arms around his neck. *Praise be!*

They entered the kitchen and Rachel placed a hearty breakfast in front of Freeman, while her *daed* and *opa* tried to convince him to go to Lake Erie just for the day. Freeman was steadfast in wanting to stay with Rachel, until the mention of ten-pound walleyes being caught, along with enough perch to pickle that would give them many meals.

Rachel pictured married life with Freeman.

Would she hold him back? Of course not. Many times, a husband and wife had to be apart. She did not want to be like her *Mammi Fern* pouting when her husband did anything she didn't approve of. *Which was everything!*

She made up her mind. "Freeman, you go fishing while I study my baptismal material. The family could use all that fish, and you'd enjoy yourself." She leaned down and whispered for only him to hear. "And get to know my *daed*. We'll be family."

Jeb took another swig of coffee. "Rachel, you've asked me to take you ice fishing plenty a time. Now that you have the chance, why not go?"

How could she ice skate on a pond, yet be petrified walking on the ice of a deep lake? "I'm sorry, *Opa*. I'm afraid to go out on the lake."

Freeman started to blush. "If Rachel doesn't want to go, can I stay here with her? Help her study her lessons?"

Jeb slapped Freeman on the back. "Young love. I remember the day when I filled the one-room schoolhouse Deborah was teaching at with flowers to give her spring. It was a blustery winter, but in that schoolhouse, every inch was covered with vases of flowers. Got some side jobs to pay for it all."

"And that's where you proposed, *jah*?" Rachel asked, knowing the story but loved seeing the gleam in her *opa's* eyes.

"*Jah*. That's when Deborah Byler committed

herself to marrying me. Best day of my life."

Rachel hugged her *opa*. "You're so romantic to do that for *Oma!*"

~*~

After the van left with eager fishermen, Freeman took Rachel's hand. "Is there any place private to talk?"

Rachel noticed her *mamm* was buzzing like a bee around her kitchen. "*Mamm*, are we getting visitors today?"

Sarah was all smiles. "When the men are away, we women folk like to have a *gut* long visit. The van is filled with seven men, and seven women will be here today for lunch, potluck style. Didn't I tell you that?"

"I forgot. This house is always busy."

"Go out to your *daed's* fishing cabin if you want privacy," Sarah suggested.

"Sounds *gut*," Freeman said, heading to the door. "I'll go out and make a fire in the stove to heat it up."

"I'll pack a picnic," Rachel said with a skip in her step as she went to the refrigerator.

"We just finished breakfast," Sarah informed.

"We'll be out there all day, I suppose," Rachel quipped. "*Mamm*, can you believe how sweet Freeman is to give up ice fishing for me?"

"It shows me something," Sarah said in a flat tone. "You're ready to get married." Her chin quivered.

"I'm sorry. I've tried to be cheerful, but you'll be moving to Smicksburg and I'll miss you so."

Rachel held her *mamm.* How close they'd become since Thanksgiving. Since her parents started dating again, love permeated the family, and she wanted to stay.

But then something dawned on her. "*Mamm*, why did *Daed* move out here by your people. Why didn't you settle near his kin?"

Sarah grew rigid. "I felt guilty leaving my *daed.* Now that you're older, we can talk plainly. You can clearly see that he's been such an unhappy man. I was closest to him, and he cried at just the thought of me leaving."

Sarah turned to fill the tea kettle. "It was hard on your *daed,* and I wonder if he's been resentful deep down. But, if he is, he'll tell me, and I'll move to wherever he wants. Rachel, never let anyone become first place in your life over your spouse." She put on a brave smile. "I'll miss you, but you must go where Freeman is."

Sorrow mixed with an odd joy filled Rachel. Her *mamm's* love for her was evident, something she hadn't seen in years. But so sorry that they'd be apart…

~*~

Rachel entered the warm, cozy cabin with a picnic basket, offering Freeman a smile.

"What's wrong, Rachel. Your eyes look swollen." He took the basket from her. "You've been crying."

They embraced, Rachel holding him as if for dear life. He kissed the top of her prayer *kapp*. "Tell me what's wrong."

He led her to one of the rockers and held her, rocking her like a child. "Now, whatever concerns you concerns me. Tell me."

Rachel let out a hiccup. "Oops, I hiccup when too emotional."

Their eyes met and they both let out nervous laughter.

"My *mamm* is crying since I'll be moving to Smicksburg."

"Maybe. We haven't talked about it," Freeman said. "My parents said to live where we feel is best."

"But, isn't a woman to follow her husband, putting him first?" Rachel asked quizzically.

He held her tight and resumed rocking. "The two shall become one, *jah*? We both need to make the decision. What if we were to move to a new settlement altogether? Many do."

"*Ach,* I wouldn't like that at all," Rachel said.

"Well, neither do I. New settlements are hard, from what I hear. Many don't make it. We can move where we have kin. I have kin in Lancaster, Indiana, even Colorado. How about you?"

"They're in Montana, Indiana, and Pennsylvania, but I think my one uncle might move to Maine."

The creaking of the rocker on the floorboards was

relaxing and Freeman had been up since four o'clock to catch the van to Holmes County. His eyelids felt heavy, but he wanted to make this day with Rachel special. "You wouldn't move to New York with Jared. You're too attached to Millersburg?"

"He wanted life in a big city and not live plain," she said. "My family was surprised that when he wrote me I had not a drop of emotion towards him." She touched his face. "I told you about his letter, *jah*?"

"*Jah,*" Freeman said, kissing her hand. "Not one doubt at all about me?"

Rachel turned to cup his cheeks. With glistening eyes, she said, "Not one. I never knew what real love was until I met you."

Freeman was so choked with emotion, he wanted to take this beautiful girl, his gift from God, and propose the most outlandish thing, but she'd think him impulsive.

The bewilderment on her face grew. "You have doubts?"

"*Nee*, not at all. Just thinking. What if we got married before next wedding season in November?

Rachel's eyes flashed in delight. "I'd love it."

He squeezed her. "Then how about we wait until my *daed* is up and around and we have it here after you get baptized? Have a spring wedding? I know my *mamm* loved hosting my sisters' weddings and I wouldn't take that away from your *mamm*."

Rachel kissed him soundly. "Freeman Yoder, you are the kindest man I know. Always thinking of others."

He drew her in for another kiss and they spent the day in the cabin planning their lives together and eating. By the end of the day, Freeman knew he made the right decision to not go fishing.

~*~

The next day the men deboned and sliced the many pounds of perch and walleye caught in Lake Erie, while the women pickled the meat. Freeman and Rachel weren't assigned any tasks, other than spending time alone.

Freeman was ready to meet Rachel at the fishing cabin, when Ruby popped in, breathless. "Freeman, I need to talk to you. Now, I don't care about you like I did, and I realize I never did, because I only care for Tall Billy."

Trying to keep his mind up to speed with her speech, he soon realized Ruby wanted to be friends. "*Gut.* Glad to hear it."

She shifted. "Can I talk to you about Rachel?"

"Sure thing."

Ruby settled herself in a rocker while Freeman put another log in the woodstove. "You see, Freeman, Rachel talks in her sleep. And some of the things she says worry me. She was crying last night."

Taking a seat in the other rocker, Freeman asked her to go on.

"Well, it woke me up. So, I went to her and talked to her like I always do when she talks in her sleep. She kept saying she loved Holmes County and how could she leave the family. I said that Freeman lives in Smicksburg, and our *oma* and *opa* did, too. Rachel sobbed harder, so I just held her and smoothed her hair. She fell back to sleep, but I thought you'd want to know."

Freeman knew Ruby didn't want Rachel to leave since any siblings that shared a room were usually inseparable. "She'll visit you often. Smicksburg is only three hours away."

Ruby laid her head back on the rocker. "I've lived through the hard times here over the past three years. *Mamm* and Rachel fought like cats and dogs. Now, since *Mamm* is happier and Rachel is really Amish, they have a bond that's special. I know *Mamm* wishes she could make up for lost time but would never say so. And then there's the problems with my *brieder*!"

Freeman thought Ruby's animated ways comical, although this gave him much to ponder. "What's wrong with your *brieder*. They seem like *gut* young men."

"They'd be better with a big *bruder* around. I can't snitch, but let's just say they need some guidance from an older Amish man, and I think you'd be the best."

Freeman leaned forward. "They have a *gut daed* and men at *Gmay*."

"Well," Ruby started, "they did so much better when you were here. After you left, they fell back into bad habits. Mostly the twins, not Benjamin. We need a big *bruder* around here. When you have a family, I'd be around to babysit all the time. Wouldn't you like that?"

Freeman wanted to say his sister could babysit but held his tongue. Ruby's words held a hidden meaning. Was the whole family falling apart over Rachel's potential move to Smicksburg? He didn't want to hurt the Weaver family. "I'll be praying on all you said. If we commit our way to God, he'll establish our thoughts."

Looking puzzled, Ruby frowned. "That's in the Bible, *jah*?'

"*Jah*. It's one of my life verses."

"What's that?" Ruby asked.

Now Freeman was puzzled. She didn't have any life verses? "Well, it's a Bible verse that directs your life. I have many. Like when my *opa* died, I took it hard. My life verse was, 'Come to me all that are weary and heavy-laden, and I will give you rest for your souls.' I was on my knees going to God more than usual. It was like an invitation to meet with him and it was a real healing time. I was so close with my *opa* and didn't think I'd recover. Now, I know that anytime a tragedy comes along, I can go to God and have that special time and be all right." He swept his blonde bangs out of his eyes. "Am I making sense?"

Ruby's eyes were bugged. "I thought my *opa* from Smicksburg was the most spiritual man on the planet. I think you beat him."

Raising a hand in protest, Ruby refused to be contradicted, mumbling that "we need someone like you around these parts."

"We'll take our time in making a decision. Where's Rachel, anyhow. Does she have to help pickle the fish?"

Ruby threw up her hands in desperation. "She just came down to breakfast when I came out here. She was crying half the night and is all tuckered out. Truth be told, I am, too. And my tongue wags too much when I'm tired."

Freeman grinned, asking her to walk back to the house with him.

~*~

Granny finished pouring pickling brine over the diced fish, when Daniel flew into the house. "*Mamm*, Uncle Noah's in the hospital and he needs to speak to you."

Granny's heart flipped. "In the hospital? Is he all right?" All Granny saw was darkness ahead. A life without her *bruder*. "Is it bad?"

Daniel got her cape and outer bonnet and asked her to be ready in a few minutes. He called a driver to get her to the hospital, and Jeb was washing up now.

Everyone just stared at each other in shock, until Sarah turned Granny to go to her husband and put on her cape and bonnet. "Bless you, *Mamm*." She kissed Granny's cheek.

Granny grabbed on to Sarah for support. "They call in the family to say *mach's gut, jah*?"

"We don't know that, "Daniel comforted as he draped the cape on her shaking shoulders and held her close. "*Mamm*, we'll be praying."

Jeb ran in, eyes wild. "Where is she. *Ach,* Deborah, honey, we'll get through this together. He didn't ask for me to come, but I am."

Granny was in tears as Jeb scooped her up in his arms. "*Danki*, Jeb, my leaning post."

They met the driver outside in a few minutes, and then it was all a whirl to Granny. "Am I going to be with my *bruder* when he dies?" she asked Jeb.

He smoothed her hands. "I don't know. It would be an honor, though, to help escort someone into Paradise, don't you think?"

Paradise. Heaven The great Eternal Reward she'd believed in all her life, but why did she dread it? Separation from loved ones and the great unknown, she supposed. She prayed silently for Noah until they were left off at the entrance of the hospital. A gift shop was to the left, and Granny asked Jeb to go buy the brown Teddy bear that was in the window. Noah always liked watching bears come through the back woods but was never allowed a Teddy bear with eyes. Well, he'd have one now.

After getting the bear and the number of his room, which wasn't in the Emergency Room, they were relieved a tad, but still fearful. Making it to the fifth floor, Granny near ran into the room. "Noah, my dear *bruder*."

He sat in a recliner, flipping through the television stations. "Debbie, you came."

Granny looked back at Jeb, confounded.

Jeb stepped forward. "We thought there was some kind of emergency."

Noah's face shone. "I'm being released, but my doctor has been asking for a long time who my power of attorney is, and I always said for him to do what he thinks best. Well, we talked, and he suggested you, since we're kin. We can do the paperwork now for hospital records; I'll have my will done by my lawyer as soon as possible."

Granny was so relieved, she hugged him and sat at the foot of the bed. "Is that the person who makes final decisions and all?"

"Yes, it is. As for my will to my estate, I'm changing it." He reached for Granny's hand and she took it. "It'll all be left to you, dear sister. You never gave up on me when I gave up on all the Amish. Being reintroduced into the Amish community, being able to talk to old friends, has been a healing balm. I owe it all to you."

Jeb collapsed in a nearby chair. "Your whole

place? What would we do with it?"

"Run it. Help the kids who are dying have some fun. Make memories. That's what the place is really for. Yes, a wedding here and there, but it's an extension of the children's cancer wing."

Granny was dazed. "But we're Amish. How could we show Englishers a *gut* time when we can't do anything that's fancy? And Noah, you won't be leaving us soon, will you? Did you get a bad report?"

"No, the same. I can live to be a hundred if the Lord wills, but then I could have a year or two."

Jeb slapped his knee. "You said if the Lord wills. I thought you didn't believe in God anymore."

Noah pulled a book out of his computer bag. "Read the book you dropped by."

"Mere Christianity!" Jeb boomed. "What do you think?"

"Well, I downloaded several of C.S. Lewis books to my Kindle, and I have to say he has a way of making you feel your own doubts with him, since he was such a skeptic. He explains Christianity in ways that I've never thought of, and well, he made a believer out of me."

Jeb raised a hand. "Praise be. I can get you some Max Lucado."

"I need a list of books, but I prefer my Kindle." He paused, as if not being understood. "A Kindle is an electronic device that you read from. Mine has over a thousand books on it. The best part is that books written over sixty-some years are free."

"Little Men," Granny said. "You have to read *Little Women* and then Little Men. They're some of my favorites. Brings back memories of our childhood since the March family didn't have electricity and lived like we did when we were *kinner*."

A tall, young doctor entered the room. Noah introduced everyone, and they started the paperwork for Granny to be the power of attorney. And she felt ever so close to this *bruder* of hers.

Chapter 17

When they got Noah to the farmhouse, he sampled the pickled fish, and was quite impressed. Ruby and May took turns playing checkers with him, and Noah let them win. Their confidence got high, and they asked for more rounds, and then he went in and beat them both, double and triple jumping at times. Granny hated to interrupt them, but she needed a private word with him, so they retired to her bedroom.

Taking a seat in the rockers, they relished a while in each other's presence, desperately trying to make up for decades of lost time. After a cheerful long chat, Granny broached the subject she wanted to speak to him about.

"Noah, I got a letter from Mary Miller. Fern King has been corresponding with her…even though she's shunned."

Noah slowly lowered his head and then lifted it, like a tired rooster. "Shunned? She left the People?"

"Her whole family did. They moved out of these parts to Lancaster, not agreeing with Old Order ways. They were Beachy Amish, and then left the plain life all together."

Noah's eyes misted. "Did she get married?"

"*Nee.* She's a retired nurse. Went to college, like you did."

"I need to see her," Noah gushed.

Granny picked up her new knitting project, since her *bruder* speaking of death unnerved her. "She offered to drive out. Would you like her to do that?"

"Debbie, I never loved anyone but Mary. Came close to loving a woman I worked with, but I could only compare her to Mary. No one ever matched up. Maybe she never married for the same reasons. Mary's a beautiful woman."

Granny contemplated how *wunderbar gut* it would be to have this medical woman and Noah get married, Mary being able to care for Noah; but she had an overactive imagination when it came to romance. "She said she drives in the snow, so I think she's eager to see you soon."

"I don't want her driving so far in the winter. The roads may be icy," he said, cracking a few knuckles. "I could take the bus out to see her."

"Not by yourself," Granny cautioned. "How about I write Mary and tell her your concerns. Wait until spring."

"I can't!' Noah exclaimed. "I've waited decades to make things right with her. Ask forgiveness for breaking her heart."

Granny knew Mary wanted to come out in less than two weeks, but she wouldn't spill the beans.

"Okay, Noah, how about we look into a bus to take you to Lancaster in March. The weather always breaks in March."

He inhaled and sighed audibly. "I do have some appointments coming up I can't miss. We have my place decorated for Valentine's Day and lots of children with terminal cancer have the time of their lives. After the party, then?"

Loving to prepare for a party, Granny offered to help, but Noah said he paid an event coordinator to take care of it all. "You can never have too many pies," Granny quipped. "Can't I help with making pies?"

Noah, still visibly shaken with excitement, told her that it was her birthday and she needed to stay home. Granny dismissed his idea. "We do what I want on my birthday, and I want to meet these *kinner* and make pies for them." She froze. "Do the girls need hats? Cancer patient hats?"

Noah nodded. "Sadly yes. But many wear scarves and such."

In her mind, Granny ran through all the hat designs in Suzy's store. "I need to go to Walmart for hat patterns.

Noah threw her a loving gaze. "You haven't changed a bit, Debbie. You were always full of spunk and still are. If you want to make some hats, go for it. And if you want to come, it's up to Jeb."

"It's my birthday," she repeated.

"It's also Valentine's Day, and Jeb may have something up his sleeve to surprise you. You know, Debbie, I never knew I could like Jeb so much. It's not that I never liked him, but I was leery. At your wedding, he seemed too serious, but he's changed. You made the difference in him."

Granny felt heat rise, and as she rarely blushed, she wondered if it was her blood pressure. "Well, Jeb's changed me. We call each other leaning posts." She snuck a glance at Noah to see if he was up to her suggestion. He was. "We all need a leaning post. It's not *gut* for man to be alone, Noah."

He chuckled. "Remember when we were in grade school and you wanted to find an Amish man for our pretty teacher?"

"Lavina Troyer!"

"Yes. She was a beauty. Do you remember feeling sorry for her? Wanting to find her a beau. You're doing it again."

"Sorry," Granny said sheepishly.

"Oh, I don't mind. Seeing Mary again will be one of the joys in my old age."

Granny wondered if Mary Miller would be *gut* medicine for Noah.

~*~

Freeman was disturbed by all that Ruby relayed about how sad his Rachel was, and that night, they took their skates to the pond to have a quiet talk. There was a full moon that reflected off the pond, giving it an otherworldly sheen. The night seemed magical and Rachel did ballet moves, spinning around to the point where he feared her skates would drill a hole into the ice. She assured him the ice was seven inches thick.

They held hands, and sometimes Freeman stole a kiss, until they were tuckered out and needed to rest on the bench. Freeman poured hot chocolate from a thermos, and they sipped down the piping hot liquid.

"Is it less cold in Smicksburg in February since the mountains stop the wind? The wind off the lakes, and it being flat here, is what I won't miss."

"What will you miss?" Freeman asked sincerely.

"*Ach*, I love Holmes County, but home is wherever you are. We need to make our own life."

He placed an arm around her. "It's okay to miss your home. Does it make you cry sometimes?"

Rachel's eyes near popped out. "Ruby had no right to tell you."

"Never mind Ruby. I need to know the truth."

She buried her face in his chest, like a cornered animal wanting to hide. "The truth is, I love you and will live in Smicksburg. We'll take over the family house, your younger sister will live with us, and we'll build a *dawdyhaus*."

"I called my *daed* and had a long talk about not only my future, but our whole family's future."

Freeman looked up into the clear winter sky, pondering how to talk about his sister without giving Rachel the wrong impression. "You see, Lily's had a rough *Rumspringa*. She's not baptized at nineteen, which concerns *Daed*. She thinks the Amish in Smicksburg are too rigid. When I told her that Amish ride bikes, mix with the English for charity and all, she said maybe she'd bow the knee and be baptized."

Rachel offered him a hopeful smile. "I'll talk to her. She's not settled yet, is all. But we are more 'liberal' out here, and she should visit."

"Well, she's been out to shop several times and likes it. *Daed* also said there would be more opportunity for our woodworking out here. I filled him in on the area, and he's interested. Land taxes back home have skyrocketed, too. It's getting as bad as New York, so *Daed* said he'd talk to *Mamm*. She has cousins out here but would miss her sisters."

Rachel gripped his frigid hand tight. "So, would they sell the farmhouse and business? Have money to set up shop right here?"

He cocked his head back. "Right here, as in right here?"

"*Jah*. I should have told you, but I'll inherit two acres, including this pond, if I decide to settle here. I didn't want to sway you though."

Freeman wanted to throw his hat up and let out a whoop again, but only nodded, noticing that concern was etched too deeply into Rachel's brow.

"That's generous of your folks. But do you think it's a *gut* idea? Too many businesses?" He tucked a chestnut strand of hair back under her prayer *kapp*, and then kissed her, wisps of vapor rising around them. "What are you so concerned about? Do you want to live near your *oma* and *opa* in *Smicksburg*? Was Ruby exaggerating?"

She flung her arms around him. "My home is where you are."

Again, he tried to pry out what was concerning her so, but she got up and fiercely skated a circle around the pond. When he caught up to her, she said, "I refuse to wear the pants in the house, like *Mammi Fern*. I want to be a *gut* wife…"

He slowed them down and he held her close. "Do you know how much you're like your *oma* from Smicksburg? The whole town calls her Granny, ever since she started her knitting circles. She's so giving and kind, and Jeb, well, he's the wisest man I know, besides my *daed*. I want a marriage like theirs."

Rachel let out happy tears. "You think I'm like my *oma*?"

Freeman rubbed her back. "When I met you years ago, I saw you were like her. It's the main reason I came out. To see if you still were. And you are, for sure and certain."

"*Ach*, that's sweet," Rachel said, crying and

laughing at the same time. "I'm exhausted. Need to get a grip."

"We'll go inside and get warmed up and talk about this some more. I can't feel my toes."

"Me, neither," Rachel said, lacing her fingers through his.

Hand in hand they climbed out of the so-called valley that Freeman envisioned he'd build a home in. He loved Smicksburg, but never felt more at home than in Holmes County. Home was where Rachel was, and he was ever so grateful to be able to marry this precious woman.

~*~

Knowing that Valentine's Day was in just two days, Granny decided to pay a visit to Fern, fulfilling her promise to Rachel. It was an unseasonably warm winter day; Granny was grateful that the pond had stayed frozen for Rachel and Freeman to skate on. Over the past week, the phone calls between Rachel and Freeman were all too frequent, but they had many decisions. One thing Rachel wanted was to have her wedding, whenever it was, to be filled with peace and no strife. She hinted that Fern needed a talking to.

So, wanting to stretch her legs, she walked along the road to Fern's, dodging puddles everywhere. A flock of Canadian Geese flew over in their V formation, which she found unusual, since they didn't return until warmer weather. A buggy came in the opposite direction and she waved a cheery hello to someone in their new *Gmay*. Their new *Gmay*? Is that want it would be? She missed her church district in Smicksburg, along with her Baptist and Englisher friends, but she and Jeb committed themselves to not fret.

The mailman deposited Fern's mail when she arrived, and she decided to retrieve it, saving her a trip. Not wanting to be nosey, she avoided looking at letters addressed to Fern, but she couldn't help but see one return address; Mary Miller from Lancaster. Was she discouraging Mary from coming out, not being very fond of her *bruder*? She hoped not!

She went to the side door, knocked and went into the kitchen. Fern had flour all over the table, and much of her black apron. "What are you making?" she asked, placing the mail in the wall basket.

"Cookies for the *kinner*, as usual. Nothing changes around here."

Granny decided to stay clear of the mess and sat in a wooden chair near the window. "I saw Canadian Geese on the way over. It never ceases to amaze me how they work as a team to make their long flights."

"They're like our frolics and bees. Many hands make less work." She sifted the dry ingredients a bit too fast and a cloud of flour, salt and baking powder erupted. "I don't know what's wrong with me. This new sifter beats all! It's so big, you'd think it could be filled to the top, but I suppose not."

"Fill it half-way and sift. Always works for me," Granny suggested. "Not that I haven't had my own kitchen full of flour before." She tried to slow her speech, soften her tone, to make for a calmer atmosphere to talk. "Did you hear that Rachel and Freeman will be getting married?"

Fern wiped her brow, making a streak of powder. "Well, I'd be the last to know."

"Well, it just happened," Granny said with a lilt in her voice. "He's a fine man. Jeb invited him out here to meet Rachel, but Freeman remembered her from a visit to our place. He liked her then."

Fern tilted her head. "Rachel isn't even baptized. How can they be engaged?"

Granny cringed at Fern's bluntness. "Jeb is a bishop and has been giving her instruction. Bishop Andy will consider baptizing her on New Birth Sunday, and a spring wedding will follow."

Fern plunked herself down on the bench. "What's the hurry. Why not get married with all the others in November?"

Granny winced. "They love each other, and their long-distance courtship is hard on them. Did you know that Freeman's whole family might be moving out here? Build a house on the land inherited by Rachel?"

Fern's frown softened. "She wants to live near us?"

Granny nodded. "But she wants everyone to get along."

"We get along," Fern said. "Sarah and I talk more often now. What are you talking about?"

Granny looked out the window, seeing two snowbirds. The little gray and cream-colored birds always soothed her as they hopped around on the ground, snatching up millet and thistle seeds that fell from the big feeders the blue jays and cardinals dominated. She felt like those little birds being towered over by Fern. But she would be brave.

"Fern, I gave Rachel some marriage advice she never heard before. Have you ever heard of the little foxes that spoil the vine?"

"Foxes are in the Bible?"

"*Jah*. Well, I told Rachel that it's not the big things in life that tear us apart, but the little day to day annoyances. The bickering, snide remarks, and not having a…humble spirit. Not putting others first."

Shaking her head, Fern harrumphed. "Rachel can have a sharp tongue. You spoil that girl, Deborah Weaver."

Granny's dander was now way up, and she knew she needed to get to the point and leave. Fern understood her meaning. "Fern, Rachel wants you and Matthew to work on patching up your vines. The foxes have bitten into them, and we all see the strife between you. This is what she wants before she'll accept her inheritance and live behind you."

Fern beat her chest. "Me? She thinks she's too *gut* to live near me? Matthew and I may have our faults, but- "

"Rachel's afraid all your fussing will affect her marriage. Daniel and Sarah took advice and have a nice, *gut* marriage now. Stop being a fool and take the same advice. Spend time together, confess the wrongs you've done to each other, and put on love like a garment, like the Bible says to do."

Granny rose, ignoring daggers of harsh words from Fern. The truth did indeed hurt! She refused to slam the door shut when she left, but stomped most of the way home, until she twisted her ankle while avoiding a puddle and fell.

~*~

Granny was rescued by an Englisher neighbor who saw her fall and drove her home. She had a nasty bruise on her hip, and her palms were bandaged up, which meant no baking for a spell. She mumbled under her breath that Fern was one of the most stubborn creatures on God's green earth. Sarah was coming to her bedroom with a tray of food and heard her.

"Jah, my *mamm* is stubborn, but my *daed* needed to stand up to her. He's timid, you know. A lot of the child rearing was on *Mamm's* shoulders."

"*Ach*, Sarah, I'm sorry you overheard. You were always your *daed's* shadow, so this surprises me that you're defending your *mamm*."

Sarah placed the little tray of sandwiches and tea on the nightstand. "I've talked to *Mamm*, trying to hear her side of the quarrel; there are two sides to every coin."

"*Jah*, it there is," Granny said, holding her tongue. It was hard to see two sides in Fern's marriage because of her huge, interfering personality that made Matthew timid. Fern was a drip, drip, drip, nagging wife who plum tuckered out her husband. "Sarah, your *daed* needs to put his foot down."

"He did. He went to Pinecraft and is still paying for it."

"Not a big thing like that, but in little things, like you did. They have to move a mountain bit by bit, don't you think?"

Sarah's eyes blinked in disbelief. "Like my *daed* standing up to my *mamm* in little things like visiting with friends to play Dutch Blitz when *Mamm* insists he stay home?"

Granny's head was spinning. "She does that?"

"*Jah*, she says he overworks the horse."

Granny hadn't calmed down yet; her mind was cranked up in full gear. "What if he walked over to your place and played Dutch Blitz with Jeb and Daniel and the *kinner*?"

Sarah straightened. "I'll invite him over. *Gut* idea, but *Mamm* will come, too."

Granny's brows rose in disbelief. "I doubt she'll

come here anytime soon. She'll avoid me, for sure. But invite your *daed* over as soon as possible. Rachel wants harmony between them, like you know."

"I know. And Rachel sees it's possible since her parents changed," Sarah replied.

Granny saw the glow on Sarah's face, and it calmed and warmed her heart. *Lord, do the same for that stubborn as a mule Fern and her long-suffering husband, Matthew!*

Rachel and Ruby rushed into the room, having just returned from going to the store. "*Oma*, we heard you fell!" Rachel cried out. "Are you badly hurt?"

Granny lifted her bandaged palms. "Still have my fingers free and clear to knit or crochet," she said with a forced smile. "It could have been worse."

"But, why are you in bed?" Ruby asked. "Are your legs hurt?"

Granny motioned to Sarah. "Your *Mamm* insisted. I bruised my hip, so I've been ordered to stay off my feet today."

Sarah told the girls they could visit their *oma* for a little while, but chores still needed to be done. But as she left the room, Sarah doubled over, crying out in pain. She held her abdomen and sank to the floor. Granny sprang out of bed, told the girls to get their *daed*…and a midwife.

Fear was etched into Sarah's pretty face as she screamed, "Not my *boppli*! *Nee*. It cannot be!"

~*~

The day of Sarah's miscarriage was a dark night that lasted into the next day. Daniel tried to comfort his wife, but she couldn't be. She kept blaming herself, and no one could tell her otherwise. On Valentine's Day, she asked for her parents. When they entered her room, they took her hands and wept.

Sarah sputtered out, "*Mamm*, how did you do it?"

Fern gasped, but then collected herself. "Do what?"

Choking back tears, Sarah said, "We knew you were pregnant many times, but no *bopplin* came home. As Amish, we don't ask about pregnancy, but I'm asking now."

Fern had several miscarriages, but how would Sarah know? She never showed. Shame, that old enemy strangled her, and all she could get out was, "You're tired, Sarah. You rest."

"Tell her," Matthew said gently.

"Fern straightened. "It's all in the past."

Sarah always knew her *Mamm* had a wounded spirit but hid it. "We saw your stomach swell and...how many?"

"Several," Matthew said. "That's why we only have three *kinner*. Would have had ten if..."

"How did you do it, Mamm? Sarah cried out, clinging to Fern for dear life. "I feel so horrible."

Fern withdrew her hand as if it hurt and went to

straighten her prayer *kapp* in the small mirror. "You just move on."

All was a hush in the room, Fern's response was too calculated, not seeming like the heart of a mamm.

Matthew rose to stand close to his wife. "You haven't moved on. You've buried your grief, and along with it, that young girl I courted and married."

She spun around. "That's nonsense! I've been strong."

Her husband took her by her now trembling shoulders. "*Jah*, you have been. But you're so angry."

Fern felt such rage deep within, and she didn't want to upset Sarah, so she dashed out the door. Matthew followed, catching up in the empty kitchen.

Fern could hold down the volcanic hot indignation no longer. "I *am* angry! How can I ever forgive…?"

"Me?" Matthew prodded.

"*Nee*," she screamed. "God! He took my *bopplin*." She shook her fist at heaven. "And my *kinner* that are alive hate me."

Matthew pulled her close and she near collapsed in his arms. She kept asking for forgiveness over and over. She'd been a bad wife, bad *mamm*, bad person. God took away her *bopplin* because she was bad!

Years of pain seemed to pour out of her, but

Matthew held on tight. And she realized after her tears dried up, what a comfort her husband was.

Chapter 18

Melody hugged Granny after depositing her at her brother's place. "Do you want me to walk you to the door? Don't want you to…fall…"

"Again? There's nothing wrong with my balance." Granny pinched Melody's cheek. "You're looking rather chipper lately."

Eyes glistening, Melody said, "Kenny. It's all good now."

"I'm so happy for you- "

"I think I'm pregnant," she let out, fist pumping the air. "Have to see my doc to verify. Those pregnancy tests aren't one-hundred percent accurate."

Granny grabbed Melody's hands. "How do you feel in the morning?"

"Great. No nausea. No change at all."

Granny doubted the tests bought at the store could tell for sure. And as happy as she was for Melody, talking about babies today was the last thing she wanted. Memories of her own miscarriage, a still-born daughter…her only daughter…plagued her as she tried to calm Sarah.

This pain of losing her little wee one she'd take to the grave, but with God's grace, she could bear it.

"What is it, Granny?" Melody asked.

She forced a smile. "*Ach*, getting old. A memory popped into my head and got stuck there."

Melody lowered her head, eyes questioning. "You said we help carry each other's burdens, right? We're knit pickers? We knit and pick each other up?"

Granny was glad to see Noah standing behind the storm door, waving. She kissed Melody on the cheek. "Some other time. Noah's waiting."

Melody hugged her. "Have a great Birthday breakfast."

Thanking Melody, she made her way up to the porch, where Noah met her with open arms. "Happy Birthday, Debbie. Don't look a day over fifty."

She chuckled. "Don't feel like it. But, Noah, I had no time for making pies or hats for the *kinner* with cancer. Sarah's miscarriage set the household into a whirl, and I fell and scraped my hands but *gut*."

He gently took her bandaged hands, extended his sympathies, and led her into the house. "You and *Mamm* always made the best pies, but maybe another time you can make one just for me."

Granny heard his Penn Dutch accent when saying '*Mamm*' and it took her back to childhood days.

What was wrong with her today? Was this aging? So reminiscent of the past. But the smells also played on her mind. It was the smell of an Amish breakfast. Her *mamm's* fabulous breakfast.

Noah opened the door into his lovely kitchen, and suggested they sit in the nook. But how could they have separate tables? They'd always eaten on trays. Well, her conscience didn't bother her, so she slid into the bench and Noah did the same on his side.

Kimberly ran into the kitchen. "Oh, don't be burnt!" She pulled out the tray and let out a sigh of relief. "They're perfect."

Granny bit back tears. They were sticky buns, their *mamm's* specialty. "*Danki* Noah. Did you get *Mamm's* recipe?"

"I have her recipe box," he said, one eyebrow arched.

As Kimberly laid out a spread of sticky buns, scrambled eggs, bacon, berry muffins and sausage, the menu for a special Off-Sunday morning, the longing to have one day with her dear deceased family ran through her heart. "Ach, Noah. What memories!"

"I have this breakfast on special occasions, with fond memories of *Mamm* and the family." He rubbed his hands together. "Let's dig in."

Granny savored every taste along with every memory. Noah shared childhood memories which sparked her memory to share some of hers, and they spent a leisurely time eating good Amish food.

When done, he led her into the west side of his house, which was filled with windows.

"See that plot of land behind the row of cedar trees? There's a gardener's cottage. Came with the house. Do you see it?"

Granny spied a small white house. "*Jah*, I see it."

He put an arm around her. "Happy Birthday."

"What?"

"It's for you and Jeb. Perfect size for a *dawdyhaus…jah*?"

His Penn Dutch accent, along with the present caused an avalanche of emotion. She pulled a handkerchief from her pocket to wipe the rapid onset of tears. She leaned her head on his shoulder and he embraced her. "Don't you like it?" he teased.

"It's…too…much."

"It didn't cost me anything. Like I said, it came with the house."

Granny was feeling rather fatigued from all the emotions running through her. "I need to sit down," she said, resting her hand on one of the many Queen Anne leather chairs and settling herself in it.

Noah pulled up a caned chair. "Debbie, I talked to Daniel. He said he was building a *dawdyhaus* for you to live in and I must say, I got excited. I told him about this cottage, and he said it was okay, although a few things needed to be changed to make it follow the rules of the People. Electricity lines and all that." His eyes were so hopeful. "Do you like it?"

Granny nodded. "Nice location and in the same church district as Daniel. Nice place to stay for a visit."

"Visit?" Noah asked. "I thought you were moving to Ohio."

His tone fell flat, and Granny could hear the disappointment. But she could not wrap her brain around the idea of leaving Smicksburg permanently. She instantly thought of the Amish snowbirds that flocked to Florida for the winter. "Noah, a long visit like snowbirds. But we'd come from Smicksburg not only in the winter." She was fumbling for words. "I've had several visits from folks back home since we came out in November. We can come and stay for weeks at a time whenever we feel like it."

Noah took her hand. "Well, I hope it's often. We could play badminton again." He winked. "You always beat me, and I want a chance to redeem myself."

Kimberly cautiously entered the room. "Noah, I hope I'm not interrupting, but there's a lady here who said she came from Pennsylvania to see you."

Noah darted a stare Granny's way. "Do you know about this? Oh my. I look so old. What will I say to Mary?

"Mary?" Granny echoed. "She said in one letter it

would be a *gut* surprise. Did she write back to you?"

"*Nee*. I mean, no. My heart's skipping beats." He turned to Kimberly. "Tell whoever it is that I'll be out in..."

"A few minutes," Granny added. "You need to calm down.

Kimberly left them, and Noah, visibly shaken, looked out of the massive windows. "I'm afraid, Debbie. I've dreamt of seeing her, but now that she's here..."

Granny was afraid of Noah's behavior. Too much emotion could set him back. "I'll go out and see who it is for starters. You don't know if it's her." She patted him on the back and went into the so-called waiting room where Noah received guests. A pretty woman who appeared to be in her sixties sat on one of the many chairs, biting her lower lip and fidgeting with her colorful scarf.

Granny cleared her throat. "I'm Noah's sister. He's...resting. Can I help you?"

She spryly sprang up, extending a hand, but staring hard at Granny. She squinted. "Debbie Byler? Do you remember me? I think you were a few grades ahead of me in school."

"Mary Miller?" Granny asked, her face vaguely familiar. Her dark brown eyes always made her a beauty.

"Yes. Debbie Byler? You look the same!"

Granny guffawed. "You're sweet, but I know I look as old as dirt."

"You don't," Mary protested. "Your skin. No wrinkles?" She pressed her hands into her cheeks. "You look younger than me! Does Noah look the same?"

A shuffling of feet became audible, and Noah, leaning on his cane, stared at Mary in disbelief. As he neared her, their eyes locked and then they fell into a mutual embrace. Soon there were tears and Granny left the room, not wanting to intrude on this almost sacred moment.

~*~

Rachel eyed her sisters while making sugar cookie dough. Something in Ruby's eyes spelt mischief.

Ruby put a hand on her hip. "*Mamm* isn't home, *jah*?"

"*Nee*. Still over at our *groosseldre* getting lots of well-deserved pampering. Why do you ask?"

"So, how long will she be gone?" Ruby continued.

Rachel shrugged. "When she feels rested, I suppose. They asked *Daed* to come over for dinner, so I'm in charge for today."

"The whole day?" Ruby asked.

Not knowing what Ruby was getting at, Rachel spun around. "Don't go running off with anyone."

Ruby pursed her lips, which slowly grew into a smile. "When was the last time we had a flour fight?" At that, she flung a heaping fistful of flour at Rachel's face.

Memories of the three girls having flour fights rushed through Rachel's mind with glee, so she flung what little was left in the flour canister at Ruby. May joined in and they were all soon covered in white. They howled with laughter until their ribs hurt, and then sat at the table, tuckered out.

"Remember when *Mamm* let us do that?" May asked. "It's been a long time."

"Sometimes I miss being a kid like you," Ruby said to May. "To only be in third grade and my biggest worry was learning the multiplication table."

Rachel handed out tea towels so they could wipe off their faces. "What big problem do you have, Ruby? *Rumspringa*?"

Ruby nodded. "I don't know if I like it. I know we're supposed to see what the English have to offer and all, before we make a vow to the Amish church, but I'm doing things forbidden. It doesn't make sense."

"Like what?" May asked, curiosity peaked.

"Going in a car with Englishers. Making Englisher friends."

Alarm bells went off in Rachel. "You have English girlfriends, not boys, *jah*?"

"It's a mixed group. I'm glad Tall Billy's there, though, along with Beth Klein. I could never go out with all Englishers."

"Well, stay in a group. They'll be your buddy

group for the rest of your life. I know I let down mine, and they're glad *Opa* had Freeman come out. I never knew how much pain I caused them, almost jumping the fence."

"Will you jump the fence?" May asked Ruby.

Ruby's cheeks filled with air and she let it out slowly. "*Nee*. The thing is, I feel like I don't need *Rumspringa*. I want to be Amish the more I'm out 'running around' having fun. It's not fun to do things I feel shameful about."

"Ruby, what on earth are you talking about?" Rachel felt perspiration forming on her upper lip.

"We all went to see a movie since Ainsley Atkins said it was *gut*. There was a scene in it that made me want to come home and take a bath."

Rachel shook her head and put a finger to her lips. "Not for little ears."

"I know what she means," May said, rolling her eyes. "There was swearing."

Rachel was relieved May didn't know that Ruby possibly saw an immoral movie. What a sweet, tender mind May had. "Ruby, maybe you need to talk to your Amish friends and not run around with these Englishers."

Ruby's eyes drooped. "I'm afraid Tall Billy has a crush on Ainsley. I see how he looks at her and will do anything she wants."

"Then he doesn't deserve you," Rachel snapped. "Young boys can be so daft."

"He never asks me to go home from Singings

anymore, so he doesn't have me."

May raised her hand as if in school. "I think boys have caused too much trouble for my sisters. I miss how we used to do so much together. Why don't you just pray and ask God to bring the right man to you when it's time to get married."

Rachel and Ruby applauded, clapping up a storm. "*Gut* for you, May. You're smarter than us all," Ruby proclaimed. "Who needs men when we have sisters."

"We'll find husbands, with a little help from *Opa*," Rachel said with a laugh. "*Ach*, I miss Freeman so much, especially today. But, he's worth the wait. I've never been so content. Ruby, don't follow in my footsteps, believing the grass is greener on the other side. Or that a man will magically make all your problems go away."

May let her chin rest on her index finger. "Seems like *Mamm* and *Daed* got happier since *Oma* and *Opa* came from Smicksburg. I sure do hope they stay. I ask them all the time if they will, but they just say they're praying. How can anyone pray so much?"

Ruby giggled and pulled at May's bandana. "We pray too little, I fear. I see how *Opa* gets his wings in the morning. 'They that wait on the Lord will renew their strength, they shall mount up with wings like an eagle, they shall run and not faint.' There, I memorized it, *Opa* says it all the time."

May smiled angelically. "Sometimes he says his wings fall off and he needs to go get them back on. Does that mean he prays more?"

Rachel nodded. "I see him taking walks and I know he's talking to God. His Bible's ready to split in half from wear and tear, too. There's lots of ways to grow wings."

Ruby reached for her sisters' hands. "And fellowship. I appreciate the way we live here the more I'm out in the world. I don't think I'll ever want to leave."

Rachel squeezed her hand. "Freeman and I are still pondering where to live. We're still not sure, but Smicksburg is only three hours away."

"May as well be the moon," Ruby said, her voice cracking.

Rachel was a bit perplexed over Ruby's open expression of sisterly affection. Was *Rumspringa* that hard on her?

"Well, I want to be like the March girls," Ruby said. "They never moved away from each other."

"Who are the Marches? That's not an Amish name," May said.

"I'm reading *Little Women*. Granny said it's one of her favorites."

Rachel inwardly delighted. This was how she acted when reading the book. It was the first book that made her know what she had in her precious family, besides *Little House on the Prairie*. Now, that was the only thing on television she missed since she quit the hotel to prepare for baptism and marriage. She gazed into the loving eyes of her dear sisters and hoped they would end up like the March girls, too. All living near each other forever.

~*~

Rachel found a new kind of love this Valentine's Day; sisterly and brotherly love. Her sisters' love for her, and Uncle Noah giving his little garden house to her *oma* and *opa*. What a glow they had, just at the offer, but would they accept it?

That night, feeling too full, she needed to write. So, she went to her bedroom desk, got paper and pen and wrote:

Dear Freeman,

Thank you so much for the beautiful Valentine's Day Card. That you had your sister and mamm custom make it, makes it even more special. I hope you received mine.

So much has gone on here. A few days ago, my mamm lost her boppli. It was so sad to hear her cry like her heart was breaking. The wee one went straight to Jesus, but mamm feels such loss. She's never lost a one of us kinner. She's been over at my groosseldre for a rest, and comfort. I always thought my Mammi Fern was so cranky, but she had many miscarriages. That's why she only has three dochders. But she held in her sadness and it made her bitter. I believe she'll be a new person now that she's letting others know her suffering. She's a softy under a tough exterior.

Freeman, I want us to have real openness in our marriage. I'm seeing how it helps people bond. Mamm is talking to me heart-to-heart like never before. And my sisters are, too. I think it's because Oma and Opa Weaver have been here, teaching us, but most importantly, living it out. They are such special people, I'm glad I'll have one relative when I move to Smicksburg. If we do, that is. I'll be happy anywhere with you. I don't want to pressure you.

Freeman, the sweetest thing in the world has happened to my oma. You know how she wanted to reconcile with her bruder, my Uncle Noah? Well, he gave her his little garden house for a birthday present! Can you believe it? He's shunned, but there's no exchange of money and so she can accept it. Also, my Uncle Noah's long-lost love came to surprise him today. Oma said she'd never seen anything like it. They still love each other without seeing each other for nearly forty years! Now, that's a romantic story for Valentine's Day.

I'm working hard on my baptismal lessons. The one thing I dreaded was Gelassenheit, but my opa said it's German for 'serenity'. Did you know that? When we trust each other in community, have faith in each other, we have serenity. It's more than submission.

In your last letter, you mentioned coming out for my baptism. Our New Birth Sunday is five weeks before Easter, did you know that? So, it's in nine days. I hope me joining the Gmay will cheer mamm up. All her fears are gone about me jumping the fence. I think my opa was mighty smart asking you to come out here and playing matchmaker.

Also, Jared hasn't written or come around. My heart is completely yours. Pray he finds what he's really looking for, though, and that he finds someone to love.

I miss you more than you know. Call me anytime. They always pick up the phone at the rocker shop during business hours.

All my love,

Rachel

Chapter 19

Granny sat up that night pondering what to do. Accept the garden house from Noah? Why was Jeb leaving the whole decision up to her? He'd been drilling the importance of *Gelassenheit* into Rachel for days, and Rachel sparked up when she realized submission meant serenity.

Jeb did seem chipper while instructing Rachel. Did he miss his ministerial duties? Was she being selfish in wanting him all to herself?

Ach, her mind was in a kerfuffle. Seeing Mary and Noah embrace like they did was astonishing. When Mary stopped by on her way to pick up more balloons for the children's event, she acted like she hadn't skipped a beat, had been here all along, and of all things, loved Noah! How could it be? Was love that strong it could span decades?

She went to the window to see the moon. The golden crescent showed only a fraction of the orb. "That's what life's like," she whispered.

Jeb stirred, and sat up. "What?"

"*Ach*, sorry Jeb. Can't sleep. Am headed downstairs to make some chamomile tea."

He put an arm around Bea and resumed snoring. Granny tip-toed down the steps and was surprised to see the glow of an oil lamp coming from the kitchen. *Ach*, Sarah's still grieving hard, Granny pondered. Maybe she should have stayed with her parent's another night.

But it was Rachel sipping peppermint tea, sitting at the head of the table, in her *daed's* spot. "Can't sleep?"

"*Nee*. Did I wake you up?" Rachel asked.

Granny headed over to Sarah's tea basket. "I can't sleep either. Too much on my mind, I suppose." She poured the remainder of the boiling water into a teacup and placed a chamomile teabag into the cup. "Too much excitement for these old bones, I suppose."

Rachel put on a brave front, asking her what was wrong, but Granny knew Rachel needed to talk. She learned long ago that you can't yank something out of a person, it had to be the right time. "Rachel, why can't you sleep?"

She sipped her tea. "I don't know, *Oma*. I feel unsettled and don't like it. Maybe I'm just being a *boppli*."

"Go on," Granny prodded.

"Well, I miss Freeman so much, but I know my big weakness is being impulsive. I shudder to think what I could have done, running off with Jared and all. It scares me."

"But that's in the past and you've grown quite a bit since we arrived. Jeb's mighty happy with your progress. He loved teaching you all you need to be baptized."

Rachel stared into the oil lamp. "He's a *gut* teacher. He's given me more to think about."

The pendulum clock began chiming to twelve. Midnight! Rachel just sat, too pensive, so Granny said she'd finish her tea and let her be alone with her thoughts.

Rachel protested. "I'm glad you're here. I have a question. Do you think it's wrong of me to want to be married in November, during wedding season? Deep down, I realize that I've always dreamt of being married at the traditional time."

"Did you make plans with Freeman for an earlier date?" Granny asked.

"Not really. We talked about this spring, but somehow, I feel sad about it."

Granny sipped her tea. "You know my love story, *jah*? I got married in the spring because that was my dream. You need to speak up and tell Freeman. A wedding day is something to remember your whole life, and it's not all about the couple, but the families as well. Is your *mamm* in any shape to host your wedding in the spring?"

Rachel licked her lips. "*Mamm* and I talk a lot now. She said two weeks is all she needs if everyone pitches in, as is our tradition."

Granny felt that something much deeper was stirring beneath the waters. "Rachel, are you having doubts about Freeman?"

"I love him. I'm so honored he loves me," Rachel blurted. "But I'm afraid if we have a long-distance relationship, that…"

"That?"

"*Ach, Oma*, you'll think I'm a *boppli*, but I'm afraid he'll fall for that Jane girl. His parents like her and she lives in Smicksburg. There'd be no reason for him to move out here."

So it was that old enemy of the soul: fear. "Rachel, there is no fear in love, *jah*? You need to tell this all to Freeman. When you marry, you'll have many decisions and you can't be afraid of not pleasing him. You need to speak up. Freeman would want you to."

Rachel's eyes brimmed with tears. "What if I lose him?"

"*Ach*, honey," Granny said, rising to massage Rachel's careworn shoulders. "I know he loves you. I've known that boy since he was in diapers and I've never seen him look at any woman like he does you. Now, I know it's hard, but you need to tell him. I did the same with Jeb, and he was so kind. A *gut* husband wants what's best for his wife. Jeb gave me my spring wedding right here in Ohio."

"*Opa's* so romantic," Rachel said.

"Freeman is, too. He can't read your mind, so you need to tell him. Will you do that for me?"

"But, how can we stay in touch? Just by letters?"

Granny squeezed Rachel's neck. "You'll find a way. I have a lot of confidence in you two."

"Really? Why is that?" Rachel asked.

"Because Jeb matched you up." Granny snickered. "He's mighty proud of that, in a *gut* way, you know."

Rachel embraced her *oma*. "*Danki* ever so much. What would I do without you and *Opa*?"

Granny's heart was filled to overflowing. The *kinner* did need them. It was nice to be needed.

They both decided to get some shut eye but before Granny fell to sleep, the advice she gave to Rachel rippled through her mind. *You need to speak up*. This is what she needed to do with her decision whether to move to Ohio or not. She had fears of her own to overcome, and Granny decided to make it a matter of prayer and casting her concerns on God.

~*~

Fern felt born anew as she filled her birdfeeders. The robins had returned, and the air smelt like spring, even though it was the end of February. How thankful she was this morning. She was cleaned out by Sarah's grief, poor child. Deep wounds sparked open conversation between her husband and daughters. She had to confess to them that bitterness had taken root long ago, and it choked out good fruit in her life.

But they forgave her, freely and sincerely. A boulder lifted from her chest. How she wished she'd let out her sorrow long ago, not letting it build up. She was like a dam holding back floodwaters. She'd built a wall around her, but no more.

She knew now why Deborah Weaver got under her skin. Deborah was an open book, the opposite of her, and happily married. Well, the late-night talk she had with Matthew let the remaining walls around her fall and she hoped that their years together would be happy. When she agreed to go to Florida for his arthritis after Christmas, the look on Matthew's face would be forever fixed in her mind. Like a man who'd gone through a long drought and saw a cup of water. Maybe she'd surprise him and say she'd go south for four months, or a longer extended stay next winter.

A small tan car pulled into her driveway and out flew Charlotte and Juliet. The two sisters had made such an impression on her, their joy despite hardship, got her to thinking she suffered from too much self-pity.

"Hello, girls. Can I help you with something?"

They both gave Fern quick hugs. "We were driving by and saw you," Charlotte started.

"And we have a question," Juliet said. "Can you teach us how to knit better?"

The glow from these two girls gave her the inkling that they enjoyed spending time with her. Or, did Deborah Weaver send them over, trying to mix their sugar with her vinegar ways. "Well, Granny started the circle, so you best ask her."

"Who's Granny?" Juliet asked. "Was she the little old lady at circle?"

"She's only in her seventies," Fern replied.

"Well, it's old to us. You're not seventy yet, are you?" Charlotte asked.

Fern's chest filled with pride, so she redirected the question. "Age is only a number, *jah*? Do you want to come in for some cookies? I bake a lot, you know."

The girls eagerly agreed and followed Fern into her house. Charlotte covered her cheeks as she stared at the living room and then the kitchen. "It's like a dollhouse!"

"I love it," Juliet continued. "No clutter anywhere." She dramatically sat at the table, hand to her forehead. "Being in a spotless house when you have two rambunctious boys at home puts me in shock. How do you do it?"

Fern didn't understand Juliet's meaning. "I'm sure your house is clean."

"No, the boys have toy cars, trucks and toys everywhere. I pick them up, and within an hour, they're all over the place again."

Memories of her three girls leaving dollhouse furniture that Matthew built all over their bedroom and her chiding them relentlessly was another thing she'd need to apologize for. "Juliet, don't be hard on your boys. They grow up fast."

Charlotte threw her sister a smile. "She's a good mom. She just needs some adult time."

"Yeah, Fern. And we drove by your house on purpose." Juliet pulled a knitted scarf from her large pink and black tote. "What do you think? I knit this by myself!"

Fern noticed the even knit and purl stitches. "It's *gut.* How'd you learn so fast?"

Juliet raised her fingers and wiggled them. "My brains are in here. I'm good with my hands. Once I see something done, I can usually do it."

Fern turned to Charlotte. "So, you need help with knitting?"

Charlotte blushed, but was able to say, "Juliet and I loved being with you. We don't know many Amish and it was so nice that Sydney invited us to knitting circle. We have so many questions about the Amish way of living."

"Such as?" Fern asked as she sat the plate of snickerdoodles and chocolate chip cookies on the table.

"I don't know where to start," Charlotte said. "But women talk over crafts, and Juliet and I thought you could help us be master knitters like you and we could ask questions."

Master knitter? Was there such a thing? "You know knitting is only two stitches: knit and purl."

Juliet pulled a magazine out of her tote, opening it to a knitting pattern. "I bought this book at Walmart. What's K2T?"

"Knit two together." Fern looked over the little boy sweater pattern. It was considered an intermediate level skill. "Do you want to make this for your boys?"

"Will you help me?" Juliet asked, her smile begging for a yes.

"Then bring it to knitting circle at Sarah's. I'll teach you."

Juliet shot her sister a look that seemed to say, 'speak up'. Charlotte cleared her throat. "We'll pay you for private lessons. Knitting calms me. It's good for my stomach issues."

Fern searched the dear girl's dark brown eyes. "You want to come here?"

Charlotte's chin trembled. "You remind us of our grandma. We miss her so much and would love to spend time with you."

Fern felt sunbeams burst in her soul. A specific prayer she and Matthew prayed was that people would come into her life so that she felt needed, not always pushing herself onto the grown children too much. And here came two beautiful girls needing her. "I'd love to help you knit and…get to know you two."

"Are you going to knitting circle Wednesday? I

know it was canceled last week because people had plans for Valentine's Day."

Fern realized that the girls didn't know about Sarah's miscarriage. She filled them in, and they said they'd stop by and visit her soon. Juliet asked if Fern could have circle at her place. Fern shuddered. Have the woman who was divorced twice come to her house? Her self-righteousness arched its ugly head, until she remembered Matthew confessing he would have asked for a divorce long ago if he wasn't Amish. Sydney's husbands left her with *kinner* to raise on her own. How could she be so unmerciful. She told the girls something would be worked out and to stop by on Wednesday.

~*~

When Wednesday rolled around, Sarah thanked her *mamm* for hosting the knitting circle. She'd been on herbal supplements recommended by Doc Martin for post-partum depression, but time, she was told, would heal the hole in her heart.

Granny, concerned for Sarah, decided to stay home. Truth be told, she had seen such a change in Fern, and didn't want to 'run' the circle. Fern was in charge today.

So, Sarah and Granny quietly crocheted, learning the feather and fan stitch.

"This stitch looks like bird wings touching in the middle," Granny said, trying to strike up a conversation with Sarah.

"I suppose it does."

Sarah's tone was pitifully flat. The herbalist from Smicksburg had told her depression meant pressed down. Sarah was so grieved, so how could she expect her to recover sooner?

"This guilt won't go away," Sarah near whispered.

"*Ach*, Sarah, you did nothing wrong."

"I overdid it. Worked too hard."

Granny knew Sarah would give her life for her *kinner*. An image came to her and she decided to share it. "Sarah, in many a barn fire we often find dead chickens."

Sarah frowned at her. "Why talk about that?"

Granny raised a hand. "That part is gruesome, but you're like those chickens."

Sarah let the ball of yarn fall from her hands and it rolled across the floor. "I need to take a nap. I'm tired."

"Wait," Granny pleaded. "Under the hens are often found a brood of baby chicks. I know you don't farm as much out here, but we know this back home. Sarah, you would have covered your *boppli* with your wings to save it. I know you. You're a *wunderbar mamm*."

Sarah fell into Granny's open arms and released her tears. Rubbing her back, Granny told her tears of sorrow needed to come out of the body. Tears of sorrow contained toxins, unlike tears of joy.

Sarah let cleansing tears continue to fall, until they heard Sydney singing out a 'yoo-hoo'. Sarah stood and wiped her face.

When Sydney found them, she lifted a gift basket. "Sarah, I have something for you. I know you're all wrung out, for good reason, but I want you to open it now."

Sydney sat at Sarah's feet. "Now, you may throw it at me, but when I've been depressed or down in life, I know keeping busy helps."

Sarah opened the bag to find beautiful quilt squares, new scissors, and a gift card to the local quilt shop. "*Danki*, Sydney. I do need to quilt more. *Gut* for the nerves."

Sydney put a hand on Sarah's knee. "Look inside again."

Sarah obeyed and pulled out paperwork. "What's this?"

"It's all the paperwork you need to start your quilt shop. I'm going to help you fill it out and show you how to run a business like mine."

Sarah twisted the papers into a tube. "I appreciate it, but…"

"But?" Sydney challenged.

"Daniel has a business. We know about starting one."

Sydney comically puffed up her already high hair. "Well, I know that. But Daniel doesn't have an Englisher helper, *jah*? Let me tell you something girlfriend. Pictures of your quilts will be plastered all over the walls of my business and online. I know the Amish do it, so don't protest. I'll help sell them online. That's what the papers are for, silly."

Granny held her breath. Sarah had always shied away from Outsiders, but this would be so good for her.

"I'll do it," Sarah said, crying and laughing at the same time. "I feel confident with you," she told Sydney.

Sarah stood to hug Sydney. Granny thought back to November when Sarah was so backwards around the English, but here she was being lifted up by one and tenderly directed. Praise be.

~*~

That night, Granny was led into the bedroom by Jeb. "Haven't had time to give you your birthday present," he said, handing her an envelope.

Only a card? Granny wondered. Jeb usually made something special or prepared a scavenger hunt of sorts to discover her present. Or he'd give it to her early, not able to contain his excitement. With so many in the house, he didn't have time. *Ach*, she was acting like a *kinner*. '*Danki*, Jeb."

She opened the envelope to see a store-bought card signed 'Love, Jeb'...and a credit card? "Jeb, I'm not complaining, but we don't use credit cards."

They sat in their rockers and silence filled the room, crowding out any emotion. "It's a gift card to Lehman's." He rubbed the back of his neck. "I had something planned the day of your birthday but got distracted. Benjamin and I went out when you visited Noah. I'm sorry, Deborah."

This was the least romantic gift Jeb had ever given her. *Distracted.* That's how she felt living among so many. She longed for her *dawdyhaus.* Her own kitchen.

"Roman called today, and I thought you'd want to know that the ground's broken for Anna and Ezekiel's new place."

"When are they moving out?" Granny held her hand to her jumping heart.

"As soon as we want to go home. Roman suggested a Pioneer Princess stove be put in Anna's new place, because she'd never leave ours."

"You're joking," Granny chirped.

"*Nee*, I'm serious. Roman misses us. So does Denny. All the *kinner* do, too. But, Deborah, I believe you like it out here. Am I right? Your *bruder* and you have a strong bond?"

"*Jah*, we do. But…" Granny thought of her advice to others. Speak up. Don't be afraid of others' reactions. Be truthful.

Jeb went on. "I'm leaving the decision up to you. We can move into Noah's little house if there's no exchange of money. I talked to the bishop and he said we'd have to take out the electricity and have the exterior match the others in the church district."

Granny felt sweat form on her forehead. Jeb was leaving it up to her? "Jeb, what do you want to do? You like being out here, don't you? You're attached to the *kinner*, especially Rachel. You gave her some fine teaching. *Ach,* she'll be baptized soon."

"*Jah*, New Birth Sunday is around the corner," Jeb said with satisfaction. "But you haven't answered my question. What should I tell Roman? Should we let Anna and Ezekiel live in our place until the *dawdyhaus* is built?"

Why was she afraid to be honest with Jeb? She'd always been honest. "I'm afraid."

"Of what?" Jeb asked, patting his lap.

Granny went to him, arms open, cuddling in his embrace. "Of Noah passing. Of saying *mach's gut* and not knowing if it'll be my last. I hate cancer, Jeb."

He laid his big hand on her face. "We all do. But, until we go to Glory, where there's no more tears, we'll have them here. You can visit Noah."

This comment piqued Granny's curiosity. He suggested visiting. Knowing her husband, he had a hankering to get back home to his ministerial duties and fishing hole. Lord, help me be brave. "Jeb, I miss Smicksburg. We can visit here often, *jah*? Maybe come out next November and stay the winter?"

Jeb let out a loud, long sigh of relief. "*Jah*, for sure. I miss Smicksburg something awful. Can we pack tonight?" he asked with a laugh.

Granny faced her dearly loved husband and kissed him soundly. "We have to wait for Rachel's baptism, *jah*?"

He nodded. "We can leave right after, though?"

Joy leapt into Granny's heart. "*Jah*, let's do that."

Chapter 20

It took Granny and Jeb a week to break the news to Daniel, but he wanted what was best for them. It was the visit to Noah that was breaking Granny's heart. He was all alone. So isolated in that big house on the hill. But Melody drove them to his house. She told them that their foster boys would arrive soon…and she was not pregnant. Further testing confirmed it. But there was no hollow tone in this barren woman's voice. She had a loving marriage and two boys to care for. Praise be.

The first day of March was mild, birds chirping all around them as they made their way to Noah's door. Why did he have such a big mansion for, anyhow? She'd have to ask.

Kimberly greeted them and told them Noah was having a bad day, but to come in and she'd see if he was up for company. Granny fidgeted with a small world globe as she took a seat. Noah traveled the planet but couldn't get Mary out of his mind. Did he get plain ways out of his mind? Why the paintings at the hospital?

Soon Noah gingerly came in, using a walker. Jeb

jumped up to help him, but Noah said he was strong enough to walk.

Granny held back tears. "Not having a *gut* day?"

"It's better than some. I don't know if it's the overcast sky, but I'm tired.

"The clouds parted," Jeb said. "We'll have sunshine this afternoon."

Noah met Granny's eyes, studying her. "You're going home, aren't you?"

Granny bit her lip. "We have things to tend to back home. We'll be back for a visit soon."

Noah's eyes misted. "I'm sure glad you came Little Debbie. I've been missing you for ages."

Granny pulled a handkerchief from her pocket to dab her tears. "Me, too," she croaked out, in the most unnatural voice. She cleared her throat. "We'd be happy to stay in your little house for a long visit."

"It's your house, Debbie," Noah corrected.

"*Danki*," Jeb said. "You're very generous."

Granny prayed for self-control, but the tears still flowed. When Noah told her he'd be fine, she couldn't help but cry out, "Why do you live in this big house all alone? It makes me sad. You need friends. Community."

Noah's brows rose sky high. "This house is an investment. It's historical, you know. I restored it and plan to flip it some day or sell it if I need the money."

Jeb scratched his chin. "I don't understand."

"Well, if I ever have to go to a nursing home, they can take the house in exchange for my stay there."

Jeb gawked. "What?"

"Nursing homes are expensive," Noah informed.

Granny knew the English had great fears of being alone in their old age. They didn't have the safety net of the community who took care of their own. How sad.

"Are you okay financially?" Jeb asked. "Do you have savings?"

Noah grimaced. "Well, it's dwindling, having to pay for in home care. Kimberly offered to do it for less, but I won't have it." His eyes lit up real unusual-like. "But Mary may be moving out here. That's something this old man never expected."

"Are you getting married?" Granny spat out, clenching her hands as if in prayer.

Noah's eyes twinkled. "We talk on the phone every day. We love each other. Always have. And there's something Mary and I both figured out. We're both plain in our thinking. We both miss the old ways."

"Will you return to the People?" Granny asked.

"Well," Noah started, "the ban being lifted has softened my heart. It was mighty hard towards the Amish, but no more."

"God softens the heart," Jeb said cautiously.

"That, too. I went around the world running from God, but he caught me. That's how Mary put it."

"Are you getting married?" Granny repeated. "Will you return to the People?"

"Well, Mary applied over at the hospital, and it looks like she can get a job there. And then, if all goes well, we've decided that we'd like to be Mennonite. Not Old Order Mennonite, with no cars. We like our cars."

Granny held her thumping heart. "So, you're happy?"

"Very," Noah said. "It's been a long while that I had real hope."

Granny ran to her brother and hugged his neck. "We'll be coming out so much, you'll get tired of us."

"I hope so," Noah said, his voice cracking.

As Granny held her brother, she had hope, too. Hope that she'd see him on many visits. Maybe see him get married. Praise be.

~*~

Granny walked around the perimeter of the front yard. Several crocuses popped their flowery heads to greet her. *Ach,* spring was coming, images of new life abounding. She watched as women climbed into their buggies to go home after a long day's work. Not only was Rachel's baptism in a few days, but it was Sarah and Daniel's turn to host church.

Granny entered the house to inspect, knowing how she checked her own house back in the day when she and Jeb hosted church with five rambunctious boys darting around trying to help. She was encouraged to see walls were washed and the whole house was spick-and-span clean.

Sarah and Rachel were resting at the kitchen table; it was apparent that joy was creeping back into Sarah's heart. A bittersweet joy, she told Granny last night, since it seemed to take a tragedy in her life to birth a new life in Fern. Visitors regularly visited Fern now, Amish and English. Sydney drove Englishers over to buy baked goods and tried to talk Fern into starting a bakery.

The weight of Rachel's *Rumspringa* also lifted from Sarah and Daniel's shoulders as together they rejoiced at what was to happen in two short days: Rachel making the vow to be Amish.

Rachel motioned for Granny to join them at the table. "What are you thinking of *Oma*?" she asked. "You look dazed."

Granny slid onto the bench next to Rachel. "Sometimes I need to pause to take in everything. So much has happened."

"Like Uncle Noah getting married to Mary?"

"*Ach*, time will tell. But, isn't it something else that their love lasted for so long? Maybe they'll be friends. Both are set in their ways."

Sarah beamed. "Marriage is a blessing, no matter how old you are."

May squealed in delight, which made all heads turn. There stood Freeman, his eyes searching until they landed on Rachel and a shy kind of grin lifted his face. Rachel ran to him and kissed him right in front of everyone.

"Did he come alone?" Sarah asked. "We invited his whole family."

Granny clasped Sarah's hand. "Don't borrow trouble. The Yoders will be fine in-laws to Rachel."

"You'd think that since Rachel may be moving out to Smicksburg that they'd come, though."

Granny saw that old battle with anxiety trying to choke Sarah again. Well, it was a lifelong battle for her, too, and that's why she had to do so many casting off prayers. "Sarah, cast all your cares on the Lord. He cares about you."

Sarah bit into a doughnut. "I know. My emotions are still up and down. But nothing is going to steal my joy at seeing Rachel get baptized. I still can't believe it all."

Granny knew it was a rocky road full of twists and turns steering Rachel and any mother would be dizzy by now. "Did Rachel ever hear back from Jared? He was a nice man, and I feel for him."

Sarah's eyes lit up. "She didn't tell you? *Ach*, she's finally confiding in me. Jared stopped in on a visit home and apologized again, saying he wanted what was best for Rachel and that Freeman was a Godsend. The poor young man was lonely and came back to Holmes County for a week, but he's back in Cleveland now. I suppose folks raised in the country find it mighty hard to adjust to city life."

Knowing that Jeb had set up the whole affair, Granny wanted to raise her hands and shout 'Hallelujah' like her Baptist friends.

~*~

Rachel's cheeks were on fire. How could she be so overcome with love in front of so many? She led Freeman to the coat rack, suggesting a trip to the pond.

They walked hand in hand until they reached the bench, and Freeman drew her close, planting a kiss on her lips. "*Gut* to see you. And just think, in two days, we can be officially engaged, published and all."

Only a baptized member could be engaged, and not many knew of her plans, outside of her immediate family. But dear Freeman didn't know of her plans either. *Be brave. Don't be afraid. Freeman needs to know how you're feeling.* Granny's words rang in her mind.

"What is it?" Freeman asked.

She put her head on his shoulder as the crisp wind whirled around them. "You know I love you, *jah*?"

He stiffened. "But?"

"I talked to my *oma.* She wanted a spring wedding."

"Just like you, *jah*?"

"Well…"

Freeman backed away. "You're having doubts?"

Was he mad? Disappointed in her? "Freeman, no doubts at all. I just want a wedding in November. All my life I've wanted a wedding during the busy wedding season."

He looked out at the pond. Two mallard duck pairs landed to glide across the waters. "Are you sure?"

"*Jah*, I am. Is that okay with you?"

He tenderly took her hand and kissed it. "I'll wait longer if you need the time."

Rachel was too full of emotion to speak. He wasn't mad at all? Love was patient, indeed.

"I plan to spend the summer with my *oma* and *opa*."

They clasped hands and watched the ducks glide side by side. "That's mighty fine, Rachel. We'll have such fun together. I'll show you everything there is to see from Smicksburg up to Punxsy."

Could she bring up all that was on her heart? About living here in Holmes County. "I'd enjoy that. It's a pretty area with so many rolling hills."

He turned her to himself. "But you want to live here, right?"

She blinked in disbelief. "How did you know?"

Freeman pursed his lips to stifle a laugh. "Jeb. I think since he matched us up, he thinks he can keep showing us what's right after we're married. And that's a *gut* thing. We want a marriage like his."

Rachel leaned in for a kiss. "I don't mind living by my *Mammi Fern* anymore. She's changed quite a bit and…"

"You love Holmes County. I know."

Rachel threw him a puzzled look. "What else do you know?"

He chuckled. "Your *daed* is expanding his shop to make room for me. Your *mamm* is going to open a quilt shop and you want to help her, and the extra income will come in handy."

Rachel laughed. "*Ach*, my *opa* told you everything?"

"Not him. Your *oma*. She wrote to let me in on a few things. Honey, never be afraid to tell me what's on your heart. When we get married, we'll become one, but we'll still be two people with different needs."

Love for this man overwhelmed her. "And what about you? Do you want to live here?"

"Well, my family will be here tomorrow to meet you…and see the area. Since Lily's leaning towards the English, they want you to mentor her if they move to these parts."

Rachel's heart leapt. "I'd love to. She can come stay with us for a while."

He collected her in his arms. "I love you so much."

"Me, too." Rachel was in pure bliss. Freeman loved her unconditionally. What freedom there was.

They sat contently watching the ducks as they

collected twigs to begin their nest.

~*~

Granny sat in awe as Jeb baptized Rachel. When she removed her *kapp* to let the water of baptism pour over her head, the tears flowed throughout the Weaver family. But, something kept interrupting Granny's attention. The way Benjamin kept looking over at Lily, Rachel's future sister-in-law, was unmistakable. Could steadfast Benjamin sway Lily to remain with the People?

Granny's mind started to crank up. Maybe Benjamin could come with Rachel to spend the summer in Smicksburg. He'd be sure to see Lily often. But then she caught herself. Her matchmaking days were over. She'd promised herself. But…Jeb was just getting started.

Her mind wandered back to Smicksburg and how hard it would be to say good-bye to her loved ones here in Holmes County. But the letters that arrived from her knitting circle once she broke the news of her return near filled the big mailbox. Janice and Suzy would pick them up on Wednesday and take the Yoders home as well. Fannie, Ella and Ruth would have her house cleaned as if it was church hosting time. Food would fill her icebox and her pantry would be full of baked good items so she could bake to her hearts delight all alone in her own kitchen, on her Pioneer Princess stove. Praise be!

Dear Readers,

Thank you from the bottom of my heart for all your encouragement. It was *you* who asked over the years for more of Granny and Jeb Weaver. They first appeared in 2011 in a serial form and it's amazing that it's still going strong. The series became a five-volume set called Smicksburg *Tales*, set in my neck of the woods here in Western Pennsylvania.

I visited Holmes County, Ohio a few years back and loved it beyond words. I made contacts with Amish and Mennonites and after many talks, some via cell phones (Amish…shocking) I learned much about them. The most outstanding thing was how active the Amish are in sending shoeboxes to Third World Countries. They hire five buses a year and go to areas where boxes are filled. They also have fifty Amish businesses that host wrapping centers in Ohio.

I never thought I'd write about Amish outside of my friends in Western PA & Western NY, places I've lived. I write from what I know and experience. Well, now I have lots of friends in Holmes County, only a short three-hour ride away!

A big thank you to Timbercrest RV park, a lovely place that Tim and I park our little seventeen-foot-long RV. We'll be back for sure and certain!

Discussion Guide

1. Granny pushed herself into new situations. Yes, she'd love to hide in her kitchen and bake on her Pioneer Princess woodstove, but she moves on. Do you feel like you need to stay in your safe place a bit too much? Do you need to go there more? Where can we find balance?
2. Jeb gets his wings in the morning, but they keep falling off. We have bald eagles across the street, and they need to really flap their wings when down low, but when their soar high, they glide. It amazes me.

Isaiah 40:31 says:

They that wait upon the Lord shall renew their strength; they shall mount up with wings as eagles; they shall run, and not be weary; and they shall walk, and not faint.

Like Jeb, I have a quiet time in the morning, but as life happens, I find my wings fall off. So, back to the Bible for verses I'm mulling over and time for silence or prayer.

What can you incorporate into your daily routine to get your wings?

3. Rachel doesn't know herself until she's asked by Jared to move to New York City. Big decisions have a way of helping us know

ourselves better. Can you remember a time when a life changing decision helped you get to the root of who you are?

4. What do you think of Sydney? Her blue eye makeup and big hair make Fern cringe, yet Granny comes to love this caring woman. Is there someone you judge by outward appearance you need to get to know? See their heart? You can never judge a book by its cover, *jah*?
5. Melody says she doesn't have many close friends. This is a common complaint in America. Are you lonely like Melody? Why not reach out like Granny did when she started her first knitting circle? It's something worth taking time for. I have groups of friends along with my close-knit immediate family, but something must go to carve in time for them. I could hole myself up and write more, but I stop myself and make time to nurture these vital connections. I fall short many times, wanting to stay home and read a book or knit or crochet, but I'm trying. Who comes to mind now? Who can you go out and have coffee with?
6. Freeman's story is true. He's my nephew who saw his dear wife and he felt the Lord whisper in his ear, "Cherish her." His story is better than fiction. He waited seven years

to marry his wife, who gave him no encouragement. His steadfast love in action finally made her see what unconditional love was and how transforming it is. Rachel keeps saying, "Love is patient." She admires this in Freeman. Read 1 Corinthians 13, the famous 'Love Chapter' in the Bible and ponder it.

7. What do you think of Fannie? Is she too needy? Too dependent on Granny? She has an unhappy relationship with her own mother. How does Granny fill that void? Is there someone who needs you to be their Granny?
8. Fern is a complex character. We know she has bottled up pain, but her tongue is so sharp. If you had tea with Fern, what advice would you give her?
9. What do you think of Granny's relationship with her brother, Noah? She pushes two tables together, so they don't eat at the same table. Is she pushing the boundaries of the *Ordnung*? She eats her birthday breakfast with him in the kitchen nook. She says her conscience is clean. Does that make a difference?
10. Jeb is a C.S. Lewis fan. So am I. I have a Pinterest board full of his quotes. Lewis

said:

God whispers to us in our pleasures, speaks in our conscience, but shouts in our pain: it is His megaphone to rouse a deaf world.

This quote is so profound, I can only ask you to ponder it or discuss it with your group. Many think God uses pain when we've turned a deaf ear to Him, while others believe God allows pain to refine us. Lewis wrote this while trying to come to terms with his wife's death.

11. Granny & Jeb will return to Holmes County next winter, Lord willing, and an Amish Knitting Circle in Holmes County will be out in 2020. Which characters would you like to explore? Freeman's pretty sister? Leah? Melody? Let me know by contacting me at:

www.karenannavogel.com/contact____or on Facebook at_www.facebook.com/VogelReaders/

HOPE TO HEAR FROM YINZ! It's such an honor to have you as readers! Blessings!

My special request:

Thank you for reading Amish Knitting Circle in Holmes County! If you liked it, please consider leaving a review on Amazon and Goodreads, if you're active there. Your help in spreading the word is gratefully appreciated and reviews make a huge difference in helping new readers find the series.

THOSE GRAMMAR ERRORS!

This book has been edited by three qualified people, yet there still might be grammar errors or typos. I'm grateful for readers who point them out to me. If you find any, please let me know, and as a thank you, I'll send you thank you gift. One Canadian reader sent me an error list and now she's a beta reader for me. *Danki*!

1. Contact me at

www.karenannavogel.com/contact

Amish Recipes

Pumpkin Cheese Pie

8 oz. cream cheese

¾ cup sugar

2 Tbsp. flour

1 tsp. cinnamon

¼ tsp. nutmeg

½ tsp. ginger

¼ tsp. vanilla

3 eggs

2 cups pumpkin puree

Beat cream cheese, sugar and flour in a large bowl. Add remaining ingredients and beat until smooth. Pour into pie crust and back at 350 degrees for 50-55 minutes. Pie is ready when a fork is inserted into center of pie and it comes out clean. Serve warm.

Ginger Cookie

1 c brown sugar
1 c. shortening (Crisco)
½ c. hot water
1 egg
2/3 molasses
1/3 c. corn syrup
1 T baking soda
1 T cinnamon
1 T Ginger
1 T vanilla
Pinch salt
1 T baking powder

Enough flour to make soft dough. Start with 4 cups to start. Add flour slowly until right consistency.

Sift flour with salt and spices. Cream shortening and sugar; add egg and beat until light. Add molasses, corn syrup and vanilla, then dry ingredients. Dissolve baking powder in hot water and add to mix. Add flour, not to exceed 9 cups. Drop by teaspoons on greased cookie sheet. Bake for 10 minutes at 350 degrees.

About the Author

Karen Anna Vogel is dusting off book outlines written thirty years ago when she was running after her four preschoolers. Having empty nest syndrome, she delved into writing. Many books and novellas later, she's passionate about portraying the Amish and small-town life in a realistic way. Being a "Trusted English Friend" to Amish in rural Western Pennsylvania and New York, she writes what she's experienced, many novels based on true stories. She also blogs at *Amish Crossings*

She's a graduate of Seton Hill University, majoring in Psychology & Elementary Education, and Andersonville Theological Seminary with a Masters in Biblical Counseling. Karen's a yarn hoarder not in therapy, knitting or crocheting something at all times. This passion leaks into her books along with hobby farming and her love of dogs. Her husband of thirty-seven years is responsible for turning her into a content country bumpkin.

Visit her at www.karenannavogel.com/contact

Karen's booklist so far (2019)

Check her Amazon author page for updates.

Continuing Series:

Amish Knitting Circle: Smicksburg Tales 1
Amish Friends Knitting Circle: Smicksburg Tales 2
Amish Knit Lit Circle: Smicksburg Tales 3
Amish Knit & Stitch Circle: Smicksburg Tales 4
Amish Knit & Crochet Circle: Smicksburg 5

Standalone Novels:

Knit Together: Amish Knitting Novel
The Amish Doll: Amish Knitting Novel
Plain Jane: A Punxsutawney Amish Novel

Amish Herb Shop Series:

Herbalist's Daughter Trilogy
Herbalist's Son Trilogy

At Home in Pennsylvania Amish Country Series:

Winter Wheat
Spring Seeds
Summer Haze
Autumn Grace (Yet to be released)

Novellas:

Amish Knitting Circle Christmas: Granny & Jeb's Love Story
Amish Pen Pals: Rachael's Confession
Christmas Union: Quaker Abolitionist of Chester County, PA
Love Came Down at Christmas
Love Came Down at Christmas 2
Love Came Down at Christmas 3

Non-fiction:

31 Days to a Simple Life the Amish Way
A Simple Christmas the Amish Way

Made in United States
Orlando, FL
18 November 2022

24704362R00233